I0452895

BROKEN FAIRWAYS

BUFFORD CLAY

Copyright © 2025 by Bufford Clay Books

All rights reserved. No part of this book may be reproduced, distributed, or transmitted in any form or by any means, including photocopying, recording, or other electronic or mechanical methods, without the prior written permission of the publisher, except in the case of brief quotations embodied in critical reviews and certain other noncommercial uses permitted by copyright law. For permission requests, write to the publisher at buffordclaybooks@gmail.com

ISBN: 979-8-9921845-2-5

This is a work of fiction. Names, characters, places, and incidents are products of the author's imagination or are used fictitiously. Any resemblance to actual events, locales, or persons, living or dead, is entirely coincidental.

Cover by: Deranged Doctor Design

BUFFORD CLAY BOOKS

Enemies In The Yard

COMING SOON

Pushed Too Far - Book One in the
High Knob Chronicles Series

Red 30 Introduction

Catastrophe doesn't wait for the perfect moment, it strikes when we least expect it. It can happen while we're at work, at home, or even in the middle of a weekend escape, enjoying time with family and friends. One moment, life is normal. The next, the world is unrecognizable.

For Logan, Ty, Owen, and Mace, what was supposed to be their annual getaway of golf and gambling turned into a fight for survival. Trapped far from home when the country falls under attack, they are faced with a choice: disappear into the chaos or rise to meet the danger head-on.

But the Red 30 Gang doesn't cower.

With nothing but their wits, skill, and an unbreakable bond, they stand against ruthless gangs and those who prey on the weak, fighting not just for themselves, but for the innocent caught in the crossfire. In a world where law and order are gone, survival is no longer about luck, it's about who has the will to fight for a future.

This is their story.

Chapter One
"The Last Retreat"

"Hand me my pack of sour ropes, Uncle Owen," Mace called out as he whipped the golf cart around a sharp curve, nearly sending Owen flying.

Owen clutched the cart's handle, his knuckles whitening. His head snapped around to the cart following behind, his eyes wide with alarm. "I can't hand you any candy! I'm too scared to let go," he shouted, raising a hand to the other cart in an exaggerated plea for help.

In the trailing cart, Owen's brother Logan and their friend Ty burst into laughter, tears streaming down their faces as they watched Owen cling for dear life. The laughter was cut short by the screech of tires as Mace stomped on the brakes, bringing the cart to an abrupt halt. He hopped out, his grin wide as he eyed Logan and Ty pulling up behind them.

"This lunatic is going to kill me on this golf course!" Owen exclaimed, a smile creeping onto his face despite his words. Ty's laughter turned into a series of wheezing coughs as he struggled to breathe, his laughter contagious.

"We're almost finished, and he's already thinking about the casino," Logan said, shaking his head. "Mace, you need to focus. Just because you've had a couple of bad shots doesn't mean you should let it frustrate you."

"Frustrate me?" Mace responded, his laugh sharp and humorless as he dug his sour ropes out of his golf bag. "Dad, I'm not frustrated. I'm pissed off! I've got to shoot par on these last two holes just to stay at 78 on the day."

1

Owen chuckled, shaking his head. "I was over 78 by hole nine. And let's not forget I'm on my second dozen of golf balls, lost so many I'm gonna go broke!" His self-deprecating humor earned chuckles from Logan and Ty, but Mace barely cracked a smile, his frustration still bubbling under the surface.

This was their annual bachelors golf trip, a tradition they had started years ago. Every year, the "Red 30 Gang", a name they coined during a particularly wild Vegas trip, gathered in Cherokee, North Carolina, for a weekend of golf and gambling. This year's tournament was "The Cherokee Cup being played at Cedar Hollow Golf Club." While the golf course brought friendly competition, the casino offered another challenge for them. Ending the trip without losing too much money.

Mason Reed, known by everyone as Mace, was the youngest of the group, and the wildcard of the bunch. A naturally talented golfer, his skills often clashed with his temper on the course. Mace can easily break par when playing, or he can let a bad shot ruin his round. Mace had been known to allow his temper to fling a club after breaking it into the air in frustration. His tall and slender frame gave him a fluid, almost poetic swing, when his emotions didn't get in the way. Today, though, his frustration was as evident as the sour ropes sticking out between his lips. Today, that candy was at least for the time, holding back the profanities from spewing from his mouth.

Mace loved the thrill of a round of golf, especially if he had a few side bets going on. He has the heart of a true high stake's gambler, whether on the course or in the casino, when he gets going, get out of his way. Never one to let the advice of his friends get in the way, Mace's bets usually go higher than they should. He is a fun gambler, his energy contagious, always quick to jump on a game and risk his money with lady luck. He will be the first to tell you that the next big win is just a spin of the wheel away, or the turn of the river card.

Mace is the life of the casino, his likeableness and energy always drawing fellow gamblers into his circle. The coastal lifestyle he enjoyed all his life adds to the laid-back way he carries himself and handles situations.

"You guys think I'll hit those people on the green?" Owen asked, looking at Logan for approval to tee off as he lined up his next shot, wiggling the club head slowly.

Logan raised an eyebrow, then glanced at Ty, who shrugged his shoulders, holding his hands up. "What people? There's no one on the green."

"Not that green, obviously there isn't a snowballs chance in Satan's world that I will hit straight. My slice, however, stands a good chance of ending up over there on that green," Owen said as he pointed to the next hole over.

"You're crazy, Owen," Ty said as he shook his head in amusement. "Aim way left, then it should be in the middle."

Logan gave Owen and Ty a slight nod toward Mace, who stood by the golf cart, oblivious to the conversation they had just discussed. His fingers worked furiously scrolling through his phone for scores and updates on sports games.

"He's checking his bets again," Logan whispered, grinning. The group chuckled as Mace finally looked up, catching on that he was now the subject of their talk.

"Y'all can laugh all you want," Mace said, slipping his phone back into his pocket. "I'm just trying to win some money this weekend to pay for the trip."

He grabbed his nine iron from his bag, and strolled over to the tee box, dropping a ball and lining up.

"Ten bucks says you're farthest from the pin on this shot," Owen said, getting a side eye from Mace before he nodded in agreement on the bet. Owen knew he was going to lose, but he also knew it would get Mace out of his own head and back into good spirits before he fired off the tee shot on the Par 3 hole. Using the beautiful stroke Mace so confidently had, he sent the ball high into the air, directly on target with the flag waving softly in the breeze.

When they reached the clubhouse, the guys began unloading their golf clubs and putting each one into its correct position in the bag. Everyone but Owen that was, he never thought it mattered as he couldn't hit any of the clubs straight so he rarely paid attention to which club he pulled for a swing.

The heat was in full force now as the midday sun beamed its rays on them relentlessly. They were all drenched in sweat as the sun seemed to be baking the course underneath them. "Let's grab a drink and some chips before we go back to the room," Ty said as he adjusted his hat, wiping away the beading sweat.

Inside the course pro shop, it was small, but well stocked with merchandise from hats and shirts to golf balls and clubs. Mace wasted no time in gravitating over and selecting a couple new hats as he was often prone to do when out. The smell of burgers sizzling on the grill was enticing, their stomachs beginning to growl loudly, but reservations at the restaurant inside the casino held them back from indulging.

"Hey guys, did you have a good round?" a voice asked, emerging from a back stockroom in the shop.

Logan was always the first to talk to strangers, immediately turning towards the voice. Although he had a serious side with his golf game, he had a respectfulness that came out regardless of how he played. "We had a good time," he said, his tone polite. "We had some good shots and a few we want to forget before the tournament starts tomorrow," he said eliciting chuckles from Ty and Owen.

"If you need someone to explain to everyone at the tournament tomorrow where not to hit their ball, I'm your guy for that job," Owen said. "I stayed in the weeds today."

Meanwhile, Ty stood in front of the television, his hands perched on each hip, his neck straining to look upward at the screen. The PGA tour was on, round one taking place of the RBC

4

Heritage at Harbor Links in Hilton Head, South Carolina. "Let's go Scheffler, I need you to win me some money this weekend." Ty said as he watched, although the chances of him actually placing a bet would be slim.

On another television, the news played continuously, catching Logan's attention. "You guys seen this? These things going on this week? It seems coordinated, too many coincidences to be random."

Owen stepped over next to Logan, turning his attention to the news as well, before asking the pro shop employee to increase the volume. The news anchor was smiling and making small talk with his co-host before he turned serious as he began to read from the teleprompter.

"We've received reports of widespread internet outages across several major cities. Officials are blaming these disruptions on technical issues with service providers. While service is being restored in some areas, experts are warning of potential delays."

"People at multiple banks are reporting issues accessing their accounts. Banks are assuring customers that their funds are secure and that these issues are being resolved quickly."

The anchorman's expression wasn't selling what he was telling but he continued to read the script regardless.

"Flights at several major airports have been delayed due to what officials are calling 'software glitches' in air traffic control systems. The FAA has stated that there is no cause for concern and expects systems to return to normal shortly."

"Several federal and state government websites are currently inaccessible. A spokesperson for the Department of Homeland Security says they are investigating a potential cyberattack but assures the public all is safe."

That all felt the unease, but really, this was America, what's the wors that could happen?

"I didn't have any trouble with my flight thankfully. If they made me miss my golf weekend I would have been pissed!" Ty said as he had now joined Logan and Owen by the golf balls.

"That's the third time this week the banks have been down. They're not telling us something," Owen said, pushing his hands together and popping his knuckles loudly.

Mace who now had two hats, a pair of golf pants and a polo shirt in hand spoke up jokingly, "Maybe some kid in his basement is hacking the world. Couldn't be worse than my hacking from the bunker today."

The pro shop cashier watched along as well, chuckling at Mace's comment as he placed the items on the counter. "Our systems seem to be working fine, we haven't had any issues."

"The credit card machine better work, I need these new clothes for the weekend," Mace said with a wide smile, clearly forgetting his earlier frustrations on the course.

"Let's get back to the room, clean up and hit the casino," Ty said, slapping his hands together enthusiastically. "We may have to make a pit stop at Red Ranch Deli before we go, my tank needs some fuel before I roll the dice."

CHAPTER TWO
"Chips, Laughs and Brotherhood"

After a few loud knocks, Logan opened the door to his hotel room, Owen smiling widely.

"We got shirts!" Owen announced tossing one to Logan and another one to Ty. Owen and Mace were already dressed in their new shirts, wearing them with pride.

"These are sweet," Logan said holding up the shirt and reading the bold print aloud. "Red 30 Gang, I love it."

Owen had gotten the shirts made with their self-proclaimed team name along with dice, poker chips and playing cards. Logan stripped his shirt off, replacing it with the new one without hesitation, smiling in the mirror.

"Looks like you already got those clubs shined up," Owen said looking at Logan's bag. The clubs neatly arranged and ready for the start of the tournament tomorrow morning.

Logan was Mace's dad, and Owen's older brother. He was a big guy, towering at 6'3" with broad shoulders. He kept his salt and pepper hair neatly trimmed and his face clean shaven, the look reflecting a man who valued discipline. Logan liked practical clothing now after retiring from the military. He still carried himself with the military precision he had been accustomed to for over twenty years. His gear, whether golf or guns, was always well maintained. He played golf with a tactical focus, playing each hole as if planning a mission, each shot well thought out before swinging his club.

Logan deeply valued the camaraderie of this annual trip, enjoying laughing with the group, but remaining grounded.

Logan was regularly trying to encourage others to stay positive, especially on the golf course where tempers flared easily. He was one of those guys who carried a multi-tool in his bag 'just in case'. Logan was a stickler for time and proper preparation whether it was on the golf course, his job or taking out the trash on garbage day. He was awake bright and early every morning by 5:30 a.m., whether he had to be or not.

"I've got some buddies that are meeting us at the casino later, maybe," Mace said as he tossed sour patch kids into his mouth. "They wanted to play in the tournament this year, it gave them an excuse to leave Florida for a few days."

"Are you expecting snow, Ty?" Logan asked as they all turned to look at Ty, who was bundled in a large pull over as if he expected severe cold weather, while the others wore only t-shirts, and in Mace's case, even shorts instead of jeans.

Ty scrunched his face, "damn it, I knew this was overkill. It's a really nice pullover and I wanted to wear it. Not to mention they keep it so cold inside the casino."

"Winter will be here in about six months, you will be able to wear it then," Owen said with a laugh before Ty removed the pullover, neatly hanging it back on the rack.

They were staying at a modest hotel about a mile away from the casino, it was a perfect spot for their needs. The rooms were clean and had friendly staff, the coffee hot and showers strong. It was in close proximity to both the casino and the golf course, and was surrounded by several eateries, which they all enjoyed very much. Their routine each day usually consisted of breakfast at the hotel, lunch at Re Ranch Deli and dinner at the casino topped off by a nightcap at The Waffle Shack to top it off. This was in addition to the snacks they would load up on at the Food Lion next door, these guys loved to eat.

Tyler Bishop, or "Ty", was a stocky 5'9" with a build that reflected a guy who enjoyed retirement. His eyebrows rose dramatically with every expression, and his ever-present grin softened his otherwise serious demeanor. Like Logan, Ty had spent years in the military and maintained some habits, including his cropped hair style.

Ty was serious but also relaxed about his golf game, his self-awareness kept him grounded. He knew his limitations and often joked at his own expense. But beneath his easygoing exterior, Ty was watchful, like a cop scanning for trouble. The location didn't matter where, he was quick to act if he sensed a threat, a "shoot-first" mentality never far from the surface.

"I'm just going to do it, I'm making a parlay bet tonight," Ty declared on the car ride over, eliciting laughter from the others. He threatens to place bets every year but usually talks himself out of it when the time comes. He once studied a baseball bet for hours, before finally asking, "who's pitching?" By the time he had made his mind up, the game had already started, so he ordered a round of drinks and went back to studying future bets.

"You can hang with me tonight, Ty. We'll just play some roulette and win some money that way," Mace said, knowing Ty wasn't likely to do that either.

Pulling into the casino parking lot, Logan directed Mace. "There's a charging station right near the door, pull in there," Mace maneuvered his Tesla into position.

"Why in the world did you buy a Tesla?" Owen asked. "I hear the batteries are crazy expensive to replace in these things?"

"See, there you go, talking about a good car," Mace snapped back, his ego hurt by the insinuation his Tesla wasn't a smart purchase. "In the long run it pays off. You're listening to the wrong people," Mace continued before taking off towards the casino entrance. He never hesitated, always in a hurry and on the move when it came time to gamble.

Logan nudged Owen. "He already told me he was sick of finding charging stations and was trading the car when we get back home."

Before getting on the elevator, the gang posed for a quick selfie in their new shirts. Mace, Logan and Owen smiled wide for the camera while Ty looked like he was already on watch duty, ready to strike.

"One more stop before we hit the casino floor," Logan said as they all paused near the escalator. "We need our Bean and Brew coffee."

"Ah hell, Dad, I thought you were serious. We don't need no Bean and Brew coffees, Uncle Owen got you guys hooked on those," Mace said with his boyish grin.

"He got me hooked on them, I'm in, let's get one," Ty said starting down the escalator.

"I'm not going down there, I'll see you guys in the sportsbook," Mace said as he began walking onward.

"What kind do you want me to bring you?" Owen called out to Mace as he walked off.

"Caramel macchiato!" Mace shouted back without turning.

Logan let out a chuckle, "you knew he would want one. His money is burning a hole in his pocket to get those bets started. He will have fifteen made by the time we get in there."

Inside the sportsbook, the guys settled into plush leather chairs, coffees in hand, watching rows of games showing on the numerous massive screens. They each sipped their coffee, their eyes darting between the various games. That was everyone except Mace, who stood at a kiosk selecting bets, his stack of bet slips growing as he placed wager after wager.

Suddenly Owen sputtered on his drink, struggling to hold back his laughter, while Logan tried to turn his face away to fight back his reactions.

"Did you just see that? What in the hell was that guy doing?" Ty asked, stone-faced.

"You okay?" Mace asked the man as he walked by him, others already helping to pick the guy up from the floor. The man riding on a motorized scooter had driven into a reclining chair, tipping himself over and spilling onto the floor. Casino staff rushed to help him up, but Owen and Logan turned away, shoulders shaking with suppressed laughter.

"Clearly drinking and driving is allowed inside this casino," Ty said, brows raised as he sipped his drink.

"With these prices on drinks, he couldn't have had that many," Owen offered, always one to complain about the price of drinks in the casino or anywhere else for that matter.

As the hours went by, failed bet slips began going into the loser pile, but the guys continued to enjoy the games, their spirits high for the next big win. They would watch sports, then navigate through the slot machines to the table games, looking for the next hot bet. Roulette was often a favorite game they enjoyed, placing chips on their numbers and watching the wheel spin, waiting for that little ball to catch and begin bouncing wildly. The thrill of where it stopped making everyone at the table hold their breath in anticipation as it held their attention.

As the night progressed, Owen found himself playing at a table with an older gentleman. While Owen would wager one-dollar chips onto the table, totaling twenty-five to thirty dollars per spin, the man would place five-hundred-dollar chips with each spin. He was a high roller and people paid attention.

"You're a big bettor," someone finally said to him. "What do you do for a living?"

The older man who hadn't spoken yet, looked at him, his eyes cold, as if contemplating his answer. As his words rolled out, he had a thick Russian accent full of menace. "I teach good people, how to kill bad people."

Owen didn't respond, turning his attention away and exchanging a glance with Logan, who chuckled. Owen played one more spin at the table before he collected his chips and stepped away, joining Logan who was watching the action.

"Did you hear what he said?" Owen asked his brother.

Logan smiled, "I think he's full of shit, he's also drunk and pissed his pants."

Owen shrugged, not sure if the man was telling the truth or not, but one thing he knew, the guy was sure throwing out some big money on the game, far more than he would do.

Ty went by the bar, getting a round of drinks for everyone except Mace, who rarely drank alcohol. He would occasionally have one of the fruity, girly drinks Owen called them, but it was usually a soda you would see in his cup. As Logan, Ty and Owen watched Mace playing roulette, his enthusiasm was contagious, everyone at the table following his lead and playing his numbers. "Let's go Red 30, hit me this time!" Mace would shout to the agreement of everyone at the table.

"Look at the television, another alert," Logan said to Ty and Owen. The screen above the roulette wheel, was showing an NBA basketball game, but underneath a scroll bar rolled along.

"The stock market has taken a sharp dip today following reports of technical disruptions, with tech and finance sectors seeing the largest losses. Economists are warning that if these issues persist, they could have ripple effects."

"There goes my 401k," Logan said with a dry chuckle, his eyes darting around the bustling casino floor. "Something's going on," he said looking back at the news flash.

The games were noisy as people tossed chips, clinking down on the table, while others were rapidly pressing buttons on the slot machines, making it hard to hear one another without leaning in close.

Ty edged nearer, his voice low but urgent as he addressed Logan and Owen. "I meant to tell you earlier, I called my brother Ethan. You know he works as a specialist for 'SIGINTL'. He said shipping companies are reporting disruptions at multiple ports as well. They suspect it's tied to software malfunctions affecting global logistics networks."

Owen's brow furrowed as he was clearly puzzled, "What is 'SIGINTL'?"

Logan answered for Ty. "His brother's got the inside track on everything. If there's a storm brewing, Ethan's the guy who knows about it."

Ty nodded and offered more clarity. "It's the Signals Intelligence Specialists. They monitor signals and interpret communications around the globe. They have quick updates on information, digging into what's credible and what's noise."

Ty's brother Ethan, was an Air Defense Officer, assigned to NORAD in Colorado Springs. He had spent his career defending U.S. air space and critical infrastructure. This made him privileged to top security information and high-level intel. Ethan was the kind of person everyone wanted to know and wanted on speed dial. For Ty, that privilege came naturally.

Owen thought about that, then tilted his head, processing the information before breaking into a grin. "That sounds like a pretty cool position to be in. Tell him to turn off Mace's credit card before he maxes it out."

This lightened the growing tension somewhat as they each laughed for a moment.

"He is going to call me back tomorrow, he wasn't in a position to talk much," Ty added as they shifted their attention back to the screen.

They watched for a few more minutes as the news from earlier was being replayed again. The gang all went back to their drinks and watched Mace sort his chips for another round. The news pushed to the back of their thoughts. Moving in to play alongside Mace now, the dealer switched out on the roulette wheel. The new dealer, a woman in her forties, with fiery red hair straight out of an '80s rock video, smiled bright.

Mace clapped his hands together and picked up a stack of chips, "bring us some luck, we need to win! Let's go Red30", he called out as she smiled.

Logan always being polite and courteous, smiled at the dealer. "Hello, what's your name?"

The woman grinned, her smile warm and genuine. "They call me Big Red. You all ready to play?"

Owen held his fingers on a chip he had slid onto the board. "What's your favorite number, Big Red? I'll bet for you."

Big Red's laugh was hearty, and her response came with a wink. "My favorite number's '69' baby, but it's not on this board."

They erupted into laughter, with Owen blushing furiously as he looked at the floor, his pale skin glowing red in the aftermath of the unexpected comment.

The gang played out the night, winning some, losing more, but having a blast of fun together as they took turns buying rounds of drinks. The laughter, fellowship, and endless rounds made the losses bearable.

When the games wound down, Logan checked his watch. "Alright, gang, the practice rounds done. The real tournament starts tomorrow. Let's hit the hotel and get some sleep."

"Not on an empty stomach," Ty declared. "Waffle Shack first! We want Waffle Shack!" he protested loudly.

The group agreed to this unanimously, filing out of the casino into the cool night air, their laughter carrying into the parking lot as they set off for one last indulgence before bed.

CHAPTER THREE

"Rumors in the Rain"

"Rise and shine," Logan announced as he pushed open the connecting door between their hotel rooms, his voice cutting through the morning stillness.

Owen groaned as he stretched, rolling his shoulders in an attempt to shake off the remnants of sleep. "Good morning, brother. You ready to take an early lead today?"

Mace sat up, grabbing his phone, focusing intently and scrolling through text messages. It was his routine, clearing work orders first thing before shifting gears to enjoy the day.

"I'm hoping we get to play today," Logan said as he scanned the weather forecast on his phone. "Rain is moving in."

Owen went downstairs to the hotel lobby to wait for the others for breakfast. They had biscuits and gravy with an assortment of cereals, yogurts and bagels, hearty enough to get the day moving forward. The rain was lightly tapping against the windows, not what the guys wanted to see before their scheduled tee times this morning. Owen took a seat by the window, sipping his coffee as he continued to wake himself.

Once everyone was downstairs, two of Mace's friends who had arrived late the previous night joined the group. One of them, was a young man named Caleb, in his mid-twenties. He was short with a slim build, wearing glasses he adjusted regularly on his face. Caleb was timid, often times indecisive in his decision making. He was easily influenced by others and lacked awareness of events and situations around him. He was a good guy, longtime friends with Mace as they had played golf together in high school.

Another friend of Mace's that came along was Dylan. He was a tall and lanky guy, somewhat awkward in his movements. Dylan often was gullible, easily duped into being the butt of most jokes. Being a good sport, he takes it all in stride and typically makes fun of himself for his attempt at jokes at the wrong time. He doesn't take things too seriously, just going with the flow of others and keeping the tension to a minimum.

Each player came well dressed for success, however, on the course that meant little when it came to actually hitting the ball. They each had high hopes for the first round of action, ready to lead their respective flights. Then there was Jordan, who emerged from the elevator with a confident stride.

"Here he comes," Logan announced. "He has the walk of a champion." Logan added with a slight chuckle.

Jordan hadn't been in Mace's circle of friends for long, they had met on the golf course a couple years ago. Their mutual shared enjoyment for golf and gambling quickly bonded the two men. Jordan was average height at 5'10" with a lean and athletic build, he carried himself with a quiet confidence. Unlike Caleb and Dylan, he was a resourceful guy, observant of his surroundings. Usually level-headed, he has a solid grasp on his life, a steady presence amid the group's mix of personalities.

Following a moment of introduction for the friends meeting Owen and Ty for the first time, they were loading up their gear, ready for the drive to the course.

Logan patted Owen on the back. "You going to be okay today, brother? I hate to leave you alone here."

Owen took the final sip of his coffee, mumbling under his breath as he wrestled pushing open the trash can lid to dispose of his napkin and half-eaten donut. "I'm good, you all go have fun. I'm going to hit the flea market. If I have time, I'll drive into Waynesville and go by the prepper store."

Owen left, rain falling lightly on his windshield, the wipers slowly clearing it away. He wanted to visit a store he had been told about selling prepping items and survival gadgets. In route, he stopped by a flea market he had seen days earlier, knowing he had some time to kill. It was typical, vendors hawking antique items, tools and second-hand clothes. The people were friendly, the conversations a welcome distraction.

Owen found something of interest as he dabbled about the market. It cost him $8 dollars, but he purchased a bag of beef jerky, tearing into it instantly and sampling the product. The jerky had a nice seasoning blend to the taste, tender and scrumptious. Owen purchased three more bags, tucking them into pockets on his cargo pants.

"Looking for anything particular, young man?" Owen was asked by an old man in overalls, reclined back in an old worn and battered chair. His long white beard rested against his chest, and his weathered eyes glinted behind thick glasses.

Owen swallowed his jerky, nodding a smile to the man. "Mainly browsing," he said. "I wouldn't mind finding an Army surplus store, know of any?"

The old-timer leaned forward, gripping the straps of his overall bibs. "You're at the right place, that next building over, has plenty of that prepper type stuff."

"I appreciate that, I'll check it out," Owen replied.

The man looked at him, curiosity in his eyes. "What do you think about these credit card machines not working today? I don't like them, never have. I do cash for all transactions."

Owen smiled, he could see the man wanted to talk. "I didn't know they stopped working today. That's interesting."

"Oh yeah, nobody here can use cards today. I think the government is up to something, they're going to pull the wool over our eyes," the man said, his eyes narrowing as he looked hard at Owen. "They grounded flights out of Ashville this morning, something about the computer networks acting up."

"I'll need to look into this, something does seem fishy," Owen said as he reached out his hand to shake the man's. "I better get moving, but it was good speaking with you."

The man shook his hand, nodding a smile in return. "You keep your eyes open, don't trust anyone."

Owen walked away, his mind wondering what might be taking place. He needed to check the news and get some more information. He looked at his phone, clicking on the internet browser but his weak signal wasn't strong enough to load the page, leaving him even more confused if he simply had a bad signal or was his service being interfered with.

"Welcome, come on in. Take a look around, the more you buy the better deal I can do for you," a man said to Owen as he entered the army surplus supply section of the market.

Owen gave a slight smile as he browsed over the items. "Thank you, from what I'm hearing this might be a good time to be stocking up supplies." Owen wanted to let this man have the opportunity to tell him what he thought about the situation taking place, was there even a situation, or simply some software problems "I'm hearing software glitches, banking issues, you hearing much about it?"

The store owner continued adjusting a few items on his counter, before giving Owen a sharp look, gauging his demeanor. Owen could tell the man wasn't a trusting person, probably wondering if Owen was an average Joe or someone with the government.

"Oh, I've heard plenty. Folks think it's just some tech hiccup, but I'm not so sure. First, it's the banks, then shipping delays." He continued looking at Owen, beginning to question himself about this stranger walking into his store.

Owen could sense his hesitation, so he offered some calming information to help ease the man's mind. "My friends are over at Cedar Hollow playing golf today. I'm no good so I came out to browse until they finished. Then it's casino time!" Owen said with a fist pump and smile at the man.

This must have helped some as the man grinned at Owens gesture. "It's interesting as well the power grid has been acting up this morning. Call me paranoid, but I've been in this business long enough to know when there's more going on that meets the eye."

"So, you think it's something bigger? That's been my thinking, just not sure what exactly," Owen said as he leaned close to the counter. He held his hand out, shaking the store owner's. "My name's Owen."

The store owner gave him a firm shake, "I'm Marty." He looked around the empty store, as if checking for eavesdroppers. "It wouldn't surprise me. Cyberattacks, government experiments gone wrong. Hell, who knows? But I'll tell you this, when the systems start failing, people get scared." Marty said, nodding to Owen, his expression becoming more serious. "Scared people do stupid things. You don't want to be out there when the panic sets in."

This man wasn't some anti-government nut, well maybe he was, but one thing Owen knew is this man realized the impact of scared people in need and their willingness to better themselves at any cost.

"That's why I'm here. Figured it's better to be prepared than caught off guard," Owen said, his eyes moving across the room of supplies.

Marty nodded in agreement. "Smart move. Most folks wait too long, thinking someone's gonna come save 'em. Ain't gonna happen. My advice? Stock up on water, ammo, and things you can trade. If this keeps up, money's not gonna mean much for long."

"What about you? You seeing more folks coming in this week with the same idea?" Owen asked him, possibly overreaching with the question.

Marty again grinned slightly, leaning on the counter. "Every day. Some just browsing, others clearing me out of MREs and first aid kits like it's the end of the world. Can't say I blame 'em. I've been stocking up myself, just in case."

"These are nice patches, I've never seen this one with the arrows," Owen said, pointing to a patch with two arrows broken.

Marty removed it from the case, holding it out to Owen. "It's a local group in Cherokee, but you've got to be a member for me to sell you one. You're not from this area so I can tell you that rules you out." The man smiled at Owen, returning the patch. "Not that you'd want to join them."

"My friends and I need a patch with our name, Red 30 Gang," Owen said, his happiness obvious.

"Red 30, like the roulette game?" Marty asked.

"That's it, it's what we call ourselves."

The rain was beginning to dance louder on the metal roof of the building. "What would you recommend, Marty? If you were, let's say, hypothetically, far from home. What would you buy here just in case something bad may be taking place?"

Marty rubbed his chin, his eyes narrowed further as he studied the question. "Depending on how much you want to spend, I'd go with MREs, water purification tablets and mess kits. I've got camping stoves and portable cooking kits on the back shelf."

Owen nodded in agreement, taking a deep breath as he looked over the shelves once more. "I tell you what, Marty. How about you walk with me and let's pick out a few things."

Marty helped Owen around the store, finding and suggesting different gear. The men talked deeper about the government and who might be behind some of the incidents taking place. It was no serious friendship, but the men developed some signs of trust and respect for one another. Marty helped Owen get the supplies he purchased outside to his truck and loaded into the back.

"It's been a pleasure, Owen, and not just because I got some of your money," Marty said with a chuckle as he shook hands once again with Owen.

Owen smiled, patting Marty on the back. "In case it gets bad, you take care of yourself, Marty. It's been a pleasure meeting as well as doing business with you."

Marty smiled faintly, his hand lingering on the edge of Owen's truck bed. "You too, son. Keep your head on a swivel and don't take anyone at face value. If you find yourself back this way, stop in. Well, if I'm still here that is."

Owen nodded, understanding the weight of Marty's words. The rain tapped steadily on the truck roof as if urging him to move along. He gave Marty a wave and pulled out.

The uneasy feeling from earlier lingered, growing with each mile. He turned on the radio, searching for news, but static dominated the airwaves. The faint voices he caught between stations only hinted at technical difficulties and vague reassurances, nothing meaty.

He tightened his grip on the steering wheel, his mind racing. If this really was more than a glitch happening, things could unravel quickly. He replayed Marty's words in his head knowing he was correct. Scared people do stupid things. Owen couldn't shake the image of crowded grocery stores, gas stations, and highways if panic set in.

Owen decided to make a few more stops before going back to the hotel, the last being at a convenient store. It was the kind of station Owen liked, small with a single attendant and a handful of old pumps. Inside, he picked up several items, cases of water, protein bars and packs of toilet tissue. The cashier, an older woman with sharp eyes, gave him a knowing look as she rang up his items.

"Storm prepping or something else?" she asked, her voice cutting through the low hum of the overhead lights. "We're only accepting cash, like the sign says on the door."

21

Owen hesitated for a moment, then offered a half-smile. "A little bit of both, you could say, seems like a good day to stock up. I do have cash, no worries."

Owen walked out, loading his supplies into the truck, before noticing a small sticker pasted on the gas pumps. The sticker, two broken arrows, same as the patch. "Neat logo."

At the hotel, Owen waited in the lobby for the guys to return from golf. The weather had rained on and off, probably making for an uncomfortable day on the course. He felt bad for them knowing how they had looked forward to playing.

"Have you been busy today?" Owen asked the receptionist at the front desk while he waited.

She looked up over the counter, her eyes showing confusion as she gently squeezed her lips together in thought. "It's been slow so far. This credit card machine won't work, and I've been trying to figure it out. I can't get ahold of customer service at the merchant so I'm unsure of what to do with it."

Owen had asked about the day, mainly being polite as he drank coffee in the lobby. His attention peaked when she told him. "It's not just here, I've heard other places lost service."

Looking out the large windows of the lobby, he seen the guys turning into the parking lot. He walked out to meet them, staying underneath the car canopy as not to get wet in the rain.

"You guys look like a hot shower might do you some good," Owen called out, laughing at the weary faces as they approached him, golf bags in tow.

Logan nodded as he approached, "how'd the flea market treat you?" His usual grin replaced with a more serious expression. "The thought of a hot shower sounds like a life saver right now."

Owen smiled, "you boys get cleaned up, I'll be here in the lobby. We'll get some food at the Red Ranch Deli and catch up on the day."

CHAPTER FOUR
"Under Heavy Skies"

After the Red 30 gang regrouped in the lobby, their smiles held a mix of both fatigue and satisfaction. The sporadic rain had been relentless, leaving them drenched and tired, but the fellowship kept their spirits high, as did the bourbon.

"Let's hear it, somebody tell me who is leading the tournament," Owen said, his tone light but curious. He didn't need an answer to know, Mace's grin said it all.

Mace spread his arms wide, his confidence radiating before he even opened his mouth. "It's like this, Uncle Owen, I didn't come here to lose." He punctuated his words with a playful practice swing into the air. "I got a two-shot lead on the suckers in 'Champ' flight after today's round."

Logan stood quietly, his proud smile the only giveaway of his thoughts. "He had a great round, even in this mess," he said, gesturing toward the window, where thick, low-hanging clouds pressed heavily against the horizon. "Ty wasn't far behind in 'B' flight, he's only three strokes back of the leader."

Ty chuckled and shook his head. "Go-ahead asshole, tell him who I'm trailing by those three strokes. Don't be shy now."

Logan's smirk widened, but he stayed silent. Owen caught the exchange immediately. "Don't tell me... you're leading the 'B' flight huh? Way to go, Big Dawg!"

"It's just day one," Logan replied with a shrug, though the hint of pride in his voice didn't go unnoticed. "Two more rounds to play," Logan replied. "Let's go see if we can win some money tonight. Loser buys drinks."

They stepped outside, their laughter lingering as they made their way to Owen's truck. A large tarp covered the bed that hadn't been there earlier in the morning.

Owen looked at the clouds as they exited, "That cloud cover has been relentless all day. It wasn't just rain, it felt like the sky itself was pushing down." He waved his hand towards the cloud, as if pushing them away.

Ty laughed, shaking off some droplets of rain from his hat. "Hell, we weren't just playing golf, on some holes we were swimming out there."

Logan joined the conversation, adding something Owen had noticed himself today. "Those clouds made it dark enough to feel like late evening instead of mid-afternoon. I think we got lucky it never came a hard downpour on us."

"What's in the truck?" Ty asked, craning his neck to look under the tarp.

Owen chuckled as he dropped the tailgate, revealing a haul of supplies. "Stopped by an Army surplus store today near the flea market. Met a guy who seemed to have his head on straight and made a few purchases."

"What kind of stuff?" Ty asked again, his curiosity piqued.

Owen gestured to the pile. "I got MREs, thermal blankets, tactical gloves, ponchos, boots, netting, tarps. There's also a box of knives, hatchets, flashlights and batteries. I got some extra for you all, the guy gave me a better deal for buying in bulk. Got some big army tents in there also."

Logan's eyebrows lifted as he scanned the supplies. "Nice haul, brother. What about first aid, did you find any?"

Owen grinned knowingly. "Not from this stop. But I got backpacks, maps, compasses, solar chargers, duct tape and fishing gear."

"That's still a solid haul," Ty said, picking up a fire starter kit and examining it.

24

Owen leaned against the truck bed. "I found first aid supplies at a prepper store in Waynesville. I got First aid kits, tourniquets and trauma gear. I have antiseptics and bandages and several different over the counter meds."

Logan gave an approving nod. "Attaboy, you're ready for the shit to hit the fan."

Mace wandered over, tossing gummy candies into his mouth. "What the hell are you expecting to happen, Uncle Owen?" he asked, smirking. "We aren't in an apocalypse."

Owen just laughed as he pulled Mace into a quick bear hug. "Just staying ready for when the world puts the squeeze on us little buddy. "The ponchos are for the storm putting the squeeze on you boys," he said chuckling with Mace.

Mace, oblivious to the severity of the underlying conversation, patted his uncle on the shoulder. "Whatever's brewing better hold off until after I get my next round in tomorrow."

Logan and Ty exchanged a glance, their expressions thoughtful. Owen caught it instantly. "What's that look about?" he asked as Mace climbed into the truck bed to rummage through the supplies.

"It was interesting, the credit card machine was down and the internet today," Logan said, pulling a yellow handwritten charge slip from his wallet. The guy at the clubhouse had us sign these instead. Said we'd settle up Sunday when the machines were back online."

Ty held up a similar slip, waving it in the air. "I bought one Gatorade," he said with a laugh. "Same deal, pay later when the system's back up, no interest."

Logan clenched his jaw and rolled his neck, a loud crack sending chills down Owen's back. "It's hard to imagine we could actually have a societal breakdown on a large scale. However it's obvious we're all thinking something, let's stay alert."

Owen nodded slowly, his face tightening. "Same thing at the stores I hit. I had to pay with cash everywhere," Owen said nodding to the items in the truck. "This is concerning me a little more and more, something is.....well, it's off."

Mace jumped down from the truck, brushing his hands together. "I just hope the casino is working, I need to win some of their money." He jabbed Logan's shoulder. "Come on, old man. We've got money to win, let's get to it."

They all carpooled together, piling into Mace's Tesla to take advantage of the reserved parking near the entrance.

"I'm not sure what's going on, but we should be safe here," Ty said, his voice touched with sarcasm. "Can't see anyone wanting to bomb Cherokee." He chuckled uneasily. "My brother is supposed to call tonight with an update."

There was no response to Ty's statement, the mood turning somber, his words sinking in. Each man wrestled with the growing unease, each one except for Mace who was counting his winnings before they had even arrived.

Inside the casino, the atmosphere was lively. Smiling patrons wandered between the sportsbook, slot machines, and table games. But beneath the surface, tensions lingered. It was easy to overhear a conversation about the recent outages, as those buzzed in small clusters. For some, it was a passing inconvenience. For others, a sign of something far worse.

"It's time for our dinner my good men, are we hungry?" Owen announced, trying to inject some normalcy.

Owen was the group's organizer, more of a self-appointed position. He really wanted the guys to relax and enjoy these weekends, trying to make sure the small details were in order. Golf was certainly not his strong suit, he only played the practice round for fun. Planning, however, that was his wheelhouse. Being sure to have the mini fridge stocked with cold beer upon everyone's arrival, well, he could handle that.

Owen was a cautious man, when it came to trusting, being burned too many times in the past. Analyzing people's movements and behaviors, paying attention to their languages, that was his routine. He saw himself as protector against anyone who threatened them. Always the competitive one, but humble, preparing for the worst.

"I'm starved, let's do it," Ty said, feeling good after being a few Crown Royal drinks deep.

The guys had chosen to eat in a different restaurant tonight, Owen had booked reservations in a brewery. The food was simple, burgers and sandwiches.

"I tell you one thing about this 'devils' mustard', seems like it's straight out of a baby's bottom," Owen said, grimacing as he wiped the sauce off his bun. "I'm gonna need to find a dog and lick it's ass to get this taste out of my mouth."

As if on que, a barking dog in a baby stroller passed by, its owner oblivious to the group's amusement. Drinks nearly spilled as they erupted into uncontrollable laughing at the coincidence. The dog's multiple barks seemed to call out to Owen that it would volunteer for the assignment.

"There is no way in hell we could ever explain that one to somebody. That was too funny," Logan said as he leaned back, patting his belly firmly. "I'm full, at least until we hit the Waffle Shack later."

Following dinner, Owen picked up the tab, paying in cash as they were warned before dining was the only option. Ty stretched and rubbed his stomach softly. "I'm gonna hit the head, meet you all in the sportsbook."

The night was going smoothly, their bets hitting as Mace racked up wins on basketball and baseball games. They made jokes about needing to get sleep, being too old for the long hours and keeping up with Mace. This was the fun of their trips, hearty ribbing on one another, bet slips, casino chips and long days on the fairways.

CHAPTER FIVE

"When Panic Strikes"

The small screen in the sportsbook had been scrolling breaking news across the ticker, *"Cybersecurity Breach Disrupts Financial Systems across the East Coast- spreading to West Coast states."*

"Look!" Ty exclaimed, grabbing Logan's sleeve and jerking his attention to the screen. "Holy shit."

The scrolling headline changed, prompting a few people to pause, though most remained glued to the games.

"China strikes Taiwan – U.S. sends multiple 'Carrier Strike Groups', guided-missile destroyers, and submarines to counter aggressions."

Logan's jaw tightened. "This leaves key areas wide open. The Coast Guard can't fill in all those gaps."

Ty looked at the screen, "you're right, we're going to have unguarded areas," he said before brushing it away from mind.

They continued their night, trying to enjoy the good times, but often checking the screens for further news. More drinks flowed, more betting slips piled up and once again Mace had disappeared into the sea of gaming tables.

The news channel had changed, its latest message going unnoticed. *"Incoming attacks imminent – Seek shelter immediately."*

"It's time for another round of drinks," Logan announced as he finished off his beer, slamming the can down with a smile.

Before Ty could respond, his phone buzzed violently in

his pocket, startling him. He fumbled to retrieve it and held it up for Logan to see: 'Little Bro – Ethan'.

"Hey, Ethan, we seen this news on China and Taiwan. What' going on?" Ty asked quickly, placing the phone on speaker and holding it between Logan and himself.

"Listen to me, Ty," Ethan's voice was tense, each word sharp and deliberate. "This should have been reported earlier. We're already at war, nobody knew it. We've been in a silent war behind the scenes for months now. China, Russia, North Korea and Iran have been plotting this against us, it's full-scale now, Ty." Ethan said, panic in his voice as he stressed each word.

"Full-scale?" Ty repeated, his voice rising above the multiple voices conversating in the sportsbook. "We're at war! Like right now, we're at war now?" Ty asked, looking at Logan who had pulled Owen into the conversation to hear for himself.

"We've been hit with cyberattacks and we have physical attacks happening now. China sent in their long-hidden Shadow Talon-9 fighter jets along with their Black Mirage-24 stealth bombers. We had no idea, they evaded all our radar detection, slipping past like ghost." Ethan replied.

"What's the plan, Ethan?" Ty asked, his fingers frantically trying to type a text as he spoke.

"They have commercial airlines, cargo planes and a shit-ton of drones swarming in our airspace now. China attacking Taiwan was the bait. They wanted us distracted while they moved on our coastlines."

"Where are you, Ethan? Are you staying put or leaving?" Ty asked, glancing at Logan.

"I'm on the base, we're about to be briefed, I'm not sure how much time I have. Listen to me, Ty, we're tracking missile strikes, cruise and ballistic. Submarines are launching them. It's chaos here. They've probably got EMPs lined up and we're bracing for ground invasions. Ty.... this is going to cripple us." Ethan said, his voice strained with concern.

Ty's voice cracked. "Stay safe, Ethan, I...," Ty was struggling to find the words he needed, stunned that this was a war developing on American soil.

"They are targeting critical infrastructure. We have mass casualties...." Ethan's voice cut off as a deafening BOOM exploded in the background, followed by static.

"Ethan! Ethan!" Ty shouted, gripping the phone tighter as his hand shook. "Are you there? Can you hear me?"

The line crackled. "I'm here." Ethan's voice returned, breathless and strained. "We've got incoming-" A sudden crash cut him off followed by muffled shouting. "Scramble! Scram..."

The call went dead.

Ty lowered the phone, his face frozen. "Logan...?" he said, looking to Logan for an answer, for anything to say this didn't just happen.

Logan stood, swallowing hard, glancing around nervously. They had a small group of men listening in now on the call, their postures rigid and military-like that had paused nearby. Without a word, they turned and disappeared down a side exit from the sportsbook.

"We don't know what happened, Ty, he's probably okay," Logan said, though his tone betrayed his own uncertainty. "The cell tower must have gone down, he'll be okay on base."

Owen grabbed their arms. "We need to find Mace. He was going to the roulette tables. Let's grab him before people panic. We can get back to the hotel and make a plan."

Logan nodded. Together, they wove through the growing commotion toward the table games.

"Hell yeah!" Mace's triumphant yell cut through the crowd as his number, Red 30, hit. It was great timing as his raised arms and loud yell made him easy to spot.

"We got to go Mace, we'll explain outside, the shit's about to hit the fan!" Logan hissed, wrapping an arm around Mace and pulling him close. "Just move."

Mace barely had time to register Logan's urgency, "what do you...." Mace began to ask when the sirens in the casino began to shrill loudly from overhead. The blaring sound halted the casino floor. Everyone's mouths were silent instantly as players and dealers looked upwards for the source of the sound.

The casino public address system began, the sirens temporarily stopping as everyone listened intently.

'This is not a drill. Please begin exiting in an orderly fashion to the nearest exit immediately."

"Orderly fashion, my ass!" someone shouted as chaos erupted.

"Hell no, we aren't leaving! Not without our money!" another man shouted as casino staff began pulling chips away from the tables, loading them onto carts.

"Take your chips, they will be good once we reopen!" a small man who was a pit boss shouted. It was of little interest as the panic was setting in for many people, the reassurances falling on deaf ears.

All the televisions were switched to breaking emergency reports showing much of the same information Ty's brother had just explained to him along with video footage.

"This is about to turn into complete chaos, it's going to be a stampede." Logan said as he held his arms in front of the guys pulling them back out of the main path.

The sirens resumed, heightening the tension and panic on the floor, some patrons had now seen the breaking news. Many others only watched the cash and chips being shuffled away, adding to their rage.

Angry players began grabbing at chips, cash and bus carts as security attempted to roll them away, heading for the safety of the casino vault. Dealers tried pushing back the rowdy gamblers, some of which were climbing across the tables now in a mad effort to claim their money. Punches were being thrown at casino security who were overwhelmed with the outbreaking

31

riot, there simply wasn't enough of them. The twenty-five or so low trained security personnel, along with the six or eight highly trained undercover guards simply weren't enough against the hundreds of angry and drunken players.

The casino wasted no time employing additional security measures, many never before seen. The ceiling panels opened in several locations, allowing multiple drones to descend. The drones buzzed ominously as they captured footage of the rioting crowd. This was an added security measure in the event of a riot on the casino floor.

Ear splitting noise beyond the sirens blaring began to penetrate the casino. It was a high frequency sound deterrent system to paralyze many players as they fell to the floor, covering their ears. This included the 'Red 30 Gang', who huddled together trying to contemplate a plan of action amongst the chaotic moment.

Logan tapped them on the shoulder, motioning to follow him as he moved along the wall. The flashing strobe lights had a disorienting effect on the patrons as many were now down on their hands and knees trying to block out all the various sounds being used against them.

Exiting the table game area and clearing most of the machines, the guys paused by a long hallway, the sound not as loud and excruciating.

"Do we try to reach the parking garage or cut through one of these hallways?" Logan shouted, pointing to a dimly lit hallway where security personnel had just scurried down.

Ty squinted as a guard at the end of the hallway activated a series of red beams that stretched floor to ceiling with a mechanical groan. The glow of a red sign illuminated brightly, "Do Not Enter – Restricted Area – High Voltage".

"I don't think that's an option," Ty said loudly, backing away as another man near them scoffed.

"High voltage, my ass," the man grumbled, sprinting toward the hallway.

Logan's eyes tightened as he watched the man, seemingly trying to escape the nightmare inside. The security measures were working in many ways, the only problem, this wasn't a simple riot, and all the various control methods were creating more havoc than help.

Red 30 froze, watching as the man reached the lasers, wobbling like a penguin as he ran. He entered into the beams, the tiny unseen wires wrapping him up like a spider web as the voltage coursed through his body like blood in his veins. His life zapped away as his body fell to the floor in a heap.

"What the hell?" Mace shouted, looking at his father with a sense of shock he had never imagined before.

Logan and Ty had seen plenty during their time in the military, but nothing quite like what they had just witnessed. "Move!" Logan commanded. Each man held a hand on the man in front as they moved in a combat crouch together, weaving through the melee and disoriented guests.

Patrons were rushing from the casino, many being trampled as they fell and were unable to get back up. The casino floor had turned into a battlefield as drones continued to whirl overhead and guards struggled to maintain order.

Exiting the casino area, the guys ran up the ramp on the long route towards the parking garage. Slightly out of shape, their lungs burned with each step. The hall was filling quickly as people were beginning to bottleneck near the elevators at the end of the ramp. They didn't hesitate, pushing their way through until exiting the doors onto the parking level two.

Finally, the deafening sound of the sirens had relented, and they stopped to catch their breath by the garage wall.

"Now what?" Ty asked, his voice trembling.

Logan scanned the garage, his expression grim. "Now. Now we figure out how to survive and we bet on ourselves."

33

CHAPTER SIX

"Inferno in the Garage"

Ty ran back to the group after inspecting the exit out of the parking garage, his expression tense. "We have a problem," he said, his jaw tightening. "We're not getting the car out."

Mace's head snapped up, his eyes narrowing as he instinctively glanced toward his car, which sat untouched. "Why not? The car's fine-we've got enough charge to move."

Ty shook his head grimly. "It's not the car. Go look at the exit ramp. The lockdown barriers have risen, blocking the way out. Probably a security measure in case of a robbery."

Logan's eyes darted around the garage. Crowds of people were streaming through the doorway and scattering into the parking structure, their frantic movements adding to the chaos. "That's bad. Really bad. The hotel's only a mile or so from here. We can hoof it on foot if we need to."

The noise around them grew, blaring car horns, the shrill wails of alarms, and angry shouts. The noise made it difficult to think. Ty added, "Even if we get past the barriers, there's a drop gate blocking the exit. If that opened, there's a pile-up, several cars that have hit one another, it's like sand in an hourglass." He slammed his fist against his palm in frustration.

Mace didn't wait. He sprinted to the edge of the garage and climbed onto a car parked near the corner. From his elevated view, he cursed. "Damn!" he grumbled, his voice echoing in the concrete space. From his vantage point, the scene below was worse than Ty described. Cars were in a tangled mess, and a growing crowd was swarming the barriers, pulling at the drop gate in desperation. Others hammered at the gates with crowbars or whatever they could find. Drivers honking furiously as if noise alone would clear the way.

People were abandoning their vehicles, forming a restless crowd near the barriers as they opted to flee on foot. They shouted at the security cameras mounted throughout the garage, demanding answers and for their cars to be released from confinement. Many began moving back into the building.

Logan peered over the edge of the second floor, assessing the height. "If I were twenty years younger, I'd try climbing over the side or rappelling down," he shouted over the noise.

A loud crash nearby made everyone flinch as a car had reversed into a pillar, its bumper crumpled as the driver screamed in frustration. Another vehicle revved aggressively, trying to ram the barriers, but only managed to damage its front end. Smoke began wafting up from the engine, adding a burnt stench to the already uncomfortable air in the chaos.

Owen's attention shifted to an elderly couple near an SUV. The woman was sobbing, clutching to her husband, who dabbed at his bloodied lip with a handkerchief. "Be right back," Owen said to the group, moving quickly toward the couple.

"Please, don't hurt us," the woman whimpered as Owen approached. "We don't have any money."

"Ma'am, I'm not here to hurt you," Owen said, his tone soft but firm. He crouched slightly to meet her eyes with his. "Are you okay? Is he hurt?" He gestured toward her husband, noting the crimson stain on the handkerchief and the split in the man's lip. "You don't have to be afraid."

The woman hesitated before wiping at her tears, a flicker of relief crossing her face. "He tried to help move the gate," she explained, her voice trembling. "Someone punched him. People have gone mad. I don't know what we should do," she sobbed.

"I'm fine," her husband interjected. "Barely felt it. Just a scratch." He gestured toward the gate with a nod. "We're stuck."

The woman clutched Owen's arm, her voice pleading. "What do we do? There's no way out."

Owen placed his hand gently over hers. "These are probably automated security steps that were triggered by mistake. They'll need to be reset or overridden, but they'll get everyone out eventually." His reassurance seemed to calm her, though the fear lingered in her eyes. "You can follow us if you want, we're going back inside."

"We're going to wait with our vehicle, if we don't get out soon, we'll come back inside," the man said to Owen, shaking his hand firmly as smoke was drifting into the garage.

Behind him, the chaos escalated with a fistfight breaking out between two men near the elevator, their shouts drawing a crowd. A teenager climbed halfway up the gate before losing his grip and crashing to the ground, his anguished cries cutting through the noise, his arm now in an unnatural broken position.

Owen glanced back at his group, seeing Mace rummaging through his car. He knew Mace well enough to guess what he was after, his handgun. That reminded Owen of his own weapon, stored in Mace's car because the casino didn't allow firearms inside. His stomach tightened as the realization hit, he'd feel a lot safer armed right now. He went to Mace's car, collecting his weapon and tucking it into his waistband.

"Hey Mace!" A voice called out, snapping Mace's attention away from the car. Turning toward the source Mace spotted Caleb approaching with Dylan and Jordan in tow. "We couldn't find you inside," Caleb said, relief evident in his voice. "Everyone's okay?"

Mace stepped forward and pulled Caleb into a quick embrace. "Glad to see you made it. You guys all good?" He nodded at Dylan and Jordan, who returned the gesture, their expression somber but steady.

"What's the plan," Caleb asked Mace, looking for answers on what to do next.

Mace pointed towards his father, Logan, who talked with Ty. "It's up to that man, I trust whatever he says to do. You guys should do the same."

The sound of glass shattering cut through the moment, followed by a sharp whoosh and a wave of heat that rushed by them. A car near the barriers had caught fire, its hood engulfed in bright orange flames that crackled as it spread under the car.

"Fire!" someone screamed, igniting a new wave of hysteria as many more scrambled to run inside from the burning vehicle, bumping into one another in their rush to flee. Some tripped and fell, only to be dragged to their feet by others.

Owen turned toward the flames, his teeth grinding. "We need to move. Now."

"Wait!" Logan shouted, his voice barely carrying over the noise. "Look!"

The fire spread quickly, jumping from one car to another. Gas tanks exploded with deafening bangs, sending shrapnel flying and thick black smoke billowing upward into the dark night sky. The harsh smell of burning rubber and metal filled the air making it hard to breathe.

The air grew hotter with every second, the smoke stinging their eyes and filling their lungs. The people had crowded the entrance, brining the line to full stop.

Logan gathered the team, his voice cutting through the chaos. "Stay close, stay together!" he bellowed, the heat radiating around them like an open furnace. The sprinkler systems were useless, leaving the growing inferno unchecked.

They moved slowly, bypassing the elevator doors and heading down the ramp that led back into the casino. The stalled escalators were clogged with panicked people, pressing and shouting as they tried to reach the hotel lobby.

Ty pushed through the mob, waving the others forward. "Forget the lobby! Keep moving, we'll exit out the valet doors near the casino."

Without hesitation, they obeyed, falling into step like soldiers retreating from a battlefield. The crowd ahead was jammed shoulder to shoulder, desperate to escape from inside the building to a safer area on this side.

Suddenly, Owen froze, spinning around. His face was a mask of panic. "No! No! No!"

Logan stopped, whipping around. "What is it?"

Owen's eyes were wide, his voice breaking. "The couple. The elderly couple in the garage. I left them there!"

A wave of realization swept over Logan. He clenched his fists, his jaw tightening as he exchanged a grim look with Ty.

"You're not going back," Logan said firmly, though the look in Owen's face told him it was a lost argument.

"I can't leave them," Owen said, already stepping away.

Mace caught the look between the two and stepped forward. "I'm going with him."

Logan hesitated, then nodded sharply. "Don't do anything stupid. We'll meet you on the bridge."

Owen and Mace didn't wait for another word, pushing back toward the parking garage at a snail's pace. The heat hit them like a solid wall as they rounded the corner. The garage was an inferno, flames devouring everything in sight. Smoke hung thick in the air, a suffocating shroud that clawed at Owen's throat with every breath. The stench of burning rubber filled his lungs, making his eyes water. Beams of flickering orange and red light danced wildly across the soot-streaked walls.

The once-intact second floor was now charred, pieces of concrete crumbling under the relentless flames. Cars exploded sporadically, the force of the blasts rattling the structure.

Owen sprinted toward the SUV where he'd left the couple, but he came to an abrupt halt, Mace nearly colliding with him.

The elderly man and his wife were slumped against the side of their car. The man's arm rested protectively around her, as her head lay nestled against his chest. Their hands entwined now in their death. The woman's face was peaceful, as though she had found solace in her final moments. In their hand, a crumpled photograph lay, a younger version of the couple, smiling under a sunlit sky.

Owen dropped to his knees, pressing two fingers to their necks, first one and then the other. "They're gone," he said, his voice breaking. "I'm sorry," he whispered, his voice barely audible over the roar of the flames.

Another explosion rocked the garage, shaking him from his grief. They had seconds, maybe less to escape. He took one final look at the couple, then pushed himself to his feet.

"We can't stay here," Mace shouted, tugging on Owen's arm. "The fire's spreading, we have to go, Uncle Owen!"

The flames leapt toward the entrance of the doors, licking at the walls and consuming Mace's Tesla in a fiery grip. With their exit cut off, the heat intensified, the air searing their lungs.

Mace darted to the edge of the structure, peering over the side. "We're trapped!" he said as sweat poured down his face, smudging the soot across his skin. "Owen, it's too late! The fire's spreading faster than we can move!"

A deafening crack split the air, and Owen froze as a chunk of the second floor collapsed, sending vehicles tumbling into the inferno below. Sparks and embers erupted in a deadly storm, and the ground beneath them trembled.

Owen scanned their surroundings, his gaze landing on the fire hose encased in glass. He smashed it with his elbow, yanking the hose free. He held it with his hands trembling, feeling the heat pressing against him, like a relentless force driving him back.

"Take this," he said, thrusting it into Mace's hands. "Drop it over the side and slide down."

The air burned their throats, each breath like swallowing fire. The structure groaned, threatening to collapse entirely.

Mace stared at the hose, then at Owen. "What about you?"

"Just go!" Owen snapped, giving him a shove.

Mace didn't argue. He threw the hose over the edge and began to slide down. The material burned against his raw skin as he dropped rapidly, his descent swift and jerky. "I'm down!" he yelled from below, trying to look back through the smoke.

Owen followed, gripping the hose tightly and lowering himself. The heat from the flames licked at his skin, the harsh smoke stinging his eyes. He landed with a jarring thud, pain shooting through his knees and hips as he hit the ground below.

Mace helped him to his feet. "We made it." He said as another chunk of the garage collapsed. Mace helped him away from the structure, stumbling into the open air, coughing and gasping. The fresh air felt like salvation against their overheated skin and smoke-filled lungs.

Owen didn't feel like he had made it, collapsing to his knees, staring at the burning structure. His body ached, and his mind was haunted by the image of the couple he couldn't save. He turned, vomiting into the grass, the taste of smoke and bile mingling in his throat.

Mace gave him a moment before tugging his arm urgently. "We have to go. You did what you could."

CHAPTER SEVEN

"Valet of Vengeance"

The fire from the parking structure had leapt into the hallway, its flames curling upward and quickly igniting the carpet on the walk ramp like a fuse. With no staff in sight, a handful of patrons, desperate and determined, rushed into action. They yanked fire extinguishers from the walls and sprayed a blast of foam that pushed back the encroaching flames. The fire seemed alive, hungry and relentless.

At the opposite end, near the casino, Logan and Ty had fought their way through the chaotic crowd, emerging into the valet car lane. They paused, leaning against a pillar, their lungs burning, hearts pounding and breaths ragged. Their clothes were damp with sweat and ash, sticking to their skin. The sounds of screams and frantic shouting echoed around them, as people swarmed from the doors like panicked wasps, confused, looking for something or someone to vent their fury upon.

The flames from the parking garage, hundreds of feet away, were strong enough to cast an eerie orange glow over the area, lighting up the night. The faint light from backup emergency lamps flickered weakly across the pavement. On the other side of the road, at nearby hotels, the darkened landscape was punctuated by the shaky beams of flashlights, adding to the sense of impending doom.

Inside the casino hotel, the lights began to flicker, their brief bursts of light illuminating the growing desperation of those still inside. The strain on the generators was unmistakable, their groans and faltering hum a stark reminder of how fragile the systems of safety had become. The smell of smoke and burning rubber, clung to everything.

Ty glanced at Logan, his eyes betraying the tension gnawing at him. He gave a subtle fist bump to Logan before speaking, his voice low but urgent. "We need to get to the bridge. Try to find Owen and Mace," he said, pointing toward the bridge crossing Soco Creek. "We don't know how bad this is... but we need to move. Before it gets worse."

Around them, the scene was unfolding like a nightmare. Hundreds of people stumbled through the valet lanes, as if in a trance, unable to process what had just happened. Injured individuals sat in agony on the sidewalk, tending to wounds, clutching at makeshift bandages. Some cried openly, their faces contorted in fear and helplessness, as panic spread like a contagious disease.

The parking structure was collapsing in slow, painful increments. The deafening sound of metal beams twisting and snapping repeated through the air, like a warning of worse things to come. The Cherokee fire trucks had arrived, but their attention was focused on the hotel rather than the parking garage. Their water streams pounded into the side of the building, trying to prevent the flames from spreading further, but it was clear that time was running out.

The few firefighters on the scene had set up a makeshift pumping system, drawing water from Soco Creek to feed their hoses. The firefighters were simply overwhelmed. Despite their efforts, chaos raged all around them. Agitated patrons, angry and desperate, screamed at the firefighters, demanding they save their belongings and get the hell out of the way.

Along with a light drizzle of rain, a heavy silence settled over the crowd for a moment. Many gazing into the darkness, their faces blank, their minds just as empty. They had no clue what was happening, no news, no updates. They couldn't get a signal on their phones, and some believed it was because of the power outage, others suspected it was crowding on the network.

"Back up! Stay back!" A voice, loud and furious, cut through the air, snapping Logan and Ty from their thoughts. They turned sharply, their bodies tensing, instincts on high alert. Near the valet lane, a different kind of conflict was brewing. The source of the shout was a man, frantically attempting to enter his car, only to be surrounded by several enraged individuals. They wanted the car, and they weren't going to ask for it nicely.

"We need a ride," one man growled, stepping closer, his face twisted in anger. "You can take us with you, or we can take your car. Either way, we're getting in it."

Caleb, usually the easygoing one, had other ideas. He moved forward, hands raised in a calming gesture. "Let's all just stay calm, alright?" His voice was soothing, but the tension grew. "We don't need any violence." He pleaded calmly.

The driver, sensing an opening, took advantage of the distraction. He jerked his door open and bolted into the car, hitting the ignition button with shaking hands. The men lunged at the car, desperate to stop him, their bodies slamming into the vehicle. Caleb was caught off-guard and shoved violently to the pavement, his head hitting with a sickening thud. The angry men banged their elbows against the side window, the glass shattering with a loud crack.

Logan's heart pounded in his chest as he sprinted forward, desperate to reach Caleb. His eyes were locked on the man's limp form sprawled on the ground, and every muscle in his body screamed for action.

The car jerked into gear, its tires screeching, and slammed into the canopy post with a gut-wrenching crash. Several men hung on to the car like frenzied predators, trying to prevent the driver from escaping. The chaos reached its peak as people began fleeing on foot, wanting to escape the turmoil.

"Logan, watch out!" Ty shouted, yanking Logan backward just as the car reversed wildly. Caleb, still motionless on the ground, was directly in its path.

The horrible sound of bone and flesh meeting the car's tire resonated above the chaos as the car rolled over Caleb's body. Logan's stomach twisted as he darted forward, but before he could act, the car accelerated again, running over Caleb a second time before screeching away.

Logan knelt beside Caleb, his breath ragged, his hands trembling as he reached out for a pulse. There was none. Logan's eyes scanned Caleb's face, but there was nothing, nothing but the vacant stillness. Caleb's life had been snuffed out by the angry men and the car they had been trying to take.

Rage exploded inside Logan's chest, a fury roaring to life like a second fire. Without thinking, his hand went to the weapon at his side, pulling it free, his finger instinctively tightening on the trigger. He would make them pay for Caleb.

Before he could aim, Ty's hand shot out, grabbing his wrist and jerking him back with a force that nearly sent Logan stumbling. "No, Logan," Ty's voice was sharp, his eyes locked onto Logan's. "There's a baby in that car. He was trying to get his family out of here, not hurt Caleb."

Logan's grip tightened on the pistol, the weight of Ty's words crashing into him. He understood, he did. But it didn't change the gut-wrenching pain that burned in his chest. The car sped away, its flat tire sending sparks into the night, the sound of its engine roaring into the distance. The rage inside Logan was a beast, gnawing at his insides, but he knew Ty was right. The pistol slipped from his hands, and for a moment, the world around him seemed to spin.

Ty helped Logan to his feet, his hand on Logan's shoulder steadying him. Together, they pulled Caleb's body out of the valet lane, dragging him away from the chaos. The sound of screams, the squealing tires from cars, and the crackling of fire followed them as they placed Caleb's body on the sidewalk. The world felt unreal, the devastation so overwhelming it was hard to process. Someone was going to answer for Caleb's life.

Logan turned to the man who had started the fight. Their eyes locking, and the man squared his shoulders, fists raising. Logan said nothing, his fist shot out, connecting with the man's mouth and sending him sprawling backward over a bench.

Two of the man's companions tensed, their confidence faltering as Ty stepped up behind them. With a brutal efficiency, Ty struck one man in the lower back, dropping him, and swept the leg of the other, sending him crumpling to the ground.

The last man, young and wiry, threw up his hands. "I just came to play blackjack! I'm out of here!" He bolted into the darkness, avoiding the wrath of Logan and Ty.

Logan grabbed one of the downed men by the collar, dragging him toward the creek. With a grunt, he hurled him into the water. Ty dealt with the other, delivering several swift punches before letting him collapse.

Breathing heavily, Ty joined Logan. "I didn't expect that," he said, shaking out his sore hand. "But they deserved it."

Logan crouched beside Caleb's body one last time. "What do we do with him?"

"We can't stay here, that's for sure," Ty said, his voice quiet but urgent. "We have to go while we can."

Leaving Caleb behind was a hard thought to process, but the moment didn't offer options, and they had to move. Logan could barely look at the body as they turned to scan for threats.

Then, a hand touched Logan's shoulder. He whipped around, his reflexes lightning-fast, grabbing the wrist of the intruder in a defensive grip. He was ready to strike, but stopped himself. The man, elderly, his skin wrinkled with age, wore a shirt with the casino logo. His eyes held no threat, only kindness, and he lifted his other hand, showing he meant no harm.

"I saw your friend try to help the family in the car," the man said, his voice gravelly but calm. "I'll take care of his body, troublesome times are ahead. I will treat him with dignity."

Logan and Ty exchanged a quick look. They couldn't argue with that. The man seemed sincere, his eyes honest.

"Thank you," Logan said, his voice tight as he extended a hand. "We appreciate your kindness greatly."

The man nodded. "Help me put him in the truck. I'll take him to the hospital for holding."

They carried Caleb to the nearby truck, the casino logo visible on its side. They placed him in the back, the final act of respect they could offer at least for now.

"Do you know what's happening?" Ty asked, shaking the man's hand before he turned to leave.

The man looked to the burning fires, his face serious. "The United States has angered many people. Now, they want revenge. They've brought war to this land. It will be long, and there will be many deaths. Someone will stand for good."

The weight of the man's words settled on them like a cold, heavy fog. The world around them was collapsing, and it was only just beginning. Would it be a long war?

"What's your name?" Ty asked softly.

The man spread his arms wide, a gesture of openness. "I am Ahyvnvwi," (ah-huh-nuh-WEE), he said, his accent heavy with tradition. "It means 'spiritual person.' But, call me, Dale."

As Logan glanced behind him, he saw the flickering glow of the fire from the parking structure. His thoughts were consumed by the need to find Mace and Owen. But when he turned to thank Dale, the man was gone, and the truck carrying Caleb already pulling away into the night.

Before they could process what had just happened, one of the men they'd fought with staggered to his feet, blood dripping from his face. He looked up at Logan and Ty, an angry sneer curling on his lips.

"I'm gonna—"

Logan didn't let him finish. His fist crashed into the man's face, sending him back onto the pavement. "You're going to sleep," Logan said, his voice unyielding.

Ty moved quickly, his eyes scanning for any further threats. "Let's keep moving."

They stayed low and quick, slipping through the crowd with urgency, heading for the bridge. As they approached, they saw Dylan and Jordan, their faces blending confusion and fear.

"You guys left us," Logan said, his voice tight.

Jordan stammered, clearly afraid of Logan's cold stare. "We thought the plan was to get to the bridge," he said, glancing at Dylan. "Where's Caleb? Have you seen him?"

Logan met their gaze, his expression hard. "Caleb didn't make it," he said bluntly. "There was an accident."

Dylan froze, shock creeping over his face. "What do you mean he didn't make it?"

Ty stepped in, giving Logan relief. "He was hit by a car. He didn't survive. They've taken his body to the hospital."

Dylan's body shook with grief, his voice barely above a whisper. "We should've stayed together. It's our fault."

Logan's voice cut through the air like steel. "It wasn't anyone's fault. It was the wrong place, the wrong time. We need to focus right now. We need to stay together."

Mace and Owen joined them, Mace's expression distraught as he overheard the news on Caleb.

Logan turned sharply, "I'm sorry, Son." He said before motioning for them to follow. "Let's get across the road."

They huddled near an old steakhouse restaurant. Ty took charge. "Let's get inside and figure out our next move." He said as he broke a window out to unlock the door. "There is too much random gun fire right now, we need to hunker down." The group nodded in agreement, the weight of the night pressing down on them as they prepared for whatever came next.

CHAPTER EIGHT
"Broken Arrows"

***

Ty tapped his watch, the green backlight glowing faintly in the darkness. "3:15 a.m.," he announced quietly.

"Moment of truth," Owen muttered under his breath.

Logan let out a soft snicker. "I remember that movie. Good one. But yeah, you're right, it's our moment of truth." His eyes turned to the others. "Wake up," he said as they had dozed out, fatigue gripping them tightly. "You ready for this? If the worst happens, there can't be any hesitation you." His voice hardened as he clenched his fist.

Ty nodded, his gaze sweeping across the group, assessing their determination. "Hesitation could get us all killed," he said firmly, his eyes lingering on Dylan, who looked the most uneasy.

"Do you hear that?" Owen interrupted, tilting his head. "Listen, I hear shouting over a megaphone."

They all froze, straining to listen. Distantly, the sound of a voice carried on the cool night air, growing louder with each second. A convoy approached, their headlights flickering as they bounced along Paint Town Road toward the casino.

Logan's sharp eyes scanned the area. "There's a ladder to the roof. Let's get up there for a better view," he instructed, already moving.

"I'm staying down here," Dylan stammered, backing away. "I'm-uh-afraid of heights." He darted toward a storage room, wedging himself between shelves and a wall.

Logan, Ty, Owen, Mace, and Jordan climbed the ladder quickly, one by one, settling into a prone position on the roof of the restaurant to stay concealed. The sound of engines and voices grew clearer as the convoy closed in.

"*We are the Broken Arrows,*" a voice boomed from a megaphone, harsh and commanding. "*Martial Law is in effect. All supplies, food, water, fuel, and weapons are to be surrendered immediately. Resistance will not be tolerated.*"

Ty shot Logan a grim look. The announcement confirmed an earlier talk. Opportunistic groups exploiting the chaos.

"Broken Arrows?" Ty whispered with a hint of mockery. "Who came up with that name?"

"*Join us, and you'll be protected,*" the voice continued, dripping with menace. "*We are the law. Hiding won't help you. We will find everyone. There's no one else coming to save you.*"

"Stay low," Logan ordered, his voice barely audible as they pressed closer to the roofline.

The flickering glow of distant fires lit up the street below, casting an eerie orange haze over the scene. As the convoy came into view, the group could make out five trucks in line. There were two lifted diesel pickups painted black and army green, their exhaust pipes growling menacingly. Another truck, a modified flatbed carrying cargo that appeared to be fuel drums and some items covered by strapped down tarps. The fourth truck was a larger, military-style truck with a mounted machine gun. The last truck was an armored Humvee, likely stolen.

Around two dozen men accompanied the vehicles, some riding in the trucks, others walking alongside. They wore mismatched gear, camouflage pants, tactical vests, and hooded jackets. Every one of them sported an armband, though the design wasn't visible from the roof. A few wore bandanas or caps, one even had on a cowboy hat tilted low over his face.

"They've got AR's and Ak's. Shotguns, too," Ty whispered as he surveyed the convoy through tightened eyes. "Nobody panic or do anything stupid."

"That looks like sniper rifles the two guys kneeling on the flatbed are holding," Mace whispered, pointing at the men.

The trucks rumbled closer, the engines snarling and popping as they idled into position at the intersection. Voices barked orders below, though the words were muffled.

Suddenly, in a hotel parking lot, a car's headlights flared to life. Its engine roared, tires screeching as it peeled out, trying to escape the group of militia.

The machine gunner on the military truck reacted instantly. The weapon roaring to life, spitting fire and chewing through the car's flimsy sheet metal and fiberglass. The vehicle swerved violently before veering off the road and slamming into a tree. Flames erupted from the crashed wreckage.

One of the armed militia men jogged to the car and peered inside. He turned back to the convoy, dragging his thumb across his throat, a signal: the occupants were dead.

Ty's eyes widened, his breath catching as he looked at Logan. "These pistols aren't matching up with that," he grumbled, rubbing his hand across his face in frustration.

The militiamen stopped an oncoming car, people unaware they weren't the U.S. military. They yanked the occupants out with rough efficiency. An elderly couple, their faces pale with fear. The woman clutched a young boy tightly to her chest, her arms trembling. One of the men tore the child away. She screamed, striking out at him with desperate slaps.

The man holding the boy passed him off to another militiaman with a cruel detachment, then turned back to the woman. Her cries were cut short by the sharp crack of his hand across her face, sending her to the pavement.

Her husband lunged forward in rage, fists raised in futile defense, but the butt of a rifle smashed into his chest, knocking him to the ground. Two guards forced the couple onto their knees, ignoring their groans of pain as the child's wails echoed through the mountain pass.

The man with the megaphone strode forward, his presence commanding attention. He surveyed the small crowd with cold, predatory eyes before raising the device to his lips.

"You need examples?" his voice boomed, reverberating off the surrounding ridges. *"Do not disobey our orders! Do not attempt to fight us! You will not be given a second chance!"*

"For all of you watching, do not look away. I want everyone here to witness our authority."

As the child was carried off, his terrified cries fading into the night, two guards stepped behind the kneeling couple. Without hesitation, they leveled their weapons. The crack of gunfire rang out, sudden and final. The couple's bodies crumpled to the ground, lifeless. Gasps and muffled cries rippled through the crowd, but no one dared move.

"Damn it," Logan hissed through clenched teeth from his hiding spot. His fists were balled tight, veins bulging against his skin. "Nobody makes a sound. There's nothing we can do."

The next victim of show was a teenage boy, hiding between two parked cars. He was grabbed by one of the guards and dragged to the intersection, his pleas ignored. They dropped him in front of the traffic light pole, kicking him viciously, taking his breath away. A noose was thrown over a crossbeam and looped around his neck without hesitation or doubt. The guards pulled the rope together, hoisting him into the air as his legs kicked frantically. The struggling ceased, leaving only the grotesque sway of his lifeless body.

"Our orders will only be given once!" the man with the megaphone declared. *"Follow them, or face the consequences."*

The guards repeated the gruesome act with the elderly couple, their bodies hung beside the boy's as a grisly warning to others. Blood pooled beneath them, spreading across the cracked asphalt slowly as others feared to look away.

One of the militia guards spray-painted, "BROKEN ARROWS LAND", in bold letters on the pavement beneath the hanging bodies, shouting out a war cry afterwards.

Logan swallowed hard, his jaw tightening, grinding his teeth. Owen's hands trembled, as he turned his back to the scene, unable to watch any longer. "We have to get to the hotel," Owen whispered. "I got a couple weapons in my truck, AR's."

Logan nodded grimly. "If they clear out, we move."

The trucks rumbled to life, their engines a rough, menacing growl once again. Slowly, they began to roll out of the intersection, one guard firing rounds into the air as their laughter filled the night.

"Look," Mace whispered, pointing. "Two guards are staying behind. There on the corner."

"Probably to secure the area," Ty said, his face grim. "Look at the casino security coming out, why aren't they doing anything? Just standing guard over there."

Logan watched briefly, "it's like they're only protecting the casino and hotel. Their not part of these Broken Arrows."

Owen offered a quick plan, his voice steady despite the tension. After a brief debate, the group agreed.

Owen approached the guards casually, hands raised. "Excuse me," he called, drawing their attention.

The guards spun to face him, rifles raised. "What's your business?" one of them barked.

"I was here on vacation," Owen said, pointing to the smoking parking garage across the street. "My car's destroyed. I've got nowhere to go. I thought maybe... I could join the Broken Arrows?" He flashed a nervous smile.

The guards exchanged looks before breaking into laughter. "You think it's that easy?" one sneered.

"Just thought I'd try," Owen said with a shrug. "I've got supplies and weapons. There, by the dumpster. Didn't want to scare you by carrying them."

51

"Scare us," one scoffed with laughter. "Show us," the other ordered, then gestured for him to lead the way. As they approached the dumpster, Owen knelt by the boxes, glancing over his shoulder. "All right, guys, you're up."

"What did you say?" the guard demanded.

Owen smiled coldly. "You bastards are going to die."

Logan and Ty struck from behind, each grabbing a guard in a brutal chokehold. Logan whispered harshly, "Stay quiet," as his arm constricted the man's throat. Using a sharp twist of his neck, the guard went limp, slumping down.

Ty struggled with his target, who clawed at his arms. Owen stepped in, delivering a powerful punch to the guard's jaw. The man crumpled, and Ty finished him with a precise snap of the neck. The sound was quick, an audible snap in the stillness of the night. The guard's body went slack as Ty lowered him gently onto the ground. He crouched there for a moment, breathing heavily, his hands trembling slightly.

"Hide them," Logan ordered, his voice tight with suppressed rage. "Put them in the dumpster," he said leaning back on the dumpster, both men catching their breath.

The group worked quickly, taking their weapons and gear before disposing of the bodies in the dumpster.

They turned back toward the intersection, where the bodies still hung. Logan hesitated, then grumbled, "We can't leave them like that. Let's go."

They sprinted to the poles, lowering the bodies gently to the ground and moving them to the roadside.

"They'll know someone did this," Ty warned.

"Let them," Logan growled.

With the guards gear, Red 30 began the mile-long trek to the hotel, sticking to the darkness. Logan's voice was a low whisper in the dark. "If you see lights, hide in the trees."

They moved swiftly, the night thick with tension and the promise of more violence to come.

CHAPTER NINE

"Whispers in the Dark"

They ran and walked nearly half a mile without incident, the faint hum of crickets and distant hoots of owls their only company. As they neared Don Lambert Road, Logan raised a hand, signaling the group to stop. The faint rustling of leaves came from behind the trees that separated Casino Trail from Don Lambert Road.

"Wait here," Logan whispered, his voice low but firm. He slipped into the trees, moving carefully between the dense trunks. He stepped cautiously as not to alert his presence.

Don Lambert Road wasn't much more than a long driveway leading to nearby homes. As Logan edged closer, he spotted a Jeep Wrangler parked under the cover of trees, its hood raised. A man stood by the open engine compartment, fiddling with something inside. The engine sputtered once before going silent again, accompanied only by the dry clicking of a starter motor refusing to cooperate.

"Hey," Logan called softly, his voice cutting through the stillness. "Don't be scared."

The woman was startled, she let out a low, stifled gasp as she spun around, scanning the shadows for the voice.

"I'm not here to hurt you," Logan added quickly, keeping his tone calm.

The man bolted upright, struggling to pull a pistol, holding it nervously in hand, his eyes darting toward the sound. "Who's out there?" he demanded in a hushed but urgent tone.

Logan remained concealed behind a tree, his hands raising slightly. "I mean you no harm. I just want to talk."

"Show yourself," the man growled, his grip on the gun tightening. "Or I'll shoot."

Logan exhaled slowly, choosing his words carefully. "Alright, I'm coming out. Keep your lights off, and don't shoot. If I wanted to hurt you, I could have done it already." He stepped forward, hands visible but ready to react if things went south.

As Logan emerged, the man squinted, his pistol still raised but wavering slightly. "Who are you? What do you want?"

"My names Logan. I'm not from around here," Logan began, his voice steady. "I was at the casino when everything went to hell. I ran into some bad people earlier. I'm trying to figure out who they are. I only want to ask you some questions."

"What questions?" the man asked again, panic growing in his voice.

Logan stepped closer, "who are the Broken Arrows?"

The man glanced over his shoulder at the woman, who hovered nervously by the Jeep. "Emily, it's okay. Come here."

The woman hesitated, then moved to stand beside him. "I'm Brian Dawson," the man said cautiously, his gaze flicking between Logan and the dark woods behind him. "This is my wife, Emily."

"Do you know a group of military looking people in the area, goes by Broken Arrows?" Logan asked, deciding to get straight to the point.

Brian and Emily exchanged uneasy glances before Brian answered. "They call themselves the 'Broken Arrows'. They're locking down the area, attempting to take control. You don't want to mess with them. They're a nasty group of people."

Logan nodded grimly. "Where are they from? What do they want?"

Before Brian could respond, the rumble of an approaching engine broke the quiet. Headlights flickered through the tress, prompting all three to duck behind the Jeep for cover. The vehicle sped past, its taillights disappearing down the road toward the casino.

"Nothing good that way," Logan said. "We just came from there. There were guards at the casino, but they didn't engage with the Broken Arrows."

Brian frowned. "They won't engage unless the Broken Arrows come across the creek or fire on them. But wait, you said, we?" He questioned Logan curiously.

Logan hesitated, realizing his slip. "Yeah, I'm not alone. My group is waiting, I came alone to avoid scaring you."

Brian's expression softened slightly. "You should re-think that, you're a pretty scary looking dude by yourself. How many of you are there? Where are you headed?"

"Six of us," Logan replied, gesturing vaguely in the direction of the hotel. "It's just up the road a short distance."

Brian sighed, looking at his Jeep. "I'd offer you a ride if we weren't packed with supplies, not to mention the damn thing won't start. Lights went out, then I lost power."

Logan eyed the Jeep, its interior brimming with supplies. Though rugged in appearance, the vehicle was remarkably clean, as if it hadn't seen much off-road action. Equipped with a winch, beefy tires, and full-length running boards, it looked the part of an adventurer's ride. Extra gas cans and a first aid kit were neatly attached on the rear. It was a sharp-looking Jeep, but Logan couldn't shake the feeling it had been more of a showpiece than a workhorse.

"You got one of these pavement princess Jeeps," Logan said, slightly smiling.

Emily snickered at the comment, looking at her husband. "I tell him we should be taking it off road more."

"Oh goodness, leave me alone," Brian said jokingly, easing his nerves slightly.

Logan moved closer, peering under the raised hood. With a beam of his flashlight, he spotted the problem almost immediately. "Here's your issue," he said, grabbing the loose battery cable and pressing it firmly onto the terminal. "Do you have a wrench?"

Emily hurried to the back of the Jeep, returning with a crescent wrench. Logan tightened the cable securely, then nodded toward Emily. "Try it now."

She slid into the driver's seat and turned the key. The engine roared to life, purring smoothly.

Brian grinned, lowering the hood and securing the latches. "Thanks, Logan. I appreciate the help. I can drive but never was much of a mechanic."

Logan shook his hand. "Do you think you could help us out? Maybe give us a lift to the hotel?"

Brian hesitated, his face hardening again. He glanced at Emily, who mirrored his concern. "We can stand on the running boards," Logan added quickly. "You won't need to stop, just slow down and we'll hop off."

After a brief pause, Brian nodded. "Alright, but hang on tight."

Logan whistled and waved for his group to join him. They emerged from the trees, climbing onto the sides of the Jeep, three to a side. "We're ready," Logan called.

The short drive to the hotel passed without incident, and the Red 30 gang jumped off as the Jeep rolled to a stop. "Thanks, Brian, thank you Emily," Logan said sincerely.

Brian glanced at Logan, offering a smile that suggested there was still some good left in humanity. "We'll make a few trips this morning to get our supplies to our friend's house," Brian said. "You all take care of yourselves. Avoid anything marked with the Broken Arrows."

Logan nodded, watching the Jeep disappear into the night before leading his group toward the hotel. They moved swiftly, relieved to find Owen's truck untouched, the tarp still secured over the contents underneath.

Owen peaked under the tarp with a relieved breath. "Yes! It's all here."

"The hotel has lanterns and emergency hall lights," Mace said, pointing toward the side door. They entered quickly, climbing the stairs to their second-floor rooms, their footsteps echoing in the stillness.

Ty pulled a key card from his wallet, nervously testing the lock. The green light blinked, and the door clicked open.

"Guess the batteries still work," Ty murmured low.

Inside, the group huddled together, their exhaustion evident as they tried to fight it off. The weight of fatigue pressed down on them as they tried to make sense of their situation. But the plans needed to be made, and Logan was already lost in thought as he peaked through the curtains.

"We've got three cars, Owen's truck, Ty's rental, and Jordan's car, assuming you've still got yours?" Mace asked.

Jordan shook his head. "Nope. Mine's gone too. It was in the garage at the casino, burnt to a crisp now."

Ty stood up, pulling a pillow from its case. "I'm heading to the vending machine. See if I can scrounge some snacks up." He tossed it onto his shoulder. "Logan, work on the plan, I'll be back soon. Fight or flight, make our decision. I'm with you."

"I'll go with you, TY," Owen said as they slipped back out the door into the hallway.

The hallway stretched dark and silent, except for the faint glow of emergency lights that drew shadows against the walls. They moved quickly toward the stairwell, their feet quiet on the worn carpet as they descended to the lobby.

Ty's gaze flicked to the parking lot, headlights moving about, people trying to leave he assumed. Suddenly, they were met by a startled young woman at the front desk. Ty and Owen both froze, both of them taken aback by her sudden appearance. It was Becky, one of the employees they recognized.

"We didn't expect anyone to be here," Ty said, his voice low. "Why are you still here?"

Becky placed a hand over her heart. "You about scared the life out of me! I didn't expect anyone to show up." Her eyes darted nervously around the lobby. "I actually live here."

"Sorry we spooked you, Becky," Ty replied, his tone softer. "Do you know what's happening? Is there any news?"

Becky looked over her shoulder, her eyes moving to the office behind her before scanning the hallway. "The news said China, Russia... and some other countries. They showed cities burning, bombs going off. It was crazy, like a movie. We lost power shortly after that and I didn't see anymore."

Ty stepped closer, his gaze sweeping the parking lot through the front doors. "Is safe to stay here at the hotel for now? Anything going on we should know?" His voice was tense, searching for anything that might help them.

Becky glanced toward the lights outside, her face tightening. "You aren't safe here," she said, her voice low and filled with fear. "There's a group... The Broken Arrows. They're taking control of this area, locking it down. They've declared martial law. One soldier came here, told me they would be back at daylight with more men. Any outsiders here would be killed."

"Tell us everything you can, Becky," Ty said softly.

Becky nodded and told them everything she knew and that she could think of, holding nothing back. Ty's breath caught in his throat as he listened closely.

Becky's words were a warning, words that carried more weight than he had anticipated. "You've been kind to me every year you guys come here," she continued, a faint smile before she gestured toward a storage door. "Fill up your bag with food before it's all gone," she said, her voice urgent but calm. She

58

opened the door to the supply room, revealing packaged food and supplies.

Ty quickly filled the pillowcase with whatever he could, cereal bars, cans of fruit, fresh fruit and water bottles. He turned to Becky, his expression softening. "Thank you for the food and the information. Are you sure you'll be okay here?"

Before she could respond, the sound of glass breaking echoed through the lobby. Ty spun around to see Owen holding his hands up, a mischievous grin on his face as he stood in front of a vending machine.

"Oops," Owen said with a chuckle.

Becky looked at him, shaking her head but offering an amused smile. "I'm sure that was an accident," she said with a sigh. "Grab what you need but leave me those coconut donuts."

Ty looked back to Becky, "do you need us to help you with anything? You want to board this place up?"

Becky shook her head, "no, no. You guys just get away from here, they won't hurt me, I know many of them. They will kill you all, don't let them find you."

Ty nodded, "thank you, keep yourself safe as well."

"Good luck, Becky," Owen called as he and Ty turned to head back upstairs.

CHAPTER TEN
"Checkpoints and Chases"

Ty and Owen returned to the room, their expressions tense as they prepared to fill the others in on what they'd learned. Inside, Logan, Mace, and the others had already packed their belongings, ready to hit the road and leave Cherokee behind in a cloud of dust.

"We're packed and good to go," Mace said, dropping his duffel bag near the door. "Let's get the hell out of here. The Broken Arrows can have this place."

Ty glanced at Owen, then both of them turned their attention to Logan, their silence speaking volumes.

"That look doesn't seem to agree, are you not on board?" Logan asked, narrowing his eyes. "What's going on?"

Ty sank onto the edge of the bed, rubbing the back of his neck. "Owen and I talked to Becky downstairs. You know her, she is the one always working the check-in desk." He gestured at Owen. "You tell them. I'm beat."

Owen took a deep breath, dragging a hand down his face as the others gathered around. He and Ty began to explain in turns, piecing together what they'd uncovered.

"The Broken Arrows," Owen started, "are a militia group that's been clashing with the local tribes for years. We got a lot of details, and it's clear they've been waiting for the right moment to take control."

Ty picked up where Owen left off. "Becky told us she caught some news reports before communications went down. The whole country is under attack as we seen ourselves.

Bombings in major cities, chaos everywhere. While everyone here was still scrambling to figure out what was happening, the Broken Arrows made their move."

"They started with the police," Owen said grimly. "They had loyalists embedded in the department, waiting for orders. As soon as the attack hit, they turned on anyone still loyal to the police chief. Now the department's completely under their control with nobody to stop them."

"That makes sense," Logan said, his tone cold as he rubbed his chin. "You want martial law, you start by seizing the cops. Scare the people into submission. But what does that mean for us getting out of here?"

Ty's shoulders slumped. "Every exit route is blocked. They've set up armed checkpoints on the highways and major roads. Even the backroads and trails are being watched by scouts. They've destroyed bridges to make escape harder. Becky said if we're caught trying to leave, we're dead unless we have something they want, and it's still likely we'll be killed."

"They've got this place locked down," Owen added. "Gas stations are under their control. Grocery stores and supply warehouses are next, if they haven't already taken them. No cell towers, no internet, no radios. Even if we could call for help, who would come?"

Mace ran his hands over his head, his pacing growing more frantic. "How is this even possible? This is America, the land of the free!"

Jordan spoke up, after staying silent and listening the whole time, "The Indians once thought it was the land of the free as well."

The group looked at him, some nodding the statement made sense, but no one furthering the discussion.

Owen's face darkened. "Not anymore. Becky said they're making public examples out of people to show their authority. They've already killed two community leaders, hanged them in front of the police station as a warning. A curfew is coming, probably by tonight. Penalty for breaking it? Death."

"And there's more," Ty said, his voice heavy. "Becky warned us to watch for signs, two broken arrows with red feathers. It's their symbol. They're recruiting locals, too. Using coercion, bribery, whatever works. They're targeting the young and desperate, and some people are already siding with them. That's how they've taken over so fast. They will grow quickly."

"They're aiming to take the casino next," Owen continued. "Becky thinks it'll become their headquarters. Once they control the money and resources, they'll own this place completely. It's the main target on their list, the casino."

Logan exhaled sharply, his jaw tight. "They must have been planning this for months, years even. They were waiting for an opportunity and this attack has sped things up. That also explains what we just witnessed with the guards protecting the casino."

"That's exactly what Becky said," Ty confirmed. "She told us there were rumors for weeks that they were preparing to make their move. The attack on the country just gave them the push they needed."

Mace stopped pacing and stared out the window, his eyes scanning the horizon. "There's got to be a way out, has to be."

"Becky said not to trust anyone," Owen warned. "They've got informants everywhere, trading information for safety and privileges."

Logan leaned back against the wall, his mind racing. "They're smart. They've thought this through, and they've got firepower to back it up. If we're going to escape, we'll need a plan, and we'll need it fast."

The group fell silent, each person lost in their thoughts, weighing their next moves. Fatigue pressed heavily on them, but the idea of sleep felt too dangerous right now.

Owen exhaled deeply, breaking the quiet. "You ready for the rest of the story?" His voice carried a weight that made everyone look up, dreading what more he might say. "Becky says people like us, outsiders, had better hide. She said the mountains might be our best bet, but even there, we'd have to be careful. They're watching everywhere."

Logan turned his head slowly toward Ty, his expression grim but shaded with sarcasm. "Have we fallen into Red Dawn?" He gave a smirk. "I mean, are we supposed to be the Wolverines, hiding out in the mountains?"

Ty snickered softly, but Owen didn't share in the humor. He stood, took a long swig of water, and squared his shoulders. "Screw it," he said firmly. "You guys are ex-military. I've got nothing to lose, and Mace and the boys are young enough to get excited about this. Let's fight back. We'll give em' hell."

Logan raised a hand, cutting him off. "Hang on a minute." His voice was steady, trying to rein in the group's rising tension. "We can't just go charging into a fight. Not against a group this size. There's six of us, Owen. Six. We've got to be smart. We need to lay low and figure out a plan."

Mace nodded thoughtfully before speaking. "What about the golf course? There's no reason for anyone to be there. We could find a spot nearby and camp out for a while."

Ty turned to Logan, gauging his reaction, then added, "I like it. Mace has a point. We could hike just off the course and set up a campsite."

Owen rubbed his chin, nodding as an idea formed. "I've got tents in the truck, got them from the Army surplus store. Plenty of supplies, too. We'll figure things out once we've had time to get our heads straight."

Logan stood, rubbing a hand over his face as if laying out words in his mind. "Unless anyone objects, I say we do it." His agreement surprised the others, but he wasn't done. "We've got two vehicles: Owen's truck and Ty's rental car. "Let's pack up and move. The sun's coming up soon and sitting here isn't an option anymore."

They packed quickly, tossing their gear into the back of Owen's truck and even grabbing linens from the hotel. Becky saw them off, her expressions a mix of worry and acceptance. "Good luck," she said softly. "I hope you make it, but I don't think you will find it easy anywhere."

Becky, a local tribal member, knew the area better than many. She warned them that surviving in the wilderness was one thing, but surviving the Broken Arrows, a ruthless group now controlling the town, well that was another entirely.

Just as they loaded the last of their supplies, the blare of a Jeep's horn shattered the tense silence. Brian and Emily Dawson sped by, hauling more supplies in their vehicle.

"Let's catch up to them," Owen said, already climbing into the driver's seat. "They might know a good place to hide."

As Owen started the truck, the screech of tires tore through the morning air. A lifted Dodge truck roared out of a nearby parking lot, following the Dawson's Jeep.

Logan looked at Owen and Mace. His expression hardened. "Looks like it's starting. Let's go."

They peeled out of the parking lot, Owens' truck speeding onto the empty highway with Ty's rental car struggling to keep up. Ahead, the Dodge truck stayed hot on the heels of the Jeep, weaving recklessly down Highway 441. Another truck, this one with a Broken Arrows logo, darted out from a side lot, falling in behind Owen's truck.

"We're being followed," Owen called out, his eyes darting to the rearview mirror.

The chase intensified as the vehicles veered onto Shoal Creek Road, a narrow two-lane stretch flanked by trees. Ty's rental car fell further behind, its small engine no match for the powerful trucks ahead. Suddenly, the truck behind Owen slammed on its brakes, skidding to a screeching halt.

Two men jumped out, rifles raised and approached Ty's car who came to a stop behind them.

"Stay calm," Ty muttered to Jordan and Dylan, who sat frozen in the back seat. He opened his door slowly, stepping out with his hands visible.

"Why are you following us?" one of the men barked, his weapon aimed directly at Ty.

"I saw everyone rushing this way," Ty said, keeping his tone level. "I thought this was where we needed to go. I'm with you guys, a Broken Arrow is who I want to be."

The men exchanged a look, then burst into laughter. "You're not with us, Little Man," one of them sneered.

Ty's jaw tightened at the insult, but he kept his composure. The moment their attention wavered though, as they once again laughed, he struck. His hand darted to his concealed pistol, muscle memory taking over as he fired two shots into the first man. The second barely had time to react before Ty fired three more rounds in rapid succession. Both men crumpled to the ground, clutching at their wounds.

Without hesitation, Ty moved around the car and delivered a final, precise shot to each man's head. He grabbed their rifles and ammo, climbed back into the car, and sped off, weaving around the abandoned truck.

Dylan's eyes were wide with shock, "you have got to teach me how to do that," he said enthusiastically, Ty's eyes locking with his in the rearview mirror.

Ty nodded, "I'll teach you, but right now, keep your eyes open and help me find where the others went."

The morning sun was trying to peak through the clouds, offering a break from the rain throughout the night that had left a wet blanket over the golf course. As the Dawson's continued to lead the way, Brian and Emily veered hard to their left, turning onto one of the golf course holes. The Dodge truck followed behind them, bouncing hard over a small drainage ditch. Owen,

Logan and Mace followed as well, bringing up the rear of the chase.

Brian and Emily's Jeep roared ahead, tires tearing into the soft, manicured fairways. The Dodge truck behind them was relentless, its lifted suspension and roaring engine giving it an ominous presence as it pursued the Jeep through the sprawling course.

Inside Owen's truck, the tension was growing as Owen pressed hard on the gas pedal, his truck leaving its own deep ruts on the course. The growl of the Dodge truck's engine echoed through the open air, punctuated by the distant crackle of gunfire from an unseen source. Owen gripped the wheel tightly, his knuckles white as he tried to keep up with the chaos ahead.

"Hold on!" Owen shouted as he swerved to avoid a sand bunker. The tires skidded, spraying clumps of dirt and grass as the truck fought for traction on the wet green of a hole. In the back seat, Mace clung to the seatbelt, his face pale but determined. Logan leaned out of the passenger window, scanning the truck ahead with his rifle at the ready.

"Brian's taking them up the hill!" Logan shouted. His voice was barely audible over the roaring engines.

The Jeep hit a sharp incline near the 14th hole, bouncing violently as it crested the hill. The Dodge followed, its driver clearly more interested in catching his prey than maintaining control. Behind them, Owen's truck climbed the same slope, jostling its passengers.

"They're gaining on the Jeep!" Mace called out, his voice filled with excitement and urgency.

From his vantage point in the Dodge, the passenger leaned out the window, aiming his rifle as steadily as he could. A burst of gunfire erupted, ripping through the quiet morning air. Bullets pinged off the Jeep's rear bumper, sending sparks flying.

"Damn it!" Emily screamed from inside the Jeep. Brian swerved erratically, throwing the shooter's aim off, but the Dodge closed the distance with alarming speed.

"Logan, take the shot!" Owen barked, his voice sharp with command. Logan steadied his rifle on the window frame, exhaled slowly, and fired. The crack of the rifle echoed like thunder inside the truck. The Dodge's passenger slumped forward, his weapon clattering uselessly to the ground as the truck swerved violently.

"He's down!" Logan shouted, but the victory was short-lived. The Dodge's driver floored the accelerator, the massive vehicle lunging forward like a predator closing in for the kill.

Up ahead, the Jeep approached the creek that snaked through the course, its waters glistening under the morning light. Brian didn't hesitate, plowing through the shallow stream with a spray of water and mud. The Jeep jolted as it hit the embankment on the other side, its tires spinning for a moment before finding traction.

The Dodge barreled into the creek seconds later, but the heavier vehicle struggled against the soft mud beneath the water. Its oversized tires churned the muddy bottom, sending up geysers of filth as it clawed its way forward.

"Here we go!" Logan shouted as Owen slammed the gas. His truck hit the creek at full speed, the impact sending a shockwave through the cab. Water splashed up the windshield, temporarily blinding him. The truck coming to a stop at the embankment, the tires spinning uselessly. Owen gave a quick spin of the 4x4 control, moving the truck in four-wheel drive mode, then easily climbing the embankment out of the creek.

The course was getting more difficult and treacherous as narrow paths wound between bunkers and water hazards, forcing split second decisions. A sudden dip in the ground sent the Dodge truck airborne before it slammed back down, the suspension groaning in protest. Smoke began billowing from underneath the hood.

"Keep up!" Logan barked. "Get me a shot!"

Owen surged forward, pulling alongside the Dodge, chasing down the middle of a fairway. Logan leaned out, aiming directly for the Dodge's front tire. "Come on, you son of a ---" His shot rang out, striking true. The tire exploded with a loud pop, and the Dodge veered wildly to the left. The truck entered a sand bunker, flipping onto it's side, the metal crunching and glass shattering as the truck slid before catching and rolling over, coming to rest on its wheels.

The silence that followed was intense, as Owen and Logan looked at one another momentarily, both releasing long held breaths. They leapt from the truck, the engine ticking as the water steamed off. Brian and Emily's Jeep parked just ahead, both already climbing out, visibly shaken but unharmed.

Logan's boots squished on the damp grass as he surveyed the wreckage, the eerie sound of steam hissing from the warped hood on the Dodge. He moved with precision, his Glock 19 already in his hand as he approached the wreck.

The Dodge's driver door creaked open, and a man stumbled out, collapsing to his knees. Blood streamed down his temple, pooling on the wet grass. His chest heaved with shallow breaths, pain etched across his face.

Logan pressed his gun to the man's head, his voice low and cold. "Is anyone coming? Did you call this in?"

The driver coughed, blood trickling from the corner of his mouth. "No... we didn't," he mumbled weakly.

"Lies," Logan growled, his finger tightening on the trigger. The gunshot echoed across the golf course, startling a flock of birds from the trees.

Brian came sprinting over, his face pale but filled with relief. "I'm sure glad to see you guys! How in the world did you find us?" he asked, clapping his hands together, his voice trembling with adrenaline.

Logan turned at the sound of an approaching engine. Ty's small SUV rolling over the crest of the hill, moving slowly across the fairway. Logan raised a hand to signal they were okay before turning back to Brian.

You went past our hotel," Logan said. "We saw the truck pull out behind you and figured they were coming for you."

Brian let out a shaky laugh and gripped Logan's hand, shaking it vigorously. "I don't know how this would've ended if you hadn't shown up," he said, gratitude evident in his voice.

One by one, he shook hands with Owen and Mace, who climbed out of the truck, his face still pale from the harrowing chase.

Ty pulled up and rolled down his window, his usual humor cutting through the tension. "Fore!" he called out, mimicking a golfer on the tee.

Owen gave a faint smirk but didn't lose focus. "We were warned the Broken Arrows were blocking roads, killing anyone they came across. Do you know of a place where we can lay low? At least until we figure out what to do."

Brian exchanged a glance with Emily, who nodded silently. Turning back to Logan, Brian's voice grew firm. "We're in debt to you. Come with us to a friend's place. He's got room, might be in the barn, but there's security, and plenty of food."

Logan studied them both, sensing Brian's trusting nature but noting the cautious suspicion in Emily's eyes. She seemed reluctant but willing to help, her protective instincts fighting with her sense of obligation.

"That would be great," Logan said after a moment, looking to Owen and Mace, who both nodded in agreement.

Emily finally spoke, her voice colored with regret. "We should've invited you this morning when we ran into you. I'm sorry we didn't. I am thankful to you for helping us, again."

Logan gave a reassuring smile. "Don't worry about it. Honestly, I wouldn't have invited us either."

Mace glanced back at the ruined fairways, the chaos of the chase laid bare in the torn grass and rutted greens. "Doesn't look like we'll be playing golf anytime soon," he complained, his voice heavy with the realization of how much their world had changed.

Ty pointed toward the tracks rutted into the course. "We need to move. Those tracks are like a neon sign. They'll know where to look." His eyes lingered on the wrecked Dodge. "I left one of their trucks back on the road. It won't be long before someone finds it."

Brian nodded sharply. "I know a way out. Follow me." He and Emily ran back to their Jeep, urgency in their every step.

As Owen climbed into the truck, he took one last look at the carnage. The pristine course they'd walked just days ago, playing a simple game of golf, was now a battlefield. Trails of broken fairways lay silent under the morning sun. The contrast hit him hard, but he didn't have time to dwell on it.

The engine growled to life, and they followed Brian and Emily, leaving the shattered remnants of the course, and their former lives, behind.

CHAPTER ELEVEN
"Hidden Refuge"

Owen steered the truck carefully along the winding trail that wove through the dense pines, their towering forms creating a cover across the path. The forest closed in around them like a protective cocoon, the earthy scent of pine needles mingling with the fresh rain. Brian and Emily's Jeep led the way, its brake lights flashing occasionally as they navigated the rugged terrain.

Logan sat in the passenger seat, his gaze fixed on the passing trees, though his thoughts were far from serene. His mind churned with worry over what they'd escaped and what lay ahead. "This place is really tucked away," he said, his voice thoughtful. "Under different circumstances, this would be the kind of drive I'd actually enjoy, peaceful, quiet."

"Yeah, if it weren't for the world going to hell," Owen replied, keeping his eyes on the trail.

In the back seat, Mace leaned forward slightly, his eyes flicking between the road and the side mirrors. "This is the kind of hidden setup someone would dream of in a world without power or law," he spoke softly, glancing at Ty's SUV in the rearview. He shifted in his seat, the faint clink of his holstered pistol catching Logan's attention. "Let's hope this turns out to be the safe haven it looks like," Mace added, double-checking that his weapon was ready if things went south.

Ahead, the trees parted to reveal a wide metal gate flanked by thick posts. The large solitary figure standing beside it let his rifle lay casually over one shoulder. The man's build was imposing, easily six feet tall and pushing three hundred pounds, much of it muscle. As Brian's Jeep slowed, the guard broke into a grin, offering a wave before swinging the gate open with a routine ease. The metal creaked as it swung wide, the bottom edge grazing the embankment.

"Friendly so far," Logan remarked, watching the interaction between the guard and Brian ahead.

The guard motioned for Owen to pull up next and he approached with his rifle pointed downward, a stance that felt deliberate and non-threatening, but firm.

Brian had clearly vouched for them, but the man's piercing gaze lingered on the truck and its passengers. When he spoke, his voice carried an unexpected warmth. "Brian says you're with him. Welcome to Yona Haven." He gestured toward the trail behind him, though the name was swallowed by the low hum of their idling engine. "If you've got weapons, keep them holstered, and you're welcome to hold onto them."

Owen extended a hand in a friendly fist bump. "Fair enough. I'm Owen. This is my brother Logan and my nephew Mace. Did you say Yona Haven?"

"I did. It means Bear Haven," he said as he met Owen's gesture, his smile broadening. "Name's Crackhead," he said, chuckling at their raised eyebrows. "And no, it's not drugs. Back in the day, I was the guy they brought in to 'crack heads' when things got ugly." His laughter was deep and genuine. "Hell, I miss those days right about now."

Owen chuckled, appreciating the man's humor. "We miss the old days, too. Though for us, the 'good ole' days' were just yesterday." He shifted the truck into gear. "Feel free to mess with the guys behind us, they can take it."

Crackhead grinned mischievously. "Oh, I'll mess with 'em all right. Y'all go on ahead; I'll see you around."

Ty's SUV pulled up next, its engine idling softly as it came to a halt. Crackhead's demeanor shifted as he approached, his face hardening into something almost menacing.

"What's your business here?" Crackhead asked, his tone sharp.

Ty stiffened, caught off guard by the sudden hostility. "We're with the two cars ahead of us. All one group."

Crackhead's eyes swept over the passengers, his expression unreadable. He lingered for a moment before shaking his head. "We're full up. Turn around and head back."

Dylan and Jordan exchanged uneasy glances, and Ty's jaw tightened. "Wait, what? We need to let our friends know," Ty protested, his voice rising in frustration.

Crackhead turned back, his expression cold and unwavering. "I said..." His words halted as his serious mask broke into a wide grin. "Just messing with you, man. Go on through." He laughed deeply, slapping the side of Ty's SUV.

Ty exhaled sharply, his anger melting into relief. "Damn, man, you got me. Not the time for jokes, though, I was about to panic. Whipping your ass wasn't really an option." He grinned despite himself, and Crackhead's laughter boomed.

"Lighten up, brother. You'll live longer," Crackhead replied, waving them forward. "Go on through. I'll see you around lunch."

As the gate swung closed behind them, Ty glanced at Dylan in the rearview mirror, shaking his head. "That guy's something else."

"Yeah," Dylan mumbled, still uneasy. "Let's hope this place is worth the trip up here."

Once all three vehicles were back together, Brian led the convoy further along the rugged trail to the cabin. The group soon found themselves in an open stretch of the mountain, where the dense trees gave way to a stunning view of rolling peaks and valleys. The late morning sunbathed the scene in golden light, glinting off the surface of a distant river winding its way through the valley below.

As the vehicles came to a stop, everyone got out, stretching tired limbs and taking in the view. Brian gestured for the group to gather near the Jeep. "We didn't have much time to talk earlier, but there are a few things you need to know," he began, his tone serious yet reassuring. "Grant's okay with me sharing this, but he'll fill you in on more details himself later."

He pointed towards a large pine tree near the edge of the clearing. "See that camera up there? It's solar-powered, and its signal runs up to the cabin, which is just around the last curve in the road."

Brian and Emily exchanged glances before continuing. "Grant and Julia Whitlock are good people," Brian said, his voice softening slightly. "But they're former members of the Broken Arrows Clan. I know that might be concerning, but they left that life behind a long time ago. You can trust them, they've built something solid here. They help people in need, a haven."

The group exchanged wary looks but nodded. Given the circumstances, trust was a luxury they couldn't afford to withhold, but each knew it had to be given sparingly.

Brian went on to describe the property's defenses. "The gate and guard you saw earlier are just the beginning. There are cameras hidden all over the property, along with tripwire alarms, some mechanical, others as simple as bells. There are also spike strips hidden along the trail, logs and boulders rigged to roll out and block vehicles if necessary."

Mace raised an eyebrow, his exhaustion momentarily giving way to curiosity. "Sounds like a fortress," he expressed.

"It is," Brian replied, his expression grim. "If the Broken Arrows ever come here, they'll have a hell of a fight on their hands."

He continued, explaining that the property was littered with both lethal and non-lethal booby traps like camouflaged

74

pits, spiked barricades, steel cable traps, and more. "You might see signs on the road like 'Keep Out,' 'Danger,' things like that. Ignore them. They're meant to mislead outsiders. Same with any signs pointing to a 'Barn' or something similar. Those are decoys."

The cabin itself, Brian explained, was well-equipped for defense. Solar-powered floodlights surrounded the structure, ready to bathe the area in blinding light at a moment's notice. The windows and doors were reinforced, and there was a panic room and armory on property.

As Brian spoke, the group listened intently, fatigue etched into their faces but replaced momentarily by a growing sense of security.

"Lastly," Brian added, "there are gun ports built into the cabin, the barn, and a few other strategic locations. Clear firing lanes make it easy to deal with anyone coming in."

Emily stepped forward, her voice gentle. "They're probably worn out, Brian. Maybe we should take them to meet Grant and Julia and let them rest?"

Brian nodded. "You're right. We can go over the property's markings and other details later."

The vehicles rumbled back to life as they rounded the final curve. The cabin came into view, nestled snugly against the mountain. A sturdy, two-story structure with a weathered log exterior, it exuded both charm and fortitude. Grant and Julia stood on the porch, waving as the group pulled up.

Grant was tall and lean, his frame hinting at years of hard work. His sharp eyes scanned the newcomers with quiet intensity, but his slight nod and outstretched hand were welcoming. Julia, standing beside him, exuded warmth. Her protective nature was evident in the way she positioned herself just slightly in front of her husband, her gaze assessing but kind.

"Welcome," Grant said, his voice calm but firm. "Come on in. Let's get you settled."

He led them to the barn, entering through a side door into an attached addition. Inside was a modest but functional living space. A small kitchen area occupied one corner, with a table and mismatched chairs nearby. A well-worn couch and a couple of armchairs created a small sitting area. At the back of the room, two doors led to a compact bathroom and a bunkroom filled with neatly made beds.

"This is what we can offer for now," Grant said, his tone matter-of-fact. "Our other bunkhouses are already full. While you're here, we ask that you pull your weight around the property and be ready to fight if it comes to that."

Logan glanced at the others, who gave subtle nods of agreement. "We're grateful," he said, shaking Grant's hand firmly. "We'll do whatever we can while we're here, but I don't think we'll be staying long. I'd like to get on the road and away from Cherokee as soon as possible."

Grant's expression darkened slightly. "I understand that, but you should know the exit roads are barricaded. It's not going to be easy to leave." The weight of his words settled over the group as they exchanged uneasy glances. "When I say barricaded, I basically mean they will kill you."

Logan and Ty both raised their brows at that, but they were simply too tired to question it.

"For now," Grant added, "get some rest. We'll talk more later."

As they began to settle in, sleep was needed, their fatigue showing in each of them. Although the sun was bright and the rain had stopped, giving way to a beautiful day, the mountain air seemed a little colder. Whatever safety this place offered, it was clear they were far from out of danger.

"Let's get some rest while we can, we can start planning later today when everyone's energized," Ty said as they all staked claim to a cot and quickly went to sleep.

CHAPTER TWELVE
"The Wolf Among Us"

Owen jolted awake, sitting upright on the thin mattress. His heart pounded as his eyes adjusted to the dim light seeping through the room's windows. The younger guys were still sprawled across their bunks, their steady breathing filling the space. He rubbed the back of his neck, wincing at the lingering stiffness, before slipping quietly into the next room.

The rich aroma of coffee drew him in. Logan and Ty were seated at a makeshift table, their faces weary but alert. Ty rose immediately, grabbing a chipped mug and pouring him a cup.

"How you feeling, brother?" Logan asked, his voice low and tired, but steady.

Owen took the cup, nodding his thanks to Ty as he settled into a chair. "Like I got hit by a truck. And I guess it's safe to say this isn't some weird dream."

Logan cracked a smile, glancing at the sunlight streaming through a grimy window. Dust motes floated lazily in the beam, painting the space with a strange, fragile beauty.

"You got that right," Logan replied.

Owen's eyes swept over the barn's interior. Supplies were meticulously organized along one wall, every item sorted into neat piles. "Looks like you two have been busy," he said, tipping his mug toward the neatly arranged gear.

Ty grinned, setting his cup down with a soft clink. "Yes, sir. And let me just say, you did one hell of a job on that supply run." He reached across the table for a fist bump.

Owen met it with a small smile. "If I'd known this was coming, I would've cleaned out the whole damn store." He took a slow sip, savoring the warmth of the coffee. "Any plans yet?"

Logan leaned back, rummaging through a pack at his feet. "Grant said to head over to the house once everyone's up. They've got lunch ready. After that, we'll talk, figure out what's next."

Ty stood, grabbing a dented kettle and a large spoon. "Guess it's time to wake the troops." He banged them together, the clamor echoing through the barn. "Rise and shine, soldiers! We got work to do!"

Groans and muffled complaints followed as the others stirred, rubbing sleep from their eyes. Mace shuffled over to join them, his face uncharacteristically somber. The mischievous spark that usually lit his expression was absent, replaced by a heaviness that settled around him like a cloak.

Logan noticed it immediately. Mace's jaw was tight, his eyes distant. The weight of Ethan's death was pressing hard, and Logan could see his son struggling to find his footing beneath it.

Mace broke the silence, his voice barely above a whisper. "Yesterday, we were waking up to play golf. Ethan poured sweet and sour sauce on my pancakes when I went to get juice." He paused, biting his lip. "I took a bite and gagged so hard I almost choked."

Ty let out a low chuckle, shaking his head. "Yeah, he got a kick out of that one."

Mace's mouth twitched in a fleeting smile, but it quickly faded. "I told him I'd beat his ass for it." His voice cracked, the humor draining away. "We were joking, you know? And now... now we're hiding on a mountain, and he's gone."

Logan placed a steadying hand on Mace's shoulder. "There's no making sense of this, son. Not now. Don't try to figure it out." His tone was gentle. "It hurts, I know it does. But right now, we've got the six of us. That's who we lean on, who we trust. Red 30 has never been more real than now."

Owen pushed his chair back and stood. "Mace, I'm sorry about Ethan. There'll be a time to grieve him, but today isn't that day. We've got something else to focus on."

Mace stared at the floor for a long moment before his head lifted, his gaze hard. "Revenge," he moaned, the word sharp and cold. "We might not be able to touch Russia, China, or whoever else pulled the trigger on this attack. But the Broken Arrows? We can make damn sure they pay."

He didn't wait for a reply, heading for the barn door. Outside, the sun showered the mountainside in golden light, the air crisp and alive. Mace stretched, his jaw set, the lines of his face drawn with determination.

Inside the house, the group settled at the long wooden table, their chatter subsiding as hunger took over. Sandwiches and leftover breakfast items disappeared rapidly, the sound of clinking plates and the occasional buzz of approval filling the room. Grant watched the scene with a small, approving smile, his weathered hands resting on the back of a chair.

"I'm glad to see you gentlemen have a hearty appetite," Grant said, his voice a low rumble. "Now that you're fed, Brian asked me to fill you in on our situation." He adjusted his stance, his presence commanding the room. "As you know, I'm Grant Whitlock. But now, I'm going to tell you about who Grant Whitlock was... and who I am today."

The group leaned forward slightly, curiosity and unease carved on their faces. Grant's tone shifted, taking on the cadence of a storyteller, and the room fell silent as his words began to paint a picture of the past.

"The Broken Arrows Clan," Grant began, his voice steady, "started as a group of locals fed up with the economic disparity brought on by the casino. The casino, owned and operated by the Eastern Band of Cherokee Indians, enriched the tribe and

79

nearby businesses. But it left others in this community feeling exploited and forgotten."

Grant's words hung heavy in the air. He paused, drawing in a deep breath before continuing. "The leader of the Broken Arrows was a man named Gideon 'Wolf' Thorne. He had one foot in two worlds, a Cherokee mother and a white father. Despite his heritage, Wolf's family was excluded from tribal rolls decades ago due to politics. That exclusion cut him off from the lucrative tribal dividends."

The room listened intently as Grant described the bitterness that shaped Wolf's life. "Wolf grew up poor, watching his peers thrive as the casino flourished. His resentment festered, fueled by the devastation he saw gambling bring to the community. Families losing homes. Marriages falling apart. Lives torn apart by addiction. To Wolf, the casino wasn't a blessing, it was a parasite."

Grant walked over to a cabinet, pulling out a bottle of bourbon and several glasses. He poured himself a drink and gestured for anyone else to help themselves. Ty stepped forward, filling his glass as he spoke. "This Wolf guy... sounds like someone who wasn't born bad, but his situation pushed him to the edge."

Grant nodded gravely. "That's a fair way to put it. The Broken Arrows started as a grassroots political group, pushing for change through legal means. They petitioned the tribal council, protested outside the casino, even tried to run candidates in local elections. Their demands were fair, profit-sharing with non-tribal members and stricter gambling regulations. But their efforts culminated in a bitter legal battle. The courts sided with tribal sovereignty, and the case was dismissed. I will add that some of this is second-hand information, I can't vouch for it being entirely accurate."

Logan swirled the bourbon in his glass thoughtfully. "That must've been the tipping point," he said.

"You're right," Grant replied. "After that loss, Wolf's ideology shifted. He began preaching that the system was corrupt and that anyone who gambled was complicit in the exploitation. His words ignited a fire in his followers."

Grant's voice hardened as he recounted the group's descent into extremism. "Wolf turned the Broken Arrows into a paramilitary force. He recruited disillusioned locals, unemployed laborers, and veterans. They trained in the mountains, sharpening survival and combat skills. Their symbol, two broken arrows with red feathers, started appearing as warnings across the community."

Julia's soft voice interrupted, trembling with emotion. "We listened. He inspired us. We joined." She dabbed at her eyes with a towel, her memories clearly weighing heavily on her.

Grant placed a hand on her shoulder, his own face clouded with shame. "We followed Wolf," he admitted. "I'm not proud of it, actually very ashamed, but we did. At first, his cause seemed just. But his methods grew brutal. He ruled through fear, silencing dissent, blackmailing his own men, and punishing those who tried to leave."

"Julia and I made a pact," Grant said, his voice steady but his eyes telling the weight of their shared memory. "We decided we couldn't stay any longer. It was more than we could bear, more than anyone should have to. We approached Wolf, hoping for his understanding, asking for his blessing to leave the Broken Arrows. But we knew, deep down, he'd never let us go. So, we started working on this place in secret, keeping everything under wraps. We wanted it finished, ready, before we made our move."

Julia sat beside him, nodding quietly as his words hung in the air. The pain etched into her face spoke volumes. Despite her composure, the emotions were raw, brimming just beneath the surface.

"Wolf... he changed," Grant continued, his voice dropping. "He became... polarizing, to say the least. His bitterness turned into a driving force, pushing the group into darker, more dangerous places. It wasn't just about survival anymore; it was about proving a point, his point." Grant paused, as if weighing whether to say more.

"He'd rant about the casino," Grant said, the words sharp and heavy. "It wasn't just a business to him; it was a symbol of everything wrong with the world, greed, corruption, betrayal. He said it with such venom, like the very existence of it was an insult to him personally. And he made sure we all felt the same. Or at least... that's what he tried to do."

Julia flinched slightly, as though the memories of Wolf's tirades had clawed their way back. "Every day, his anger grew. Every day, it got harder to believe in what we were doing. That's why we had to leave." She wrapped the towel tighter in her hands, her lips pressing into a thin line.

Mace raised his hand like a schoolboy, his curiosity getting the better of him. "How did you get away?"

Grant sighed deeply, his shoulders slumping. "Wolf gave us an ultimatum. He demanded we complete a task for him in exchange for our freedom. Failure meant Julia would suffer a slow, cruel punishment... and I'd be forced to end her suffering myself. So, we did what he asked." His voice cracked as he spoke, the weight of the memory etched on his face.

Julia's expression hardened as she added, "Even after we did what he wanted, Wolf made it clear that if he ever called, we'd better come running. We know he hasn't forgotten us."

The room fell silent as the group absorbed Grant's words. Finally, Ty broke the quiet. "So, Wolf is using this national chaos as his opportunity to take over?"

Grant nodded. "Exactly. The Broken Arrows are using the attack to assert their control. They'll impose their own version of justice on anyone they see as a threat, tourists, outsiders, gamblers. No one is safe."

Ty leaned forward, his expression bleak. "We watched them murder several people last night, hanging them from the traffic light poles. Even a young boy."

Grant nodded solemnly. "That's exactly what they'll do. Nobody is safe." He leaned back slightly, his voice steady but filled with an accepting certainty. "Wolf leads the Broken Arrows, and his second-in-command is Elijah Raines. He's former military, with unwavering loyalty to Wolf, practically worships him. The third in their chain of command is Maggie Blackfeather. She's not fully on board with their methods but follows whatever Wolf orders. She's stuck, and she knows it."

The room fell into a heavy silence as Grant's words sunk in, the weight of Wolf's ruthlessness hanging over them. The group exchanged uneasy glances, each trying to process the grim reality they were up against.

Logan broke the silence with a deep exhale. "This is intense," he said. "That's the history. Now, what about today? What do we know?"

Grant reached into his shirt pocket and pulled out a small, worn notebook. "We got word this morning. Thomas Standing Oak Greyfeather, a respected tribal elder and casino representative, was found hanging at the police station." His voice was heavy with grief. "He was a pillar of the community, overseeing the casino's profits and ensuring funds went to vital community projects. Wolf saw him as a gatekeeper, someone who allowed the casino to 'exploit' the community. Killing him was a message."

Mace shifted in his chair, his discomfort visible. "What about the tribal people working with the casino? Will they fight back?"

Grant shook his head. "They'll try, but they're vastly outnumbered. Many of them are elderly or otherwise unable to fight. And those who can? A lot of them have already joined the Broken Arrows." He paused before adding, "And Greyfeather wasn't the only victim. Hanging beside him was Marissa Quiet Doe Longbow, the community outreach liaison. Wolf killed her to send a clear message, no one is safe, not even those trying to help."

Ty frowned. "What exactly was her role in the community?"

Grant tapped the edge of the notepad against the table, his stare distant. "Marissa was a unifier," he said quietly. "She had a way of rallying people, standing up for the vulnerable. She could've been a real threat to Wolf's control, and he knew it. Early this morning, she was stopped while delivering emergency supplies to families in need. They executed her as a warning to anyone who might resist or unite against them."

The room grew colder as the implications settled in.

Owen broke the silence with the question everyone had been wondering. "How many troops do they have?"

Grant met his gaze, his tone serious. "What you saw was probably just a patrol, maybe two dozen at most. Altogether, I'd estimate their numbers are close to two hundred."

The group's faces turned to stone, concern outlined their features.

"Most of them are volunteers," Grant continued. "Laborers with no real military training. But the ones who *do* have training? They're the type who overestimate their abilities, think they're some kind of Rambo. Dangerous, but also reckless. It's a mix that makes them unpredictable."

A tense silence followed as everyone absorbed the grim details. They were facing a formidable enemy, one built on fear, violence, and unrelenting control.

"What about weaponry?" Ty asked.

"That one's tricky," Grant said, glancing at Julia. "We've been away from them for a while now, so I can't be certain.

From what I know, along with rumors I've heard, they've got pistols, shotguns, and rifles, typical stuff like AR-15s and AK-47s, all semi-automatic when I was there. They also have some sniper rifles and were experimenting with homemade pipe bombs and Molotov cocktails."

Logan leaned forward. "We saw a mounted machine gun, heavy-duty. They practically shredded a car with it."

Grant exhaled sharply. "That'd be the M240. They had two of them. Wolf stole those from a National Guard depot. Those are serious firepower, but I doubt they have much ammunition for them."

Julia, who had been silent for most of the conversation, spoke up. "Tell them about the helicopter," she said, her voice steady but uneasy.

Grant's lips tightened. "Yeah, there's that too. There's a rumor that Wolf has a helicopter. It's not military-grade, more like a civilian chopper, but it's still a significant advantage, especially now." He craned his neck, stretching it as if trying to shake off the weight of his own words.

The room seemed to grow heavier as Grant laid out the details. The group exchanged tense glances, the enormity of the situation pressing down on them heavier.

Logan finally broke the silence, standing up from the table. "Grant, we appreciate your honesty about all this. We need some time to digest everything privately, if you don't mind. Give us about an hour, and I'll come find you."

Grant nodded, his expression understanding. "That's fine. You men talk it over. If you're not comfortable staying here, no hard feelings. If you decide to stay and help, Julia and I would be forever grateful."

He led them to the door, his tone sincere. "We'll be here. Come see us when you've made a decision."

The group exchanged questionable looks, the weight of the situation pressing down on them like a heavy weight. Logan exhaled deeply. "This is intense. Do you have a plan for now, how to handle them?"

Grant's face was somber. "We prepare for the worst. Wolf won't stop until he's taken everything. I'm not ready to give what we have up yet."

Mace stopped, turning sharply before walking off the porch. "What did you have to do in order to leave Wolf?"

Grant exhaled slowly, his smile leaving as his eyes drifted past Mace, as if looking into a past he wished he could forget. When he began to speak, Julia stepped next to him, wrapping an arm around him protectively.

"We've got enough information for now, Grant. We'll go discuss the situation and be back soon," Logan said. He easily sensed the dread in Grant's face at answering the question, it would be best left for another time.

Mace sensed his dad's meaning, nodded at Grant, then turned to walk away. "Catch you later, Grant," he said before bouncing off the steps of the porch.

CHAPTER THIRTEEN
"Unleashing the Wolf's Ambition"

The Broken Arrows headquarters loomed atop a rugged ridge outside of town, where the unforgiving land mirrored the men who claimed it as their domain. Nestled among towering pines and jagged outcrops of rock, the compound stood secluded, hidden from prying eyes yet close enough to cast a menacing shadow over the valley below. The sharp peaks of the ridge protruded into the sky like the serrated edges of a blade, offering a commanding view of the world beneath. The terrain was merciless: uneven ground strewn with rocks that pierced the earth like scars from a war-long past.

This was no mere hideout. The ridge was a stronghold where the Broken Arrows trained, endured, and thrived. For many, it was more than a base, it was home. A community forged in isolation and toughened by necessity. The atmosphere here was never truly silent, it carried the echoes of relentless activity. Shouts ricocheted through the trees, punctuated by the sharp cracks of gunfire and the crackle of campfires. These sounds weren't just noise, they were the heartbeat of a place where survival wasn't an option but a creed. To live here was to endure. To endure was to dominate.

Inside the compound's main building, perched perilously close to the edge of the ridge, Wolf made his entrance. The leader of the Broken Arrows, he strode into the room with a wide, self-assured smile that didn't quite reach his cold, steel-gray eyes. Standing just under six feet tall, Wolf wasn't a towering figure, but his presence more than compensated. Years of hard living had carved his body into lean, solid muscle, and every step he took radiated predatory intent. His movements were deliberate, his posture rigid, as if constantly evaluating threats and opportunities before they even materialized.

Wolf's face bore the marks of a lifetime steeped in violence. Deep-set wrinkles etched by countless battles framed a square, unyielding jaw. A perpetual scowl seemed etched into his features, the corners of his thin lips curling in disdain even in moments of quiet. His short, dark hair was streaked with silver at the temples, the only concession to his years, though a few rebellious strands hung untamed across his brow. But it was his eyes, hard, calculating, and devoid of warmth, that left the strongest impression. They carried a spark of cruelty, a glint that hinted at a man who had endured more than most and emerged on the other side stripped of mercy.

Wolf's hands, thick and scarred, told a story of their own. These were the hands of a fighter, honed through years of toil, combat, and bloodshed. They had built, destroyed, and killed with precision, a testament to his brutal efficiency. Everything about Wolf exuded a quiet menace. He didn't need to raise his voice to command respect. His soldiers followed him not out of loyalty, but out of fear, knowing that his wrath was as sudden as it was unrelenting.

The room itself reflected Wolf's character: functional, bare, and steeped in a raw masculinity. The scent of leather, smoke, and bourbon hung in the room, mingling with the faint hint of gun oil. Wolf's boots clicked against the wooden floor with a deliberate rhythm, each step asserting his authority. He approached a large, worn desk that bore the marks of countless strategies plotted and deals brokered. Pulling back a creaking leather chair, he settled into it, the seat groaning beneath the weight of his presence.

Elijah, his second-in-command, entered behind him, carrying two glasses of Buffalo Trace bourbon. He placed one in front of Wolf, who took it with a loose grip, swirling the amber liquid lazily before raising it to his lips. The bourbon burned as it went down, a familiar fire that Wolf welcomed, a reminder of his defiance against the customs others held dear.

Wolf leaned forward, setting the glass down on the desk with a deliberate clink. The ice rattled against the sides of the tumbler, the sound sharp in the otherwise quiet room. His lips twisted into a sneer as his thoughts turned to the elders. He could almost see their stern, weathered faces, hear their disapproving groans and grunts. To him, they were relics, men bound by outdated traditions and hollow rituals.

A low chuckle escaped him as he leaned back, stretching his legs and letting his gaze wander toward the room's window, which framed the valley below like a painting. "If those old bastards could see me now," he pondered, his voice a gravelly whisper, "sipping Buffalo Trace up here on their sacred ridge, they'd choke on their damn pride."

He smirked, the edges of his words cutting like a blade. "Hell, maybe I should send them a case to the casino. Let them taste the irony for themselves." His fingers tapped on the edge of the glass as the thought amused him further.

For Wolf, the bourbon wasn't just a drink, it was a statement, it was a weapon. Each sip carried defiance, rebellion, and the sharp sting of contempt. If it riled the elders, so much the better. Here, on this unforgiving ridge, Wolf was king, and the rules of the world below didn't apply.

Wolf leaned back in his chair, the dim light lying softly across his face. The room was heavy with unspoken words, the scent a mix of bourbon and smoke. Across from him, Elijah sat stiffly, his posture respectful but strained, as though aware he was perched on the edge of a knife. Wolf's fingers tapped against the arm of the chair, his cold, calculating eyes locked onto Elijah, dissecting him in silence.

Elijah shifted slightly, clasping his hands tightly around one knee, but his voice remained steady as he broke the stillness. "Boss, we've made our mark here. Fear's spreading through the streets, but I think we need something more, something to solidify our grip. What if we put our logo on every business, make it clear they answer to us now? Show them we own this town."

Wolf's lips curled into a slow, predatory smile, but there was no humor in it, only menace. "You think small, Elijah," he said, his voice low and deliberate, the sound of a blade being drawn. He leaned forward, his piercing eyes locking onto Elijah's. "Tagging businesses, shaking down locals, that's child's play. We're not petty criminals looking for scraps."

Elijah swallowed but didn't flinch, his respect evident. "Then what's the plan?"

Wolf let the question hang in the air, his silence more crushing than words. The room felt charged, the tension like a coiled snake ready to strike. Finally, he spoke, his voice a quiet storm. "We hit them where it hurts. Not just the people but the system, their foundation. We take their casino, their precious lifeline. When it's ours, we won't just control Cherokee. We'll own it all the land. By the time this country claws its way back to normal, we'll already have the whole state in our pocket."

A flicker of understanding passed through Elijah's eyes, and he nodded slowly. "You're not just talking control. You're talking domination. We take their lifeblood, and they'll have no choice but to rely on us. They'll need you to survive."

Wolf's smile widened, a wolfish grin that sent a shiver down Elijah's spine. "Exactly. They'll come begging, not for mercy, but for scraps. And I'll make them crawl for it."

Elijah nodded, his respect for Wolf evident in the sharpness of his tone. "We've got the blockades in place, patrols running the streets, and the police station under control. I'll draw up a plan for the casino. Anything else?"

Wolf finished his drink with a sharp clink of glass against wood and then reached into his desk, producing a folded sheet of paper. He slid it across to Elijah with deliberate precision.

Elijah picked up the document, unfolding it slowly. His brows rose as he read aloud, "National Guard Armory, Sylva." He looked up, a faint smirk tugging at his lips. "Ambitious. Breaking into the armory isn't exactly a smash-and-grab. It'll probably be heavily guarded."

Wolf leaned forward, his eyes glittering with calculated malice. "In normal times, you'd be right. But these aren't normal times. Security will be thin, if there's any at all. We'll strip the place bare, and eliminate anyone who gets in our way."

Elijah cracked his knuckles, his smirk widening. "You want everything. Guns, ammo...? This could really bolster our firepower. It could be a game changer."

"Everything," Wolf said, standing and pacing toward the window. He stared out at the darkened mountain, his voice rugged. "Take all the rifles, M16s, M4s, AR-15s. Sniper rifles, handguns, every bullet they have. Grenades, explosives, even the vehicles. When we hit the casino, I want them to see our full military might. No hesitation. No escape."

Elijah nodded, his excitement tempered only by his disciplined respect for Wolf. "Understood. We'll take body armor, helmets, night-vision goggles. anything useful. It'll be a hell of a haul."

Wolf turned, his gaze sharp. "No loose ends, Elijah. Make it clean. Make it fast."

Before Elijah could respond, a knock at the door broke the tension. "Come in," Wolf barked.

The door creaked open, and Maggie Blackfeather stepped inside, her expression determined and urgent. "Sorry to interrupt, sir, but I've found him."

Wolf's lips curled into a satisfied grin. "Grant Whitlock."

Elijah's brows furrowed. "Grant? Why bring him into this?"

Wolf's tone turned colder, sharper. "Grant was always my go-to for the dirty work. The Reaper, a perfectionist. He'll ensure this transition goes smoothly. Don't question it, Elijah. You're still my number two."

Elijah nodded, though unease flickered briefly in his eyes. "Understood."

Another knock shattered the moment. Wolf's expression darkened as he motioned for the intruder to enter.

A guard stepped inside, his posture stiff and his voice hesitant. "Sir, we've got a problem. Two of our men were found dead, dumped in a trash bin behind the old steakhouse across from the casino. They were stripped of their gear."

The room went deathly silent. Wolf's jaw tightened, his face reddening as fury bubbled beneath the surface. "Do we know who's responsible?"

Elijah interjected, his tone steady but cautious. "Doubt it's the casino. They wouldn't risk provoking us. This might be something else, meant to distract us."

Wolf turned slowly, his gaze cutting like a knife. "Possibly a red herring for something bigger?" he asked rhetorically. Maggie, get Grant here. Elijah, I want whoever's responsible for this made an example. Do it publicly and brutally. Make sure everyone knows what happens when they cross me."

"Yes, sir," Elijah said, rising to his feet.

Wolf poured another drink, the ice clinking ominously against the glass. He stared out the window again, his voice low but unyielding. "No one takes from me anymore. No one."

CHAPTER FOURTEEN
"A Fools Bet"

The parking garage loomed in the distance, the once-pristine structure now a grotesque monument to chaos. Its skeletal remains of twisted metal and fractured concrete clawed at the smoke-filled sky. Unpleasant fumes of burning debris thickened the air, choking out any semblance of peace. Part of the upper levels had collapsed, pancaking under the weight of destruction and leaving a jagged trail of beams extending out like broken ribs. The ground below was a wasteland of shattered glass, blackened vehicles, and scorched rubble, a grim reminder of how quickly order could dissolve into ruin.

Smoke still curled from the wreckage, stubbornly clinging to the humid air like a bad memory that refused to fade. Though the flames had mostly subsided, smoldering embers pulsed with an occasional flicker of orange, as if warning onlookers that the destruction was far from over. Waves of heat radiated outward, stifling and relentless, an intense reminder that even in death, the structure held a simmering rage. The eerie silence of the scene was broken only by the occasional groan of shifting metal or the faint hiss of a dying flame moving over the ruins.

This was no longer a place of routine and dullness. The garage, once a hub for travelers and workers, had transformed into a graveyard of steel and concrete, its smoldering remains bearing silent witness to the chaos unleashed upon the world.

The attack on the United States had been violent, swift, and unrelenting. Across the nation, cities burned, skies darkened with fighter jets, and the earth shuddered under the force of missile strikes. Here in Cherokee, however, the devastation had been quieter, no fiery barrages from the heavens, no thunder of missiles raining down. To outsiders, the people in Cherokee might have seemed lucky, but only those wearing the Broken Arrows logo would agree.

When the attack began, the casino's leadership had been blind to the larger picture. Their initial concern was riot control, theft, or a cyberattack targeting their power and communications systems. It wasn't until the news trickled in that they realized the scale of what was unfolding, a coordinated, catastrophic assault on the entire country.

Wolf Thorne's shadow loomed over their thoughts like a storm cloud. The elders had always known he was a danger, a predator circling the vulnerable. He had sought the casino's wealth and influence for years, and now, with the world in disarray, his hunger would only grow. Protecting the families of the community meant protecting the casino, their last fortress of security. Letting it fall into Wolf's hands wasn't an option. If the country ever stabilized, he would leave them in ruin, his greed stripping them of everything they had built.

Armed men patrolled the perimeter along Soco Creek, standing as a human shield against Wolf's Broken Arrows. Their weapons were a pitiful defense against the overwhelming force he could bring, but they stood firm, determined to defend what little they had left. Outside the casino's boundaries, chaos reigned, with properties abandoned or falling into Wolf's grasp.

Inside, the conditions were tense, almost suffocating. Vacationers who had sought solace in the structure before the collapse now paced the halls and empty restaurants like caged animals. Rumors spread like wildfire, Wolf's men had blocked every exit out of town, their threats of violence keeping anyone from fleeing. Supplies would dwindle, but for now, survival meant staying put.

Deep in the bowels of the casino, hidden within a secure room near the vault, the elders gathered. The space was a fortress, its walls thick and unyielding. At the center of the room stood a magnificent conference table, its oak surface carved with intricate depictions of bears, elk, and wolves. The craftsmanship was a nod to the tribe's heritage, a stark contrast to the grim reality outside. Around the table sat the leaders of the community, their faces lined with worry and the weight of impossible decisions.

David "Running Bear" Blackthorn, a council elder and cultural liaison, rested his hands on the table. His presence was commanding, even in his seventies. The lines on his face and the weariness in his dark eyes spoke of a lifetime of battles, some won, others endured.

"We have to find a way to hold onto the faith of our people," Running Bear said, his voice steady despite the tension crackling in the air. "We've fought to keep Wolf Thorne from their hearts and minds. This will be our greatest test." His gaze swept the room, searching for resolve in the faces of his peers.

Martha "Red Willow" Gentry, the casino's treasurer and financial overseer, leaned forward. Her sharp eyes revealed a lifetime of shrewd decision-making, but today, worry creased her brow. "You've been a bridge between the casino and the community for decades," she said to Running Bear. "The people trust you to guide them. They look to you for strength."

Red Willow's own burdens weighed heavily. The attack had severed their access to the profits that kept their community afloat. Without payouts, trust would erode, and with it, their fragile unity. "I'm concerned they'll lose faith in me," she admitted. "If the money stops flowing, they may turn against the casino, and against me."

Running Bear's gaze softened. "You've done more for this community than most know," he said, his tone reassuring. "Your sharp mind and meticulous planning have provided stability for years. They may grumble, but they won't forget your contributions."

Red Willow lowered her head, a flicker of shame crossing her face. She had always maintained a stoic exterior, careful to appear impartial and strong, but her heart had guided her to make choices outside the tribe's approval. Funding education programs for the youth had been a quiet act of rebellion, and love.

Running Bear smiled faintly. "We knew about the funds you diverted for education. We knew your heart was pure, Red Willow."

Her breath hitched at his words. She felt both exposed and understood, her carefully guarded secret laid bare.

"Don't feel ashamed," Running Bear said gently. "Your compassion has strengthened us in ways no one else could."

The room fell silent as his words settled over them. The weight of their responsibilities was immense, but so too was their will power. They were the guardians of their people, and they would not let Wolf Thorne, or anyone else, tear them apart.

Samuel "Iron Hawk" Greyson listened intently to the elders' discussions, but his patience wore thin. Finally, he slammed his fist onto the table with a resounding thud. "I trust, let me say, we trust, that you will put forth a favorable effort with the community. However, we must prepare for the most certain attack from Wolf and the Broken Arrows." His voice was like gravel, sharp and weighty, cutting through the room's hum.

Iron Hawk, the casino's security chief and tactical advisor, was a man of action. In his mid-sixties, he carried himself with the authority of a military veteran. Years of tactical experience had forged him into an unyielding protector of the tribe, his reputation for loyalty and decisive action well-known. Nothing incited his fury more than the name Wolf Thorne.

The elders around the table recoiled slightly, the sound of his fist on the table jolting them out of their measured discourse. "We should have dealt with Wolf when I suggested it years ago," Iron Hawk growled. "Instead, you let him build his army unchecked."

Running Bear raised his hands, palms downward, his fingers moving gently as if calming turbulent waters. "Your concerns are valid, Iron Hawk, but we must prepare for today, not dwell on yesterday's mistakes."

Iron Hawk leaned forward, his jaw tight. "If we want there to be a tomorrow, the time to act is now. We need to strike first, eliminate their patrols one by one before they gather strength. The stronger they get scavenging, the weaker we get waiting."

Running Bear exchanged a glance with Red Willow, their shared silence brimming with reluctant understanding. Their years as leaders weighed on them, steering them toward caution rather than conflict. "Patience is needed," Running Bear said, his tone calm but firm. "War will bring destruction to our land. Lives do not need to be lost in pursuit of revenge."

"Lives will be lost in our failure to act," Iron Hawk responded, his lips pressed into a thin line, the friction in his frame apparent. His frustration was evident as he spoke, his voice resonating with controlled anger. "Based on the evidence we have, war is coming whether we accept it or not. We can't hide from it. I will honor the tribe's decision, but you know where I stand."

A low hum of whispered conversations filled the room as the council members deliberated. Iron Hawk stood abruptly, his imposing figure towering over the table. "I'll check on the guards. Inform me of your decision when you're ready to act." He turned and strode out, the voices rising behind him.

The stark silence of the lobby greeted him as he moved to the main floor. The once-lively casino now seemed a hollow shell of its former self. A handful of guests lingered aimlessly, their faces etched with worry, while displaced tribal members huddled in small groups, uncertain of their futures.

Outside, the sunlight warmed his face as he surveyed the perimeter. Guards stood near the creek, their postures lax as they chatted idly. Iron Hawk's sharp eyes didn't miss the lack of vigilance. Taking a deep breath, he let the sun's warmth anchor him in the present. The bitter thought that any day could be his last to enjoy such simple comforts gnawed at him.

Back in the conference room, silence fell as Iron Hawk returned, the elders' faces heavy with the weight of their decision. Running Bear gestured for the door to be closed, his somber expression fixed on Iron Hawk.

"The council has decided," Running Bear began, his voice steady but accepting. "We will take a defensive position. Prepare our guards to defend the property and actively recruit additional members. We wish to avoid bloodshed, even against those you see as enemies."

Iron Hawk's jaw clenched, but his expression remained stoic. He met Running Bear's gaze without flinching. "I honor your decision and will dedicate myself to defending this land." His words were calculated, his tone revealing the anger simmering beneath the surface. "If there's nothing more, I'll begin the preparations."

"Iron Hawk," Running Bear called as he rose from his seat. "This casino has always been our lifeline. It is built on taking analyzed risks. Now, we must gamble on peace prevailing."

Iron Hawk paused, turning back to face the elder. The words hung in the air, their optimism feeling more like gullibility to him. Without a word, he turned and walked away, grumbling under his breath, "You're gambling with our lives. And it's a fool's bet."

CHAPTER FIFTEEN
"Fortifying the Line"

"If we're all in agreement, let's talk to Grant," Logan said, leading the group out of the barn. Their boots crunched against the gravel in a steady rhythm. Their pace like soldiers as they marched toward the house, where Grant stood waiting on the porch, arms crossed.

Grant's sharp eyes lingered on Logan, assessing him as the natural leader of the group, even if no official title had been declared. The camaraderie between the men, their unspoken unity, was undeniable, a strength Grant admired and knew he needed. He could see they moved as one cohesive unit.

"I see the jury has deliberated," Grant said, his tone light but probing. "Is there a verdict?"

Logan stepped forward, meeting Grant's with a firm handshake. "We appreciate the hospitality you've shown us today, letting us rest, fill our stomachs, and regroup." He swept a hand toward the group, his voice steady and with purpose. "This team works as one. Wherever the fight comes, we'll stand together. And if it's going to happen, if we're going to fight somewhere, we figure it might as well be here with you."

Grant's lips curved into a genuine smile, relief and gratitude flickering in his eyes. "That's great news. I can't tell you how much it means to me. We need men with training."

Logan placed his hands on his hips, his breath steady. The warmth of the late afternoon sun brought a gleam of sweat to his brow, and the weight of the commitment settled over him.

"We don't know how long this will take or what exactly we'll face, but we're in it for the long haul."

Each man stepped forward to shake Grant's hand, their grips firm and their expressions solid. When Ty's turn came, he squeezed Grant's shoulder. "Time's not on our side, so tell us what needs doing, and we'll get started."

Grant nodded, gesturing toward the yard. "Start by taking a look around the property. Fresh eyes might catch things I've missed. Let me know what we need to shore up."

Logan's brow furrowed. "Good idea. But we'll need a guide, I don't want us accidentally walking into any traps."

"I'll go with them," Brian offered from the porch. "I'll give the grand tour."

The group mounted ATVs, their engines roaring as they climbed the steep, winding trails that snaked through the nearly fifty-acre property. Towering trees formed a canopy overhead, pine needles creating a blanket on the forest floor with shifting patches of sunlight. The mountains loomed around them, blind to the chaos ravaging the world beyond. Birds chirped softly, a melody that felt almost foreign to men accustomed to the clamor of cities and the grind of survival.

They jotted notes as they went, marking vulnerabilities and areas to fortify. Each man's thoughts were heavy, their minds playing out scenarios of what could go wrong and how they might stop it.

By the time they returned to the cabin, dusk had fallen, draping the landscape in blues and purples. A small fire crackled in the clearing, where Grant and his guard, Crackhead, lounged on wooden logs arranged as seats. Sparks leapt into the air, the warm glow of the flames pushing back the darkness.

Grant rose to greet them, a grin tugging at his lips. "Got some hotdogs here. Figured you'd be hungry by now."

Ty didn't hesitate, snatching two franks and skewering them onto a stick. "You sure know the way to a man's heart," he said, patting his stomach before holding the food over the fire.

Grant chuckled, watching as the rest of the group followed suit. "So, how was the ride? Did you find much that needs fixing? I'd like to think we're in good shape."

The men took their places around the fire, the scent of roasting hotdogs mingling with the smoky air. They ate quietly, the knowledge that each meal could be their last lending an unspoken gravity to the moment. Yet, amid the tension, laughter and banter sparked.

Mace, leaning back on his log, grinned. "I guess I could play a round of golf on that course, then shoot a few Broken Arrow guys when I'm done."

Logan chuckled softly, though his stomach tightened at the comment. He cast a sidelong glance at Mace, studying the younger man's casual bravado. Mace hadn't killed before, and Logan knew that day was likely coming. He didn't want any of them to treat taking a life lightly, but neither could they afford to hesitate when the moment came. The fire snapped and crackled, as the night pressed in around them. For a while, they sat in the glow, the future uncertain but the persistence between them unshakable.

Ty fixed his stare on Grant, his tone shifting to a more serious note. "Here's what we found on our stroll," he began. "There's no medical station, no first aid equipment or supplies. One thing I can guarantee about war is there will be injuries."

Logan stepped in. "We recommend setting up a room and stocking it with essentials like bandages, antiseptics, splints, and sutures. Then we train as many of your people as possible on basic first aid, stopping bleeding, treating burns, and setting fractures."

Grant exchanged a glance with Crackhead, both men nodding in agreement. "We've got some supplies on hand.

101

Crackhead will make sure you get access to them so you can prepare. We have an extra room that would work great for that."

"The defensive fortifications here are impressive," Ty added. "Still, I'd suggest reinforcing the exterior of the living quarters with planks or metal, anything that can stop a bullet."

Grant rubbed his chin thoughtfully. "I hadn't planned on letting anyone get close enough to the house, but I realize not everything goes as planned. We'll start reinforcing tomorrow."

"I didn't see any observation towers or platforms," Owen interjected. "That's something you might want to add to your current security."

Grant cocked his head slightly, listening carefully to their advice. "Makes sense," he said.

"Overall, you're about as well-equipped as you can be," Logan noted, but the group's energy hinted they weren't quite done.

Mace raised a question. "Do you have anyone going into town? Someone patrolling or scouting the area?"

Grant stood, gesturing for them to follow. "Somewhat we do. Walk with me. I want to show you something."

They followed him into the dimly lit building tucked behind the main house. The air inside smelled of old electronics and dust. Shelves lined the walls, cluttered with manuals, tangled wires, and spare parts. At the center of the room was a desk packed with radio equipment. Transceivers, receivers, and amplifiers hummed softly, their dials glowing faintly.

A man sat at the desk, headphones on, jotting notes on a pad as he listened intently.

"This," Grant said, motioning around the room, "is one of our most critical assets. It doesn't look like much, but it keeps us informed, and hopefully alive."

He gestured toward a large, weathered radio on the desk. "This high-frequency transceiver picks up long-range signals, military bands, emergency broadcasts, and sometimes even chatter from the Broken Arrows." He nodded toward the man at the desk. "That's Daryl. He'll monitor it day and night, filtering through the noise for anything useful."

Grant pointed to a smaller, more modern radio. "This short-range system keeps us connected with patrols and anyone on the property. It's reliable over a few miles, which is all we need for now."

He tapped an antenna cable running out through a hole in the wall. "That's our external setup. It's directional, so we can pull in weaker signals. Daryl's good at this, he's got a knack for honing in on specific frequencies."

Grant's hand moved to a nearby scanner, its screen flickering as it cycled through frequencies. "This scanner automatically sweeps for active transmissions. It's not perfect, but it's caught enemy patrols a few times already."

Daryl raised a hand, motioning for quiet as he adjusted his headphones.

Grant lowered his voice. "Right now, he's mostly picking up static and emergency calls, but sometimes we intercept coded messages. Some of it's Broken Arrow, and some could be government or local groups trying to organize."

Daryl's pencil scratched across the notepad as he turned back to his work.

Grant continued, "This isn't just about listening. If we need to, we can transmit, send distress calls or relay information. But that's a last resort. Broadcasting gives away our location, and staying off their radar is critical."

Logan nodded, glancing between Grant and Daryl. "It's smart, but Daryl should train someone else to do what he does. If anything happens to him, someone needs to step up."

Grant crossed his arms. "Good point. We'll start working on that."

Ty asked, "How long have people been working here to build this compound?"

"Crackhead's here full-time," Grant replied. "The others help as needed. This was always the plan, if things went south, they'd come here, and we'd work together. It's what Brian and Emily were doing when you met them."

Grant led the group to another building, its reinforced concrete exterior painted gray to blend with the surroundings. A heavy steel door with a keypad was the only entry.

"This is where we keep the teeth of the operation," Grant said, punching in a code. The lock clicked, and he pushed the door open.

Inside, they were met with the smell of gun oil and polished metal. Pegboards lined the walls, hung with rifles, shotguns, and handguns. The workbench was cluttered with cleaning kits and spare parts as bright LED lights illuminated every corner of the room.

"We've been building this stockpile for years," Grant said. "Nothing fancy, but everything here is reliable."

He gestured to the shotguns. "Pump-action 12-gauges. Great for close-range defense."

Moving to the rifles, he continued, "Bolt-actions, Savage Axis, Ruger Americans, and a few old Winchesters. Good for long-range accuracy."

Next, he pointed to a line of AR-15s. "These are the most versatile. We've outfitted them with scopes and red dots. Perfect for mid-range."

He finished at the handguns. "Glocks, Smith & Wessons, Berettas. Everybody carries one, and we've got spares."

Grant opened a locked cabinet filled with ammunition. "We've got plenty of rounds and reloading equipment. Spare magazines, slings, cleaning kits, everything's organized for quick access."

He faced the group. "This armory isn't for show. If the Broken Arrows come, this is where we hold the line. If you're not comfortable with these weapons, now's the time to learn."

Logan ran a hand over an AR-15. "Looks like you've been ready for a while."

Grant nodded. "I didn't think it'd come to this so soon."

"You've got a strong setup here," Ty said. "Once we get a medical facility running, you'll be in good shape."

Logan crossed his arms. "But if we're not taking the fight to them, they'll eventually bring it here. Tomorrow, we need to get back into town and find out what's going on."

Before anyone could respond, Daryl burst into the room, his expression urgent. "Grant! Sorry to interrupt, but this is big. I just picked up some chatter on the radio..."

"What did you hear?" Grant's voice was calm, but there was a nervous edge to it, like a wire about to snap.

Daryl shifted uncomfortably, his hands brushing his jeans as though wiping away invisible dirt. He glanced at the others before locking eyes with Grant. "Maggie Blackfeather found out where you are," he said, each word landing heavily. "They're sending a patrol to bring you back. I don't know when, could be tonight, could be tomorrow."

Grant's brows shot up, disbelief flickering across his face. "Maggie's sending a patrol for me? Why?" His voice tightened. "To kill me? That was quick."

Daryl shook his head, his shoulders stiff. "No, not to kill you. They want you to help take the casino."

Grant ran a hand down his face, the weight of the news pressing on him like an avalanche. "I was afraid of this," he grumbled, his voice barely audible.

Daryl drew in a shaky breath, forcing himself to continue. "There's more. They're gearing up to hit the National Guard armory. They're planning to raid it for weapons, ammo, explosives, anything they can carry. From what I heard, they already sent out a patrol today to scout the place. The raid's set for after midnight."

Logan, who had been standing silently at the edge of the room, stepped forward. His voice was sharp and filled with warning. "The last thing they need is more firepower."

Daryl nodded, his breathing uneven. "It sounds like they're planning to grab you first, then hit the casino soon after. They want to make it their headquarters. Turn it into some kind of stronghold."

Grant's jaw clenched, his mind racing. "How soon?"

"Not long," Daryl replied. "A day or two at most, I think. But the armory raid is happening first. They're not being too careful with their comms, they must think they're untouchable."

Grant gave a short, bitter laugh. "They probably don't think anyone has the means to listen in. Their arrogance might be their biggest weakness."

He turned to Daryl, his expression grim. "Good work, Daryl. Stay on it. We'll figure out our next move and make sure they don't get away with this."

"We need to get ready," Logan said, his voice allowing no room for confusion of his order.

Mace coughed, then raised his hand before asking, "why did you think they were coming to kill you already?"

"Might as well go ahead, Boss," Crackhead said, the others looking at him puzzled.

Grant motioned the gang to follow him, leading everyone back to the fire pit, each taking a seat on the logs. "There is something I need to tell you, all of you. I can't ask for your help without you knowing." He said, his voice cracking as he spoke. "I spoke with Julia about it, Crackhead knows the story. I owe you all the truth before asking you to fight by my side."

Ty looked at Logan, his eyes squinting slightly as they awaited the words. Whatever it was, it was powerful as Grant struggled trying to speak about it.

"Mace you asked earlier what we did to leave the Broken Arrows and Wolf's control," Grant said making eye contact with

Mace. He leaned forward, resting his forearms on his knees. "Years ago, as we said when we knew we wanted out, Wolf came to me with a name. Said they had unfinished business. He was an old friend of mine, a man named Daniel Harlow. Years earlier, he'd walked away from the gang, vanished without a trace. I should've known they'd never let him go."

Grant swallowed, his jaw tightening. "Wolf told me they just wanted to talk, to 'make things right.' That if I could find him, let them clear the air, Julia and I could walk away as well. I wanted to believe him... so I did. I tracked Daniel down. Led Wolf and his men straight to Daniel's home."

His fingers twitched, restless, as if resisting the urge to ball into fists. "Daniel had a family. A wife, two kids. He thought he was safe in his new life. That night, he answered his door with his daughter in his arms."

Grant closed his eyes for a brief moment, exhaling through his nose. "They forced Julia and me to watch as they shot his wife right in front of him. Then Wolf put a gun in my hand and told me I had a choice, kill Daniel, or they'd kill Julia."

His voice broke, but only for a second. "I hesitated."

Grant swallowed. "Wolf didn't. He grabbed Daniel's little girl and held his knife to her throat, told me to choose. So I did."

Silence fell over the group, thick and suffocating. Grant stared at the ground, his fingers rubbing together as if trying to rid them of something unseen. "Daniel didn't beg. He just looked at me. He knew and I pulled the trigger."

His voice hardened. "But it wasn't over. I turned the gun on Wolf, he only laughed telling me he wasn't stupid enough to put more than one bullet in the gun."

Mace watched Grant struggling to speak, feeling a sense of guilt for asking the question now, seeing the emotions being stirred up in him. Logan held up a hand to Mace, a sign to let Grant finish. He too could see the pain Grant was in, but if they were putting their life on the line for him, this needed said.

107

Grant's eyes flicked up, sharp with something darker. "They set the house on fire with the kids still inside. I fought. I fought like hell. They held me down while Wolf yanked my head back with my hair, forcing me to watch while I screamed at them to stop. The last thing I heard before the flames took them was those children crying inside for their mother."

Grant finally leaned back, rubbing his hand over his face, as if trying to wipe away the memory. His voice lowered, heavy with something between rage and regret.

"After that, Wolf said we could go. I never wanted anything like that to happen, and now, I question myself as to whether I thought Wolf might kill him or not. But I did what I had to do to keep Julia alive. When they finally let us go, we ran. We ran, and we never looked back."

Grant took a slow breath, forcing himself to meet their eyes. "Now you know what I did, you deserve to know it was because of me.... It was because of me that my friend died, that his wife died and that his two children died."

Owen and Mace exchange a look, their usual sharp wit and easy banter absent, their expression filled with shock.

Logan stood, walking toward Grant, studying him, reading the years of pain carved into the lines of his face. Without a word, he reached down, grasping Grant's forearm in a firm hold. Grant returned the gesture, their grip tightening in silent understanding.

"You did what you had to do," Logan said, his voice steady and unwavering. "No man should have to make that kind of choice. That's not on you, that's on Wolf."

Grant looked away for a brief moment, nodding as he swallowed hard. "Doesn't change what I did," he whispered.

"No," Logan agreed. "But it changes what you do next."

CHAPTER SIXTEEN

"Arrival in the Night"

Ty nodded at Logan, his expression grim. Then, turning to Owen and Mace, he raised a clenched fist. "This is it, boys. It's real now." His voice carried an unbendable edge. "Mace, you're with me. Owen, stay with Logan. Jordan and Dylan, you're going with Crackhead."

Mace rubbed his eyes, the fatigue evident as he suppressed a yawn. "You really think they'll come tonight?" he asked, his voice heavy with doubt.

Grant's gaze hardened. "If she gave the order, they'll come. Wolf doesn't waste time."

Crackhead motioned for Jordan and Dylan to follow, leading them to the base of the trail that wound up the mountainside. The dark forest loomed around them, shadows stretching like silent watchmen. Crackhead gestured to a thicket near the trail's edge. "Dylan, hide there. First line of defense. If you see anything, radio it in, that's all you do."

Dylan nodded, gripping the walkie-talkie as he vanished into the woods. Crackhead brought Jordan further up the trail, stopping at a bend. He pointed toward a cluster of boulders just past a towering pine. "Take cover there. Same deal, radio if anyone passes."

Jordan hesitated, his stomach churning. He wasn't a soldier, just a man trying to pull his weight. His hands shook slightly as he adjusted his grip on his rifle, but he nodded. "Got it."

Crackhead didn't linger. He climbed back into the truck, driving up to the guard gate. There, he placed a lantern on a post, the flickering light casting a soft glow across the trail. He arranged blankets and a hat on a log, crafting a decoy to resemble a guard sleeping at his post. Satisfied, he parked the truck further up the trail and rejoined Grant.

Grant crouched beside a partially fallen tree, its massive trunk held precariously by a thick rope tied to another. He lit a cigarette, the ember briefly illuminating his face. He took a deep drag, savoring the fleeting comfort. "If they come," he whispered, exhaling a plume of smoke, "we drop the tree." He passed the cigarette to Crackhead. "Never know when it might be the last."

The men settled into the shadows, their bodies stiff with anticipation. Their breaths felt too loud, the night too quiet. The distant howl of a coyote sliced through the silence, its mournful cry lingering like a warning. The men flinched, drawing in a breath, their muscles coiling, every nerve on edge. It was the kind of sound that gnawed at the edges of their focus, making the night feel alive with dangers.

Leaves rustled faintly in the breeze, but it wasn't wind, someone or something moving in the brush. The hairs on the back of their necks stood, but they didn't move. They couldn't afford to. The distant sound of an owl hooted, the sharp call cutting through the heavy silence before fading away. Logan and Ty, hardened by countless hours in the field, told themselves it was just the wild. But even they couldn't ignore the underlying tension.

Logan shifted slightly, scanning the darkness. "You hear that?" he whispered.

Ty tilted his head, straining to catch the faint sound. "It's a chopper," he said, his voice low but urgent.

Logan closed his eyes, focusing. "Coming from the north." His head snapped back up. "The house."

110

Grant was already moving, sliding down the embankment, hoping trees and rocks. He hit the trail and into his ATV, gesturing for Crackhead to join him. The distant hum of rotor blades grew louder, vibrating through the air.

Logan grabbed his radio. "Jordan, Dylan, stay put. Stay hidden," he barked before sprinting toward another ATV with Ty close behind. The vehicles roared to life, tires spitting dirt and rocks as they sped up the trail.

Owen hesitated, torn between orders and instinct. "What do we do?" he asked Mace, his voice tight.

"Stick to the plan," Mace said, though his tone let slip his unease. He gripped his rifle tighter, glancing nervously toward the sky. "I don't like this. We should stay together."

Owen pointed skyward, his eyes widening. "There it is. See the light on the tail?" He stepped away from the trees, straining for a clearer view. The chopper was circling above the area of the cabin now, its spotlight slicing through the darkness.

At the ridge, the helicopter's spotlight flickered over Grant's property. Inside the chopper, Elijah Raines, Wolf's second-in-command, gripped a handle holding on tightly, his sharp eyes scanning the ground below. Sparse lights dotted the cabin and outbuildings. He turned to the two men seated behind him. "Go get him," he ordered over the mic. "He's coming with us."

The first man opened the door, clipped his harness to a cord, and began rappelling down. The second followed, their descent swift and silent.

"We've got movement," the pilot reported, spotting figures darting between outbuildings. The ATV headlights rounded the last bend, giving away their position as they approached the cabin.

"Taking fire!" the pilot shouted as bullets pinged off the helicopter. He yanked the controls, jerking the aircraft higher.

111

Elijah gritted his teeth, his knuckles white as he gripped the overhead bar. "Hold steady!" he snapped, but the pilot's evasive maneuvers sent the chopper lurching.

"Wolf, do you copy?" Elijah barked into his radio, tapping the headset in frustration.

"This is Wolf," came the reply, cool and steady. "Do you have him?"

"They were waiting for us," Elijah spat. "We're taking fire. I've lost visuals on the team."

Wolf's voice tightened. "Abort. Return to base. I'll send in the others. Keep my chopper safe!"

Elijah hesitated, his gaze locked on the chaos below. Grant's men were moving with precision, their ambush seemingly well-executed. Snarling, he relayed the order. The chopper banked hard, disappearing into the night.

On the ground by the house, Brian and the other men rushed out, their movements sharp and deliberate as they circled the newcomers. Guns were drawn, barrels leveled, creating a tense standoff with the men descending from the helicopter. The two groups mirrored each other, both armed, both ready to fire at the slightest provocation.

"This doesn't need to be a shootout," one of the men from the helicopter said, his voice tight with nerves as his eyes darted to the weapons aimed at him.

An ATV roared to a stop nearby, Grant and Crackhead leaping out, pistols raised and ready. Grant's voice cut through the tense air. "What's this about?"

"We're not here to harm you, Grant," one of the men replied, his tone steady but urgent. He lowered the scarf covering his face, revealing his features. "Wolf wants you at the base camp, just come with us peacefully."

Grant's eyes widened in recognition. "You..." he muttered, a flicker of familiarity crossing his face. The man before him was someone from his past, an old comrade from the days of the Broken Arrows.

"This doesn't have to end badly. Come with us," the man added, his voice calm but edged with warning.

"Lower your weapons. Now," Crackhead barked, taking a deliberate step forward.

The guards hesitated, visibly torn, but the odds weren't in their favor. Slowly, reluctantly, their rifles began to lower, though their grips remained firm.

Grant glanced at Logan and Ty, weighing the situation. "I know him," he said, motioning toward the man. "We served together in the Broken Arrows. He's dangerous, well-trained and not to be underestimated."

Ty's reply was ice cold. "Kill him."

Grant blinked at the bluntness, startled by Ty's lack of hesitation.

"One less problem if we take him out now," Ty continued, his tone leaving no room for argument.

Grant hesitated, glancing at the men in front of him. "Shouldn't we take them as hostages?"

Logan shook his head. "These guys? They don't care about anyone, not us, not each other. Nobody's coming to trade for them."

Grant straightened, his decision made. He turned back to the men. "Drop your weapons. All of them. Or you're dead where you stand."

The two guards exchanged a brief, wordless glance. Grant recognized the look, one he'd seen in battle too many times. These weren't men surrendering out of fear. They were ready to fight, to die if necessary.

Behind him, Logan and Ty shifted positions, their movements subtle but precise as they flanked the group. The guards weren't blind, they could see the practiced discipline in the two men, the unyielding focus in their eyes.

Finally, one of the guards sighed, lifting his hands away from his weapon. "Alright," he uttered, setting his rifle on the ground. His partner followed suit a moment later, their defiance tempered by survival instinct.

Crackhead wasted no time, moving in to disarm them. He stripped them of their sidearms, knives, and any gear they carried, then zip-tied their hands and feet tightly.

Grant crouched in front of the men, his voice low and demanding. "What was the plan? You drop in, invite me back to the camp, and we all sit around reminiscing about old times?"

The man smirked, his expression unapologetic. "Wolf doesn't want to kill you, Grant. He's recalling you, recalling the Reaper. He's bringing you back to where you started. This is bigger than all of us. Bigger than Wolf, even."

Grant's jaw tightened. "Spare me the speech. Wolf's out for one thing, stealing what isn't his."

"You don't get it," the man replied, his grin widening. "We've got the chance to take what's ours. To control the land these so-called elders have been bleeding dry for their profits."

Grant shook his head in disgust. "He's using you, both of you, to do his dirty work. You're nothing more than tools to him. Pawns on a chess board, able to be sacrificed."

The man let out a low chuckle, his arrogance irritating. "We're all in, Grant. There's no fighting it. Wolf's making his move, soon. He's got squads hitting the armory tonight, raiding gun shops and ammo caches. It's already happening. You can stand in the way, or you can join the winning side."

Before Grant could respond, the crackle of a walkie-talkie interrupted.

"We've got three trucks turning onto the trail," a voice reported. "It's me, Dylan if you don't know. Over and out. 10-4" Dylan said, clearly with no idea how to use the radio properly.

The tied-up guard laughed, his confidence undiminished. "You didn't think Wolf would send us alone, did you? Let us go,

Grant. Have one of your guys drive us down to meet them. It's your only chance to get out of this alive."

Grant's gaze shifted to Logan, searching for an answer. "What do we do?"

The guard's voice cut in again, smug and mocking. "Decide fast. If they get here first, you're all dead. Let us go, and everyone lives. That's the deal."

Logan snorted. "You believe that?"

Grant rubbed his chin, torn between his gut and the cold logic of the situation. "Of course not."

The walkie squawked again, this time Jordan's voice. "I see the trucks now. Three of them, moving slow but they're coming. Over and out."

The guard laughed, "what idiots have you got on the radios? Is that the soldiers you plan to take Wolf on with?""

Logan turned to Ty, his expression unreadable. A single flick of his eyes communicated everything.

Ty nodded, his reply unwavering. "Kill them."

CHAPTER SEVENTEEN

"Over the Edge"

"Tie them up, Brian. Stay here and guard the house," Grant ordered, his voice calm but firm as his attention shifted to the house. On the porch, his wife, Julia, stood silently, her hands clasped tightly together. She met his eyes, her worry evident even in the dim light. "Julia, take the women and go to the armory."

Logan grabbed Ty's arm, urgency in his voice. "Let's go, brother. We need to help Mace and Owen before the Broken Arrows reach their position."

Ty hesitated, his jaw tight. His eyes flicked toward the tied-up guards, disdain radiating from him like heat. "We should kill them now," he grumbled darkly.

Logan shot him a warning look. "This is Grant's call, Ty. We follow his lead. Now, let them know we're en-route."

Reluctantly, Ty pulled the radio to his mouth. "Owen, Mace, we're on our way. Don't engage until we get there."

Static crackled before Mace's tense voice came through. "It might be too late, we can hear them, can't see them yet."

The ATV roared as Logan floored the gas pedal, sending dirt and gravel flying in their wake. Ty's grip on the roll bar tightened, his frustration evident in the hard line of his mouth.

Ahead, the headlights of the Broken Arrows' trucks pierced the darkness like twin eyes of a predator. The vehicles bounced along the uneven trail, a forerunner of chaos to come.

Mace crouched low beside Owen, his breath shallow. "When they get closer, I'll drop the tree," Owen whispered, his hands gripping the rope tightly. "Stay down and hidden."

Mace nodded, his voice steady despite the tremor in his gut. "10-4." He wasn't a soldier. Neither of them were. As the realization sank in that he might have to fire on another human being, his stomach churned. "I hear Dad and Ty coming," he added, more to steady himself than anything else.

He was right. Logan and Ty's ATV skidded to a halt just shy of the final bend, followed closely by Grant and Crackhead. Logan killed the engine, signaling for silence.

"We go on foot from here," Logan commanded in a low voice. He and Ty leapt from the vehicle, rifles at the ready. The night closed in as they moved under the cover of darkness.

Ty took position behind a fallen tree, kneeling and steadying his rifle across the tree trunk. Logan pressed forward, weaving through the brush until he reached Mace.

"Dad, I'm here," Mace hissed, his voice barely audible. "Uncle Owen told me to move this way, further from where the tree's coming down."

Logan crouched beside him, scanning the long, straight trail. Over a hundred yards away, the trucks idled threateningly. The figures moving in and out of the headlights were little more than silhouettes, but their presence was undeniable, a flicker of movement here, the glint of metal there.

"What are they doing?" Owen muttered under his breath. From his position, fifty yards away, he could barely make out anything beyond the blinding glare of the lights.

Grant's voice crackled over the radio. "What do you see?"

Owen keyed his mic. "They're holding for now, but I can't tell what they're planning."

"Mace, stay here and cover this position," Logan instructed, placing a reassuring hand on his shoulder. "If shooting starts, this is where you stay."

Mace nodded coldly as Logan crept away, moving to join Owen. Ty shifted slightly, positioning himself to cover Mace, his rifle trained on the trucks.

The night felt alive with tension. The soft rustle of leaves and the occasional snap of a twig seemed amplified in the silence. The headlights harsh beams danced over the terrain, their relentless brightness like a searing interrogation.

"You good, Owen?" Logan whispered as he approached.

Owen didn't look up. "All good here," he replied.

The sharp crack of a high-powered rifle shattered the stillness, making every man flinch. Owen's eyes snapped to the gate. The dummy Crackhead had set up as a decoy toppled backward, the bullet tearing through its flimsy frame.

"Nice job, Crackhead," Owen whispered under his breath, but the satisfaction was fleeting. The growl of engines swelled as the trucks began to move again, their headlights carving through the darkness.

Owen pressed his mic. "They think they killed the gate guard. Here they come."

The trucks began to inch forward, their tires crunching over gravel. Each man's pulse quickened, the weight of the moment bearing down on them. They had a plan, but plans were fragile things, easily shattered by the chaos of reality.

The trucks groaned as they came to a halt at the gate, their engines idling with a low growl that rumbled through the tense night air. The passenger door of the lead truck creaked open, and a man hopped out. Owen tracked him through the glow of the headlights, the man's shadow stretching long and distorted as he crossed in front of the truck. He approached the fallen decoy with cautious steps, clicking on a flashlight that cast a harsh beam over the slumped figure.

The man froze, his flashlight illuminating the lifeless form of the dummy propped in the chair. "It's a trap!" he shouted, spinning toward the driver with wide eyes.

Owen's radio crackled to life. Logan's voice came through, sharp and urgent. "Now, Owen!"

Owen's heart thudded as he drew his knife, its blade glinting faintly in the scattered light. He slashed at the stressed nylon rope, the blade biting into the fibers. The rope quivered under the strain, holding firm despite the gash.

"Come on," Logan whispered under his breath from his hidden position. "Cut the damn rope, Owen."

Behind Mace and Ty, a thunderous crashing sound tore through the night, echoing like a landslide of boulders or a stampede of wild beasts descending the mountain. Both men froze, instinctively ducking lower into the cover of the trees. Ty turned, his rifle gripped tightly, eyes narrowing as he scanned the darkness. The dense underbrush seemed alive, shifting with each gust of wind.

"I don't know, Mace," Ty mumbled, his voice low, edged with unease. He squinted harder, trying to pierce the darkness. "Can't see anything. Maybe... maybe a tree came down."

The guards had begun pouring out of the trucks, their flashlights stabbing through the darkness. One of them grabbed the gate, yanking violently at the chain, the metal clanking against itself in the stillness. Tension coiled tighter around the group as they held their positions, their breaths shallow.

Owen reset his grip on the knife, his hands slick with sweat. With a grunt, he slashed again, the blade tearing through more of the rope. It still held, refusing to give way. He cursed under his breath, his frustration mounting as he repositioned for another strike. On the third attempt, he pulled the blade with all his strength. The rope finally snapped, the sound like a whip crack echoing into the night. Owen fell backward from the force, his body crashing into the underbrush with a loud rustle that might as well have been a shout in the silence.

A nearby guard whipped around, his flashlight darting toward the noise. The light settled on Owen's position.

"Not tonight," Mace whispered from his perch, steadying his AR-15. He exhaled slowly, just as he'd practiced on the range, and squeezed the trigger. The rifle's muzzle flashed, the sharp crack of the shot slicing through the night. The guard staggered back, clutching his shoulder as the flashlight tumbled from his grasp and clattered to the ground.

Owen scrambled to his feet, pressing his back against the massive tree trunk. "Fall!" he barked, shoving against the tree with all his strength. Logan appeared beside him, his hands gripping the trunk just above Owen's head. Together, they pushed, their muscles straining as the wood groaned and popped. The tree swayed, then toppled forward with a thunderous crash, its branches sprawling across the trail and blocking the trucks' path.

"Start firing!" a voice bellowed from the trucks.

Chaos erupted as bullets sprayed wildly into the trees, their muzzle flashes lighting up the darkness like fireflies on speed. The Red 30 gang responded from their concealed positions, firing down from the high ground. Their shots punched through the trucks' tires, releasing hissing streams of air, while others ricocheted off metal with sharp pings. Trapped between the fallen tree ahead and a sheer drop to the side, the guards had no place to retreat but behind their vehicles.

Grant worked furiously at a second rope, positioned to drop another tree behind the trucks and block their escape. The driver of the third truck slammed into reverse, the engine roaring as the vehicle skidded backward, narrowly avoiding going over the edge.

With a final snap, Grant's rope gave way, and the second tree crashed behind the first two trucks, locking them in place. He grabbed his rifle, firing a burst of rounds toward the retreating vehicle. The bullets tore through branches, but the truck veered out of range before he could land a solid hit.

Meanwhile, Logan and Owen moved cautiously through the cover of trees, their rifles barking sporadically as they closed in on the enemy. Ty and Mace focused their fire on the trucks, shattering headlights and plunging the road back into deeper darkness. The first truck's lights were extinguished entirely, but the faint glow from the second truck cast silhouettes of the guards scrambling for cover.

The gunfire slowed, turning into intermittent bursts from both sides. The silence between shots was empty, filled only by the ragged breathing of the combatants and the occasional groan of a wounded guard. High above, the stars bore silent witness, their cold light indifferent to the battle below.

"Hold your fire!" a voice shouted from the trucks, sharp and desperate. "Don't shoot!" the man pleaded.

"Grant! Is that you?" another voice called out from behind the truck, louder and more deliberate. "We're not here to hurt you! Let's talk."

Grant shifted closer to Logan's position, crouching low behind the cover of a tree. "What do you think?" he asked, his voice barely above a whisper.

Logan's expression remained hard. "Lay down your weapons and line up in front of the truck," he said firmly, his tone allowing no argument.

Grant nodded and cupped his hands around his mouth. "Do what he says! Lay all your weapons down! Line up in front of the truck!" he barked.

Silence answered the command, heavy and deliberate. The faint shuffle of boots revealed movement behind the trucks, but no one spoke. Logan could feel the hesitation, the men weighing their odds. Mace and Ty inched closer to the trucks, rifles at the ready, their silhouettes melting into the trees as they remained concealed.

"Wolf wants you to come with us, Grant," the voice called back finally, more measured now. "We don't need any more bloodshed. Come on out, let's go see Wolf."

Grant's jaw clenched as he turned to Logan, waiting for a signal. Logan's response was immediate. "Do as we said!" he shouted back. "Drop your weapons, move to the front!"

One by one, the guards obeyed, stepping into the dim glow of the truck's headlights. Each laid their rifles on the ground with deliberate slowness, forming a line in front of the vehicle, side by side.

"Okay, Grant, here we are," one of the guards said, his voice calm but edged with confidence. "You know how this will go. Wolf has too much firepower for you to take him on."

Logan's radio crackled suddenly, Ty's voice breaking the tense quiet. "Do not come out. They've got a guard behind the truck, scanning for you. We see him."

Logan didn't hesitate. "Take him out," he ordered coldly.

Through the stillness, Mace exhaled and fired. The shot cracked like thunder in the night, and the guard behind the truck dropped instantly, his body slumping against the front tire, his weapon clattering to the ground.

The line of guards flinched, some ducking into crouched positions, their movements jerky and uncertain. Only one man remained standing, the leader. He didn't so much as blink, his posture unnervingly steady, he had anticipated this outcome.

Grant glanced at Logan, nodding his approval of the swift action. He opened his mouth to speak, but Logan interrupted, his voice booming with authority.

"We're not negotiating," Logan shouted. "We give a command, you obey it. Drop all your weapons!"

"Nice shot, Mace, I thought I'd be taking it," Ty told him with a raised fist pump.

The remaining guards scrambled to comply, throwing pistols and knives into a pile at their feet. But the leader didn't move. Instead, rolling his head slowly, contemplating his move.

"Grant, I wish you hadn't done that," the man said, his tone laced with disappointment. "Wrong choice, my old friend."

Without warning, he dropped into a crouch and bolted. Sprinting around the truck, he leaped over the edge of the mountain trail, vanishing into the darkness below.

"He just jumped over the edge," Mace roared to Ty, his voice in disbelief as they watched from their angle.

The silence lingered for a moment before Ty spoke, his eyes scanning the horizon. "Morning's coming, we'll find him," he said quietly, noting the faint light in the sky.

The three remaining guards dropped to their knees, trembling as they raised their hands above their heads. The lifeless bodies of their comrades lay scattered along the trail road, twisted and broken like discarded puppets. Some were curled into unnatural positions, while others sprawled with arms and legs bent at grotesque angles. The dirt around them was smeared with streaks of dark blood.

The gang approached the kneeling men cautiously, their weapons still trained on them. "Let's get them tied up," Grant said, motioning for Ty and Mace to secure the prisoners.

Logan stepped up beside him, his stare drifting to the steep slope that descended into the shadowed woods below. "I take it you recognized the one who went over," he said grimly.

Grant nodded, his eyes narrowing as he scanned the edge. "I did. We need to go down there and confirm. He could still be alive, and that makes him a threat."

Looking over his shoulder, Grant's brow furrowed. "Where's Crackhead?"

"Haven't seen him," Ty replied, his expression clouding as he glanced at Mace.

Grant grabbed his radio and called Brian back at the house. "Brian, we need backup. We've got prisoners."

"10-4," Brian's voice crackled back.

Logan keyed his mic, his voice sharp. "Jordan, Dylan, you copy? Check in."

Silence.

Ty shifted uncomfortably. "Maybe their radios died," he said, though his uneasy expression showed his doubt.

With no time to dwell on it, the men began tying up the prisoners and searching the trucks. The situation was heavy with tension until the distant growl of approaching ATVs broke the stillness. Moments later, Brian appeared.

"Look what I found," Brian called out, jerking a thumb toward the disheveled figure climbing out of the passenger seat.

Crackhead's appearance drew every eye. His shirt was ripped nearly to shreds, dried blood streaked across his face and arms. Mud caked his pants and boots, and his hair extended out in every direction. A crude tourniquet of torn cloth was knotted tightly around his thigh, and he limped as he approached.

Grant stared at him, dumbfounded. "What the hell happened to you?"

Crackhead lowered his face, embarrassed and frustrated. "I'm real sorry, guys," he grumbled, scuffing the dirt with his boot. "I was trying to move quiet, stay outta sight. But it was so dark, I couldn't see a thing. Walked straight into a spider web."

He paused, shaking his head. "I panicked, lost my balance, and fell over the edge. Rolled all the way down and hit my head. Knocked myself out cold. When I came to, I tried to climb back up, but... I lost my guns." His voice broke with self-remorse. "Guess I'm no Navy SEAL, more like a gravy seal."

The group exchanged glances, suppressing their laughter out of respect for Crackhead's obvious shame. Owen patted him on the shoulder. "I hate spiders too," he said reassuringly.

"Go pick up the two you dropped off," Grant instructed. "After that, get yourself patched up. You've earned a break."

As they worked to clear the road, Grant's attention was drawn to the radio in the truck, which suddenly crackled to life.

"Grant, you there? Talk to me, Grant," a deep, gruff voice demanded.

The men froze momentarily, their eyes locking.

Grant picked up the mic slowly, his stomach knotting as he replied, "Wolf."

A dark, menacing laugh filled the air. "Hello, Reaper. Been a while. I hear you've been busy. Did you kill all of them?"

Grant's jaw tightened as he glanced at Logan. "How does he already know?" he grumbled.

Logan shook his head.

Wolf's voice boomed again. "Grant, you still there?"

"I'm here. Say what you need to say, Wolf."

The laugh came again, colder this time. "You don't give me orders, that's my job. You've made a grave mistake, my friend. You betrayed the Broken Arrows, and now you'll pay for it. I'll find you, Grant. You, your wife, everyone you care about. Daniel Harlow, remember him? I can reach anyone, anytime."

"Leave us in peace, Wolf," Grant said firmly. "And I'll do the same for you."

"Are my men alive? Who else you got helping you?"

"Some. I have my team."

Wolf's tone turned venomous. "Hand them over. Now. If you do, I'll only kill one of your people. If not, I'll kill them all."

"That's no deal, Wolf," Grant shot back, gripping the mic tightly.

The line went silent before Wolf's voice roared back with finality. "I'm coming for you, Grant!"

Grant tossed the mic onto the truck's seat and turned to Logan. "This isn't over."

125

Logan nodded, his expression grim. "He knows you're not cowering, and he knows you're not alone. That makes you dangerous to him."

A faint hum rose from down the trail, growing louder with every second. The uneasy quiet shattered as an ATV came roaring toward them, Crackhead and Mace gripping the vehicle like their lives depended on it. Dust billowed behind them, curling into the air in angry swirls. Mace brought the ATV to a sudden, skidding stop, the machine spitting gravel and throwing up a choking cloud. He jumped off before the dust had even begun to settle, his boots hitting the ground with a sharp thud.

"Tell them, Jordan," Mace barked, his voice rougher and more forceful than any of them had ever heard him before.

Jordan stumbled out, his face pale and streaked with dirt. Sweat dripped from his brow, cutting tracks through the grime. His chest heaved as he struggled to get his words out, each breath sounding like it was scraped from his lungs.

"It's Dylan," he rasped, his voice breaking on the name. "He's gone. I lost my radio and was heading to his position after the trucks passed. I... I heard one of them coming back and hid. I ran after it and saw Dylan up ahead... standing in the road."

"What happened?" Ty demanded, stepping forward, his tone sharp and impatient.

Jordan paused, spitting into the dirt to clear his dry mouth. His hands trembled slightly as he steadied himself.

"He was running back up the trail when we found him," Mace said harshly, cutting in, defending Jordan's pause.

Jordan nodded quickly, then forced himself to continue. "The truck stopped, and..." his voice cracked again, but he pushed through. "A group of men jumped out, grabbed Dylan, and tossed him into the truck like a ragdoll. Then they drove off. I thought maybe I could cut them off at the main road, so I ran through the trees, trying to get ahead of them."

Owen's voice snapped through the air, his frustration unmistakable. "And do what exactly? Get yourself killed?"

Jordan didn't look up, his shoulders slumping. "I made it almost to the road," he said quietly. "The truck was coming, and... and then I saw him. Another guy, in camo gear. He came out of the trees like he'd been waiting for them. He stopped the truck and climbed in, like he belonged there."

Jordan's knees buckled, and he dropped into a crouch, his hands gripping his head. "I couldn't do anything," he moaned, his voice barely audible.

Grant's jaw clenched as he studied Jordan, then turned to Logan. His voice was low and grim, each word deliberate. "That's how Wolf knew what happened here so fast. The guy who jumped over this hill? That was Lance Tayanita." Grant's lips pressed into a tight line. "Former Green Beret. Dishonorably discharged. He's a survivalist and combat instructor, a dangerous one. Morally hardened. He'll do anything to win, no matter who gets hurt."

Ty snorted, a cold grin tugging at the corner of his mouth. "Green Beret, huh? Could've fooled me."

Logan ignored the comment, his gaze shifting down the trail, then back toward the house. His mind was already working through the next steps, weighing their options. Finally, he turned back to the group, his tone firm.

"We need to move. Load up and get everything back to the house. We regroup there, figure out our next move."

Grant gave a short nod, his shoulders squaring as he began issuing orders. The others followed without hesitation, their movements brisk.

The tension hung thick in the air, unspoken but felt by everyone. As they worked, the reality of their situation began to sink in. Dylan was gone, and Wolf's men weren't just relentless, they were precise, organized, and playing a game of their own design, rules be damned.

CHAPTER EIGHTEEN

"Twisting in the Rain"

Owen's truck rumbled along Route 441, its engine a low growl against the muffled backdrop of misty rain. His tires hissed on the damp asphalt, their sound blending with the occasional squeak of wipers struggling to clear the rain-slicked windshield. Owen gripped the steering wheel tightly, his knuckles white against the coarse leather. His fingers tapped a restless rhythm as his wide, darting eyes scanned the abandoned landscape. Every building and rain-drenched vehicle seemed like a threat.

In the passenger seat, Logan sat unnervingly still, his presence calm yet charged like a coiled spring. The AR-15 rested across his lap, its black metal gleaming faintly in the soft gray light filtering through the rain. His sharp gaze moved constantly, sweeping the horizon and mirrors. He said nothing but radiated a sense of readiness, his every breath controlled.

From the backseat, Ty's voice cut through the heavy silence, low and steady but carrying an edge of tension. "We've got movement. Truck's coming out of the hotel parking lot," he announced, his sharp eyes fixed on the rear window. The vehicle emerged sluggishly from a sea of abandoned cars, headlights flicking on like predatory eyes. "It's a Broken Arrows truck. No, wait, it stopped, it's not coming."

Owen's jaw tightened, his pulse quickening. He glanced into the rearview mirror repeatedly, each glance briefer than the last as if he feared locking eyes with whatever shadow might be following them. His foot eased down on the accelerator, the truck gaining speed, though not enough to appear panicked.

The world around them felt hollow. The once-bustling highway was a lifeless stretch of cracked asphalt and scattered debris, the familiar landmarks reduced to menacing silhouettes. Even the traffic lights, once vibrant with life, hung dark and indifferent, swaying slightly in the rain-speckled breeze.

As they neared the intersection by the police station, Owen's breath hitched audibly, his fingers momentarily freezing on the wheel. "Oh no," he choked out, barely above a whisper.

Logan's sharp instincts kicked in at Owen's tone, and his eyes followed his brother's line of sight. The rifle in his hands shifted slightly, but when he saw the source of Owen's horror, his grip slackened, momentarily, not in relief, but in disbelief. It wasn't the threat of gunfire, but something far more sinister.

A body hung from the traffic light pole, twisting in the rain gently on a frayed rope. Its lifeless form was battered by the wind and rain, pale skin glistening with moisture. Dylan. His once-lively frame was stripped bare, displaying an agonizing story of torment carved into his flesh. Gashes crisscrossed his torso, some shallow, others deep enough to reveal glimpses of muscle. Two broken arrows sticking from his chest, their shafts splintered as if snapped in rage, a warning sign to others.

A crude wooden sign dangled from his neck, the letters scrawled with jagged, hateful strokes: *Enemy of the Broken Arrows.*

Owen brought the truck to a halt beneath the grim display, his tires crunching over shards of glass and twisted metal. The rhythmic sweep of the wipers seemed deafening against the silence. Ty leaned forward from the backseat, his face grim. "Get him down," he growled, his voice a low rumble.

Logan and Ty moved swiftly, their boots splashing through shallow puddles as they reached for the rope. The rain falling harder now, its cold touch biting at their exposed skin, as if the world itself recoiled at the gruesome scene.

"We've got company," Ty growled, his rifle snapping up.

Logan turned sharply, his finger instinctively brushing against the trigger guard. A police cruiser rolled out from the station parking lot, its headlights slicing through the rain like searching eyes. The vehicle stopped close, maybe twenty feet away, idling with an unnerving hum.

The silence shattered as the cruiser let out a short, mocking burst of its siren. Its blue lights began to strobe, casting eerie flashes across the intersection. The doors opened slowly, deliberately, revealing two men who stepped out.

The driver, a lean man with long black hair spilling out from beneath a tilted police hat, smirked as he leaned casually against the open car door. His uniform, if it could even be called that, was a mockery, a tattered, sleeveless shirt exposing tattooed arms, and muddy boots that completed the look.

His partner, a stocky man with a scruffy beard, clapped his hands mockingly. "You know it's illegal to mess with public property, right?" he called out, his voice thick with amusement.

Logan didn't waver, his rifle steady as he tracked the two men. Ty worked quickly to lower Dylan's body into the truck bed, his movements brisk but respectful.

"Stay focused," Logan barked, his eyes locked on the imposters. "Just keep working, Ty," he said.

The driver chuckled, his grin widening. "You hear that, buddy? Stay focused." His partner joined in, their laughter hollow and disturbing. They stayed partially concealed behind the cruiser's doors, their hands lingering near their weapons. "That's like some type of felony to be messing with the dead," he shouted, his partner shaking his head in laughter as though this was a joke.

Ty's jaw tightened as he removed his rifle from his back. "Let's drop these bastards right here," he snarled, his voice dripping with venom needing to be released.

Logan shook his head, his eyes never leaving the men. "Not today. We don't know how many more are watching."

Raising his voice, Logan addressed the men. "This man deserves better than this. We're taking him with us!"

The passenger smirked, raising a hand in mock surrender. "Deserves better, huh? Big hearts, these guys," he taunted as they continued to laugh.

Without warning, the two men retreated, climbing back into their cruiser slowly. The tires spat water as they executed a quick U-turn, disappearing into the rain-soaked gloom.

Logan exhaled sharply, his voice firm. "Let's move. We're heading to the hospital."

They climbed into the truck in silence, the weight of the moment pressing down like the heavy rain continuing to fall. Water streaked down the windows, washing over the lifeless streets like a silent witness to the horrors of the new world.

Arriving at the hospital, Owen slowly drove through the parking lot, scanning for any signs of life. The stark silence was unsettling, broken only by the sloshing of water from the tires on the asphalt. He spotted the emergency room entrance and pulled the truck to a stop near it.

"Look," Owen said, pointing to a casino pickup truck parked by the entrance. "That's the same kind that took Caleb's body. Maybe it's the same one."

"How are we handling this?" Ty asked, his eyes darting nervously between the hospital and the parking lot.

Logan turned to him. "Stick to the new plan. Prep the cargo while I go inside."

Owen reached out to stop him. "That's a bad idea, Logan. We can't split up here," he said as he grasped Logan's arm.

Logan rested a hand on the truck bed, his gaze fixed on the ground as he weighed their options. He was startled by the faint sound of wheels rolling and a voice, a voice that felt eerily familiar. "Hello, my friends. I'm sorry we meet again."

"Ahyvnvwi?" Logan said, spinning to face the man approaching them. "The spiritual person? Or should I just call you Dale?"

The elder man offered a faint smile, nodding. "It honors me that you not only remember my name but also pronounce it correctly. However, just call me Dale."

"Ay-uh-wuh-new-we?" Owen attempted, his brow furrowing as he leaned his head sideways in confusion. "Where did you come from? And why do you have a hospital bed?"

Ahyvnvwi closed his eyes, his lined face softening as he began murmuring in a low, pleasing tone. His voice barely above a whisper, like the hum of the wind through the trees.

"Tsvsgino iyuha atsadi - ayi ulihelisdi wodi. Ulitsetlohi, ugidahli, talinehvna osda kanohisdi."

His words rolled like a river, soothing yet commanding attention, as if the earth itself were leaning in to listen. The gang exchanged uneasy glances, unsure of the meaning behind the words but unable to interrupt.

Ahyvnvwi stepped to the back of the truck with deliberate movements, his fingers trembling as he lowered the tailgate. Without opening his eyes, he placed a weathered hand gently on Dylan's body, a touch filled with reverence and sorrow.

"His spirit called to me," he said finally, his voice calm and unwavering. "He sought peace but could not find it here."

He tilted his head slightly, as though listening to something far away. "The wind carried his pain to me, and I answered, I accepted his pain."

Owen frowned. "What do those words mean, the ones you just said?"

Dale's eyes opened, and he regarded them with quiet intensity. "Many arrows pierce. There is peace in the heart. Maker of all. Protector. Lead him to the good place."

Logan and Owen moved to lift Dylan's body onto the bed, following Dale's silent instruction. Without another word, the elder man wheeled the hospital bed toward the emergency room entrance, disappearing into the building.

Owen watched him go, the tailgate still in his grip. "I've got a hundred questions, but I wouldn't even know where to start," he said, slamming the tailgate shut.

Logan turned back to Ty, who was working quickly in the truck bed. "He must've seen what we brought in," Logan said, lowering his voice. "I guess he doesn't care."

Ty paused, glancing over his shoulder. "He saw, all right. Either he doesn't care, or he's on a whole different wavelength."

Before Logan could reply, a voice interrupted them.

"Easy, friend," said a man stepping out from between cars, his hands raised in a show of non-aggression. "I saw you bring in the body. Was he a friend of yours?"

Logan tightened up, his hand moving instinctively to his holstered pistol. "That's far enough," he commanded, his voice firm as he give the order.

The man stopped, offering a disarming smile. "No need for that, just curious. Did you know him well? The dead guy?"

"He was murdered," Owen said bluntly, narrowing his eyes as he felt something was off with this man.

The man's smile twisted slightly. "Murder's an ugly word in times like these. Maybe it was, maybe it wasn't. What's your name? Where you from? What do you boys do?"

Ty bristled, starting to reply, "You're a nosy mother..."

The cold press of a gun barrel against the back of his neck cut him short.

The man smirked, nodding toward his armed companion. "Now would be a good time to put your weapon down." He said to Logan, followed by a smirk wink.

Logan's eyes darted between the two strangers, noting the Broken Arrow patch on the second man's sleeve.

"Ty, you ready?" Logan asked calmly.

"Ready for what?" the man with the patch asked, pushing the gun harder into the back of Ty's neck.

Owen looked at both men, "I'm not ready." He said quickly. "What's happening?"

"That's a nice patch on your sleeve," Logan called out to the man holding the gun on Ty, while looking at the first man.

Ty acted in a blur, turning and shoving the gun barrel away as the man's weapon discharged harmlessly into the ground. Ty drew his own pistol, firing two quick shots into the man's chest. Simultaneously, Logan raised his gun and fired a single round, punching through the forehead of the other man, dropping them instantly with a thud onto the wet asphalt.

Owen smacked the truck's tailgate with frustration. "I wasn't ready!" he barked, his voice shaking. "You guys need to loop me in on this stuff."

"When I said nice patch, instincts are to look at the object, Ty reacted knowing he would," Logan said crouching by one of the bodies, searching his pockets. Finding nothing, he nodded toward the truck. "Let's move before more show up."

They piled back into the truck, leaving the hospital behind. The road stretched dark and empty as Owen gripped the wheel. "What if that guy hadn't of looked away?"

Ty winked from the backseat, "then Dale would have been wheeling me inside."

"You ready to be in the loop now?" Logan asked.

"Dang right I am," Owen snapped. "No more John Wick stunts without telling me first."

Logan smirked, motioning for Owen to stop near the traffic light. "Stop right here," Logan told Owen. "You're about to see some real John Wayne and Clint Eastwood work."

Ty got out, pulling the tarp from the truck bed, revealing three bound and gagged prisoners. It was three of the men they took during the shootout at Grant's house. He tossed a thick rope over the traffic light pole, looping it around the hitch.

Owen's stomach churned as realization dawned of what was about to happen. Logan explained, "These men killed Dylan. Retribution starts here."

Owen nodded grimly. "I'm in. Tell me what to do."

Ty worked with cold efficiency, securing the prisoners and tightening the rope. Logan motioned for Owen to move the truck forward, letting the slack disappear. The prisoners slid toward the edge of the truck bed as the rope tightened around their necks. When their feet left the bed, and their bodies well off the ground, Logan signaled for Owen to stop.

The men kicked and struggled as the ropes tightened around their necks, before their movements slowed.

Owen stared at the swaying bodies, his jaw clenched. "It's brutal," he stammered, choking out the words, "but I get it."

"It's a statement," Ty said, securing the rope. "The Broken Arrows aren't the big bad predators, Wolf, thinks they are. They're just bullies, and we don't like bullies."

Owen climbed back into the truck, his resolve hardening. "Let's go. Let em' twist in the rain for Wolf to see."

As they drove past the police station, Ty leaned back in his seat. "They're gonna flip when they see what we've done." He exhaled a deep held breath as he watched his surroundings passing by, his mind on what they had done to Dylan.

Owen drove ahead, the truck's tires kicking up water as he focused on the road back to Grant's. The entire point of this mission had been to get Dylan back, but the plan had unraveled faster than anyone had anticipated. The Broken Arrows wouldn't let this slight go unanswered. Retaliation was inevitable, and they needed to be ready.

"We left them a clear message," Logan said, his voice low and bitter. He leaned against the window, his sharp gaze fixed on the horizon as though expecting trouble to appear. "'Red 30 Gang, they'll figure it out soon enough. We've sent our signal."

Owen's jaw tightened, but he said nothing.

Logan sighed, shaking his head. "I dread telling Mace and Jordan we failed."

CHAPTER NINETEEN

"The Hunters Command"

Wolf sat at his desk as the rain intensified, battering the roof with an unrelenting rhythm, as if war drums were announcing the upcoming madness. The dark skies loomed over the camp like a suffocating shroud, and lightning intermittently illuminated the room in brief, glaring flashes. His stare was unwavering, intense, the look of a man who believed the world should already kneel at his feet. There wasn't fear in his eyes, only frustration that others failed to meet his standards.

Thunder cracked, sharp and deafening, rattling the few fragile items on his desk. Most men would flinch, but not Wolf. He stood, his thick frame silhouetted against the dim light, and strode to the doorway. Pushing it open, he stepped onto the covered porch, staring out over the camp he had spent years building.

It wasn't the vision of order and efficiency he had once dreamed of. The camp stretched haphazardly along the ridge, a mishmash of weathered wooden shacks and Army-issue tents. The wind tugged at the tents, their flapping adding a mournful tune to the storm's chaos. Lanterns glowed inside the shelters, their flickering light leaking through seams in the canvas like ghostly apparitions.

Wolf's gaze shifted to the vehicles lined up near the edge of the camp. Two jeeps and a deuce-and-a-half six-wheeled truck sat glistening with rain, their paint dulled by the storm. He scowled. This haul from the National Guard armory was pitiful, a far cry from what he'd hoped for. No doubt the Guard had stripped their own stockpiles before the attack. The realization gnawed at him, fueling the anger simmering beneath his composed exterior.

Wolf turned his gaze toward the lone helicopter sitting at the edge of the camp, its dark outline illuminated now and again by flashes of lightning. The rain drummed steadily against its fuselage, running in streams down its once-pristine surface now dulled by time and weather. The rotor blades hung motionless, glistening under the storm, as if mocking his inability to use it.

The Broken Arrows hadn't been able to stock enough fuel before the attack, and what little he had left was too precious to waste on anything but emergencies. He waned it for the attack on the casino, conserving their fuel until then. In its current state, the helicopter felt like a caged predator, capable but useless. Wolf tightened his jaw, frustration knotting in his chest. The aircraft wasn't working as an asset, but a reminder of his inability to prepare for the chaos that had swallowed the world.

His hand tightened into a fist, and with restrained force, he tapped the doorframe. "This won't do," he groaned, his voice low but filled with poison. "We need more!"

In the distance, headlights appeared, bouncing along the rough trail leading into camp. Wolf's sharp eyes followed the vehicle as it approached, its beams cutting through the rain. The truck came to a stop in front of his cabin, its headlights clicking off. The driver's door opened, and a man stepped out, flipping the hood of his poncho over his head as he trudged through the mud toward the porch.

Wolf watched the man's approach with the experienced stillness of a predator. When the figure reached the steps, Wolf stepped forward from the darkness. "Elijah," he greeted curtly. "What have you brought me?"

Elijah pushed back the hood of his poncho, water dripping from the fabric and pooling on the wooden planks of the porch. Wolf's gaze lingered on the puddle forming at his feet, his displeasure as unmistakable as the storm. Elijah shifted uncomfortably under the weight of that stare before speaking.

"I wanted to report in person, Wolf," Elijah said, his tone steady but guarded. "I've got one of our men, Colt, with me. He has information you need to hear."

Wolf glanced toward the truck, then motioned for Colt to join them. The younger man scrambled out of the vehicle and bounded up the steps, skipping the bottom one entirely.

"You got information for me, soldier?" Wolf asked, his voice calm but lined with authority.

Colt nodded but avoided meeting Wolf's eyes, staring instead at the wet planks beneath his boots. "Yes, sir. I was at the hospital today. We saw a strange truck pull up, out-of-state tags, not a rental. It was...beefed up." His voice wavered slightly as he glanced nervously at Elijah.

Wolf's jaw tightened. "Colt, I'd appreciate it if you looked at me like a man when you speak," he said, his tone sharp enough to cut through the storm. "Now, what happened?"

Colt's head snapped up. "Yes, sir. Sorry, sir. We tried to take the men prisoners, but they were well-trained. Military, by the way they moved. They took out two of us in seconds. Precision shots to the head and chest."

Wolf's face darkened, his anger barely contained. "And how did you escape their wrath?"

Colt swallowed hard. "I....I was returning from relieving myself. I came around the corner just in time to see them take us down."

Wolf's hands moved to his hips, his silhouette imposing even in the dim light. "They didn't take 'us' down," he growled. "They took down two of my men while you cowered away." His voice carried the weight of a hammer, each word striking with precision. Colt flinched, the scolding cutting deeper than the cold rain.

Sensing the rising tension, Elijah stepped in. "There's more, Wolf. Colt followed them. You'll want to hear this."

Wolf's burning gaze shifted back to Colt. "What now?"

Colt hesitated, his voice low and shaky. "The boy we....we hung from the traffic light... They took him down." He paused, swallowing hard. "And they replaced him with three of our men, the ones who went to Grant's last night."

Wolf's fists clenched, his knuckles whitening. "Elijah," he said through gritted teeth, "how many men have we lost so far?"

Elijah didn't hesitate. "Eleven confirmed dead. Seven missing. Could be hostages at Grant Whitlock's. Two were found in a dumpster, two at the hospital, three at the traffic light, four near the golf course."

Wolf's teeth pressed together. "That answers the dumpster and golf course killings. It's the same people."

Colt spoke up, his voice trembling. "I tried to follow them, but there was someone else trailing them too. I had to fall back."

Elijah placed a hand on Colt's shoulder. "You're dismissed. Hit your bunk," he said, sparing the young man from Wolf's growing fury.

Wolf turned and motioned for Elijah to follow him inside. The two men entered the dimly lit cabin, the rain hammering against the metal roof. Wolf sat at a small table, flipping through a notepad, the silence thick with tension. Lightning flashed again, illuminating the room in stark, unforgiving light.

"If it wasn't for needing every man we can get right now, I would have you shoot him for being chickenshit," Wolf said to Elijah, his words leaving no room for argument.

Elijah nodded the comments, "I understand, Sir."

"We're going to take that casino," Wolf said finally, his voice low and dangerous. "It belongs to us. But I want to know

140

who Grant has helping him. Find out everything you can about these men."

Elijah nodded. "Yes, sir."

Wolf's eyes burned with intensity. "We need to grow our army. Intensify recruitment. Any able-bodied man joins, or you show them the consequences." His voice hardened further. "Kill their families. Burn their homes. Their neighbors will know not to resist. Offer rewards for anyone who turns over these men helping Grant Whitlock."

Elijah stood, his expression unreadable. As he reached the door, Wolf stopped him with a final, chilling command. "Elijah, go at this like your life depends on it."

The unspoken threat hung heavy in the air, as sharp and relentless as the storm outside.

"Understood, Sir," Elijah replied, stepping cautiously with every word right now.

CHAPTER TWENTY
"Saving the Buffalo"

The soft hum of the generator filled the room, casting the light of survival across the polished oak desk and leather chairs. Running Bear stood behind the desk, his large hands resting on its edge, his eyes fixed on Samuel as he entered. "How is it looking, Iron Hawk?" he asked, his voice carrying the weight of a leader accustomed to difficult news.

Samuel, known as Iron Hawk, shook the man's hand firmly before taking a seat. Rather than settling into the deep, inviting leather chair, he perched on its edge, his posture rigid like a bird of prey ready to strike. His sharp eyes locked on Running Bear's. "No good," he said, his tone blunt, stripped of any added reassuring pleasantries.

"I understand a young man, most likely a tourist, was killed and left at the intersection," Running Bear said both as a statement and a question.

Iron Hawk nodded slowly, "that is correct."

Running Bear exhaled slowly and crossed the room to a tall wooden cabinet. He opened it with deliberate care, the creak of the hinges breaking the silence. From inside, he retrieved two glasses and a bottle of aged scotch, its amber liquid gleaming under the light. Pouring the drinks, he placed one glass before Iron Hawk with a tap of his finger on the desk, a silent gesture of respect. Then, he moved to the wall, where a painting hung: a herd of buffalo thundered across an open plain, pursued by cowboys on horseback. His eyes lingered on the image, as if searching for answers.

"Wolf is the cowboy. We are the buffalo," Running Bear said quietly, his gaze never leaving the painting. "The question is, who comes to save the buffalo this time?"

Iron Hawk's expression remained unchanged. His eyes shifted briefly to the painting, then back to the untouched glass of scotch. "There may be help, if you're willing to pursue it," he replied.

Running Bear turned from the painting, his dark eyes narrowing as they locked onto Iron Hawk's. He moved back to his seat, clasping his hands atop the desk. "Explain," he demanded, his voice low but commanding.

Before Iron Hawk could respond, the door opened, and Martha 'Red Willow' Gentry entered. Her steps were purposeful as she moved to sit beside Iron Hawk. Dressed in a sturdy jacket and jeans, her sharp features revealed her no-nonsense demeanor. "What's this about help?" she asked, wasting no time on pleasantries.

Iron Hawk gave her a brief nod in acknowledgment. "Wolf's men were in a battle last night with one of their own, an old soldier who left them years ago. Grant Whitlock," he began, his voice steady but grim. "Grant chose peace after leaving the Broken Arrows. He settled down with his wife, Julia. But Wolf doesn't forgive deserters."

Red Willow leaned forward, her brow furrowed. "What happened?"

Iron Hawk's eyes darkened. "The Broken Arrows tried raiding Grant's home. They lost several men in the attack, but during their escape, they captured someone. They stripped him, murdered him viciously, and hung his body from a traffic pole near the police station."

Running Bear's face twisted in anguish, his head lowering as he shook it slowly. "How can Wolf carry so much hatred?" he muttered, his voice thick with emotion. His eyes glistened, though he refused to let the tears fall.

"It wasn't one of our native people," Iron Hawk clarified. "The man was an outsider."

Red Willow's tone sharpened. "Wolf will kill every outsider he comes across. How does this affect us?"

Iron Hawk hesitated for a moment, then continued. "After the man's friends cut him down, they took his body to the hospital. While they were there, two of Wolf's guards tried to capture them. The outsiders killed both with precision, military precision. Well trained military precision."

Red Willow and Running Bear exchanged startled glances, their unease obvious at the thought of using outsiders.

"That's not all," Iron Hawk said, his voice lowering. "Our man followed them. At the traffic light, they stopped and strung up three Broken Arrow prisoners they had alive. They let them hang and die right there." His gaze drifted to the buffalo painting again. "So maybe that's who saves the buffalo this time."

Red Willow's eyes narrowed in thought. "Where did they go? How do we find them?"

Running Bear held his hand up gently, "We must consider the usage of outside men, trained soldiers." His face deepened as considered the idea. "How would our people react to us bringing in mercenaries for hire."

Martha spoke up, "If it means saving their lives, their economic lifeline, I think they will be more than willing."

Running Bear turned his attention back to Iron Hawk, "how do we communicate with these men?"

"They headed to Grant's property. Our scout lost them once they turned up the trail to his house," Iron Hawk replied. "I can send a messenger to request a meeting."

Running Bear nodded slowly, his fingers drumming on the desk. "Do it. If there's even a chance of joining forces, we need to act now, in case Wolf strikes. People with military expertise could be a huge help for us at this time."

Iron Hawk's expression tightened. "It's not a question of if, Running Bear. Wolf will attack us, it's simple when."

Red Willow leaned back, folding her arms. "Gentlemen, we can't afford to debate on this. The time for politeness is over. Wolf wants this land, and he'll do whatever it takes to get it."

Iron Hawk allowed himself a faint smile, though it didn't reach his eyes. He knew Red Willow's bluntness would unsettle Running Bear, and he relished the subtle victory.

Running Bear sighed heavily, rubbing a hand over his face. "We'll prepare for an attack. But I want this meeting arranged as soon as possible."

Red Willow raised a hand, stopping him. "We can't just ask for their help. These outsiders have no loyalty to us. If we want their support, we need to make an offering."

Running Bear leaned back in his chair, his fingers clenching and unclenching as he considered her words. Finally, he nodded. "You're right. We'll make an offering. Iron Hawk, prepare it. Red Willow, you'll go with him to present it. We need their help before it's too late."

CHAPTER TWENTY-ONE
"Gambling, Gold and Guns"

Inside the cramped barn attachment, the Red 30 gang huddled around a battered kitchen table, their faces illuminated by the glow of a single lantern. Crackhead, Daryl, and Brian joined the group, playing a little Texas Hold em'. The rain beat against the tin roof as they waited for the river card to be turned. Only Mace, Owen, and Crackhead remained in the hand, the others had already folded. The worn quarters they used as chips clinked faintly as the pot grew, their monetary worth long gone but still serving as a distraction from the weight of survival.

"There are only two guarantees in life," Mace said, smirking as he revealed his winning hand. "We're all gonna die, and Ty's gonna fold every hand he plays."

The table erupted into laughter. Owen slapped his knee, unable to stifle his amusement. "That's gold, Mace! Ty couldn't read a hand if it came with instructions!" He reached over and gave Ty a playful squeeze on the shoulder.

Logan grinned, letting their laughter wash over him. Moments like this were rare now, and he welcomed the relief. It was good for the group, especially Mace and Jordan, who were still reeling from the loss of two friends. Logan hadn't told them everything, hadn't mentioned how Dylan's body had been found, but he'd delivered the news with the same stoic determination they all now wore as armor. Dylan was gone, just like Caleb, and both were now lying cold in the makeshift morgue at the hospital.

The gang had vowed to fight back, refusing to let their fallen friends become mere statistics in this new world. But the unspoken truth lingered in the air like the smell of the animal manure in the barn, any one of them could be next.

"Rake in your winnings, Mace," Owen said, slapping the table with exaggerated cheer. "Clear the way for Ty to make another generous donation."

The table laughed again, though Ty squinted at Owen with mock annoyance. "You know what, Owen? At least I can lose my quarters knowing I had a damn good steak at Prime's Grill." He paused for effect, a wide grin breaking across his face. "Oh wait, I didn't. Because you booked the wrong city!"

The room roared with laughter, Owen burying his face in his hands. Even Logan joined in. "That's right! Asheville! Owen, you had us thinking we were getting mouthwatering ribeye steaks, and we ended up with fast food cheeseburgers!"

Owen held up his hands in mock surrender. "I tried, okay? My apologies, gentlemen. I owe you all a proper meal someday, if Prime's Grill still exists."

Crackhead didn't follow the inside joke, but the infectious laughter made him chuckle along with Brian. "Sounds like Owen really screwed the pooch on that one," Crackhead said, grinning.

"He sure did," Ty replied, shaking his head as he eyed his freshly dealt cards.

As the group bantered and played, their lightheartedness was a thin veil over heavier thoughts. Ty wondered if his brother Ethan was still alive out there. Mace and Jordan carried the weight of their friends' deaths. Logan and Owen worried about keeping the group alive, their determination to protect everyone as unrelenting as the rain pounding outside.

Daryl finally broke the cheerfulness, clearing his throat as he shuffled the deck. "Fellas, lemme tell y'all what I heard on the radio last night." His voice dropped into a grim tone, immediately grabbing their attention. "This country's goin' to hell in a handbasket. Cities are burnin'. Landmarks? Gone, like they were never there."

He set the cards down, leaning forward as the rain softened outside. "D.C.'s downtown got wiped out. The White House, Capitol Building, National Mall, just rubble and craters now. Chicago? Same deal. That shiny bean thing? Gone. And they said the Sears Tower, well, Willis Tower or whatever it's called now, collapsed like a damn house of cards."

The table fell silent. Even Crackhead looked solemn.

"Vegas didn't stand a chance either," Daryl continued. "The Strip's just a line of smolderin' ruins. Bellagio, MGM Grand, you name it, it's all gone. L.A.'s a mess. The Hollywood sign's ashes in the hills, and the ports got hit hard." He paused, taking a swig of beer. "And the Golden Gate Bridge? Gone. They're sayin' the Bay Area's a ghost town now. Hell, even the Space Needle in Seattle toppled over."

The group exchanged uneasy glances. Mace asked the question on everyone's mind. "What's the country doin' about it?"

Daryl leaned back in his chair, the weight of his news etched across his face. "It's chaos. National Guard's stretched too thin. Air Force bases are still operational in places like Edwards and Wright-Patterson, they're runnin' drone missions and bombin' anything they can. Navy's got a few ships left, tryin' to hold the coasts." He tossed a chip into the pile, his voice lowering. "But here's the kicker, they're hirin' private contractors now. Mercenaries. Payin' 'em in whatever they've got, ammo, food, medicine. And folks are turnin' on each other, like bounty hunters with no laws."

Daryl let the silence settle before delivering the worst of it. "They've got checkpoints everywhere, claimin' it's for 'containment.' But you know what that really means. Anyone tryin' to flee the big cities? They're not comin' back. Same thing

148

the Broken Arrows are doin' around here. If they catch you, you're as good as gone."

The room grew heavy, their earlier laughter now a distant memory. Outside, the rain tapered off, leaving only the sound of dripping water from the roof. Logan glanced around the table, his jaw tight.

"This country might be fightin' back," Daryl added softly, "but if you ask me? We're all just playin' a losin' hand."

For a moment, the world outside felt eerily calm, as if the rain had been a shield, and now, without it, they were exposed once again.

Crackhead's radio crackled to life, interrupting the stillness of the barn. Waylon's voice came through, low but tense. "Grant, Crackhead, either of you copy?"

Crackhead reached for his radio, but Grant beat him to it. "Go for Grant," he responded.

"I've got a truck with four members from the casino here," Waylon announced, his tone laced with unease. "They're asking to talk."

There was a brief pause before Logan said to Crackhead sharply. "Tell them we're on our way. Don't let them through." Logan was already reaching for his AR-15, his movements quick and deliberate. Ty followed suit, grabbing his rifle with equal urgency.

Crackhead clicked his mic. "Hold them at the gate. We're en route." His voice was steady, but his fumbled grip on the radio revealed his nerves.

As Crackhead exited the barn, he met Grant jogging over from the house. "Logan and Ty are headed out. Let's follow," Crackhead said, nodding toward the side-by-side. Without another word, they climbed in, the vehicle kicking up mud as they sped down the trail.

The wet ground made the ride treacherous, the tires slipping slightly as they navigated the final turn. Ahead, the faint glow of headlights illuminated the guard gate where Waylon stood, his silhouette rigid against the truck's beams.

Grant keyed the radio as they slowed. "Waylon?"

"All good. Come on down," Waylon replied, his voice calm but watchful.

They brought the side-by-side to a halt near the gate and climbed out, rifles raised and ready. The truck's passengers, clearly aware of the tension, raised their hands in submission.

"What's your business here?" Grant called out, his voice firm as he approached the vehicle.

The driver, a composed man with long, graying hair tied neatly at the nape of his neck, spoke first. "I'm Samuel Iron Hawk Greyson, but you can call me Samuel." His hands remained visible on the steering wheel. "We represent the casino. Our leader, David Running Bear Blackthorn, sent us with an offer to discuss."

Grant glanced at Logan, who stepped forward, his sharp gaze scanning the truck's interior. His eyes lingered on Samuel before shifting to the woman in the passenger seat.

"And you are?" Logan asked, his tone chilled.

"Martha Red Willow Gentry," she answered bluntly. Her expression was tight, her tone edged with impatience. "I'm the casino's treasurer and I have something to discuss."

He looked back at Samuel, "discuss it then." Logan said flatly, his stance unyielding. "Right here, right now."

Samuel raised a calming hand. "She's just on edge. This will be fine to talk right here." With deliberate slowness, he turned off the ignition, the engine ticking as it cooled.

Martha bristled, her irritation clear. "Here? Are you going to at least invite us to your house, maybe offer some coffee or something?" she snapped.

Logan's lips curved into a smirk, though the humor didn't reach his eyes. "If we wanted you over for coffee or something, you'd have gotten an invitation to come over for coffee or something," he said coldly.

Samuel shot Martha a warning glance before addressing Logan. "My apologies for her tone. Let's get to the point." He climbed out of the truck slowly, hands raised in a show of trust. Logan stepped back, granting him space.

Grant kept his rifle at the ready but spoke evenly. "What is it you came to discuss?"

Samuel adjusted his jacket against the chill. "Grant Whitlock," he began, his voice steady. "Leaving the Broken Arrows was the smartest move you've made."

Grant's eyes narrowed as he exchanged a glance with Logan. "You clearly know who I am. Now, who exactly are you?"

"I'm the chief security officer at the casino," Samuel explained. He gestured toward Martha. "As she said, she's the treasurer. And those two in the back?" He nodded toward the two stone-faced men in the rear seats. "My guards."

Logan's gaze lingered on the guards before he spoke again. "I'm Logan. This is Ty. You clearly know Grant. That big guy over there is Crackhead."

Samuel nodded respectfully. "We understand you've had... encounters with the Broken Arrows." He paused, watching their reactions. "Word is you've taken out several of their soldiers. That interests us."

Logan's expression hardened. "We're listening."

Samuel took a step closer, his boots squelching in the mud. "We're low on experienced security. We've got weapons, ammunition, food, things to trade for your services."

Grant tilted his head. "What kind of services?"

Samuel's voice dropped, his tone serious. "We need your team to stand with us against the Broken Arrows. They're planning an attack on the casino. It's imminent, and we need your help."

Martha, unable to stay silent, "We'll pay you in cash."

151

Ty let out a sharp laugh. "Cash? Might as well be toilet paper these days."

Crackhead chuckled, and Ty added, "Though Crackhead could probably use a roll of ones."

The laughter was short-lived as Logan's gaze locked back on Samuel. "How do you know this attack is coming? What proof do you have?"

Samuel's expression darkened. "Our scout overheard Wolf himself talking to Elijah, his second-in-command. This isn't just a raid. They want everything, our supplies, our weapons, even the land. They're rallying anyone they can, promising safety to those who join them."

Logan rubbed the back of his neck. "You're sure this scout is legit? This isn't just drunk talk around a fire?"

Samuel nodded firmly. "He's one of ours, deep undercover. He risked his life to get this information to us."

Silence hung heavy in the air as the group processed the situation. Finally, Logan spoke, his voice calm but commanding. "If we're going to help, we need terms."

Samuel nodded. "Name them."

Logan rattled off the list without hesitation. "Half a million in gold. Thirty AR-15s. Thirty pistols, nine-millimeter or .45. Ten thousand rounds for each. One year of food. And a thousand gallons of fuel."

Martha's jaw dropped. "That's... a lot."

Samuel faced her, his expression firm. "We'll handle it."

Ty stepped forward, adding with a smirk, "Oh, and when this country gets back on its feet, we want free rooms every year. Presidential suites. Free drinks and dinner at Prime's Grill for Crackhead here."

Samuel allowed himself a small smile. "Deal. As long as you help us keep the casino intact."

Logan nodded. "We'll be in touch."

CHAPTER TWENTY-TWO
"The Cost of Defiance"

The heat seared Maria's face, sweat dripping down her temples as she struggled against the iron grip of Wolf's soldiers. Her screams and curses fell on deaf ears, met only with cruel laughter as they watched her home engulfed in flames. The fire roared, consuming everything she owned, painting the night sky in an eerie orange glow. Neighbors peered from their windows, eyes wide with horror, but none dared to intervene. They had seen what happened to those who resisted. The gazes of the Broken Arrow soldiers met theirs with venomous warning, challenge us, and you'll burn next.

Maria Sanchez had spent years operating an underground medical clinic, treating those in need who had nowhere else to turn. The hospital was a hollow shell now, abandoned and useless without staff or supplies. Only people like Maria remained to provide care, patching up those caught in the brutal aftermath of this new world.

Wolf's orders had been clear, and Elijah carried them out with ruthless efficiency. His voice echoed through the streets via megaphone, stern with authority and malice. "Let this be a warning! The Broken Arrows control this land. You are either with us or against us, and the latter does not end well for you."

Maria's supplies had already been stripped away, antibiotics, surgical kits, every tool she needed to save lives. She was an asset too valuable to leave behind.

"You will join us, Maria," Elijah said, his grip tightening on her jaw. "Or you will burn here with your house."

She searched desperately for a savior among the silent crowd, but none came. Fear had silenced them all. Tears carved tracks down her cheeks as she choked back sobs.

"Shake your head if you understand and agree," Elijah ordered, his fingers digging painfully into her skin before giving her a sharp, humiliating jerk.

With no choice, Maria slowly nodded. She was at their mercy now.

Elijah turned back to the crowd, scanning the terrified faces. "If you are able-bodied, step forward now and join us," he commanded. "If we have to come for you..." He glanced back at Maria's burning home, then chuckled. "Well, you see the consequences."

No one moved.

Elijah motioned toward another house. "That one's next."

The door creaked open before his men reached it. A frail old man stepped onto the porch, raising a trembling hand. "I don't want any trouble," Jack Holloway said. "I'm just an old man. I'm of no use to you."

Elijah smirked. "Gramps, isn't it? That's what your grandsons call you. Joseph and Joshua."

Jack's mouth tightened. Nearing seventy, he was a Vietnam veteran, living with his daughter and two grandsons. "Leave those boys alone!" he barked. "You should be ashamed. We are the same people! You turn on your own people?"

Elijah grabbed Jack's chin, forcing his head back. "You turned on us when you backed that damn casino over your own people," he spat. "Now get your ass to the street, Gramps!"

"Stop!" a voice called. Joseph emerged from the house, eyes blazing with defiance. "Leave my grandfather alone!"

Elijah smirked. "Come here, boy. Which one are you? Joseph or Joshua?"

"Joseph," he said, trying to hold a stoic stance.

"Brave," Elijah mused, raising his megaphone. "Joshua! Come forward, or I put a bullet in your brother's head. You have five seconds." He began counting down, dropping his fingers one by one.

Joseph stood frozen, his breath shallow.

"Two. One..."

"Wait!" Joshua burst from the darkness, panting. "We'll go with you! Just don't hurt anyone!"

The soldiers shoved them both to their knees.

Elijah crouched in front of them. "Tell me what you can do," he demanded. "And don't lie."

Joshua swallowed hard. "Our grandfather's a gunsmith. He can repair any weapon, reload ammunition. Joseph's a mechanic."

"That's enough, Joshua," Jack growled. "This man isn't one of us. He's a traitor."

Elijah chuckled. "Still got some fight in you, old man." He backhanded Jack, sending his head snapping sideways. "Learn your place."

He turned to Joshua. "And you? What can you do?"

Joshua squared his shoulders. "I'm an expert shooter. Short range, long range, doesn't matter."

Elijah studied him for a moment, then sighed. "Can't have you pointing a gun at my back." He drew his pistol and without hesitation or remorse, fired a single shot.

Joshua crumpled to the ground, his eyes blank as his life was eliminated, blood pooling beneath him.

His mother's scream tore through the night as she rushed forward, collapsing over her son's lifeless body.

Joseph clenched his fists, fury blazing in his eyes.

Elijah raised his gun again, this time aiming at the back of the grieving mother's head. He said nothing, merely tilting his head in silent command. His stare at Joseph clear, was he ready for her to be next? Or was he ready to serve?

155

Joseph trembled, rage and grief colliding within him.

"We'll go," he whispered, voice thick with tears. He turned to Jack. "Let's go, Gramps."

Elijah continued his brutal campaign, house by house. Some residents surrendered willingly, others were dragged from their homes, some burned alive. Fear was working as many climbed into the trucks, one by one.

Noah "Scrap" Daniels, an electrician, was taken for his ability to restore power. Calvin Jenkins, a seasoned truck driver, offered himself in exchange for his family's safety.

Then there was Judith Calhoun. The elderly Native woman stepped forward, her dark eyes unyielding. "I am Judith Calhoun, healer of this village."

A soldier spoke up to Elijah, "She's on the list. Mama Jude. Wolf wants her dead, says she is dangerous."

Elijah hesitated. "Are you dangerous, old woman?"

Judith shook her head. "You are surrounded by darkness. The Great One no longer welcomes you. You are marked by the beast. Your soul destined for the fire of Hell."

Something twisted in Elijah's gut. His gun fired before he even registered pulling the trigger. Three rounds, center mass.

Judith fell, convulsing before growing still.

Elijah stared at the weapon in his hand. A flicker of unease crawled down his spine. What had just happened? Was she right? Was his soul black? He shook off the thoughts, turning his attention to his soldiers.

"Take everything and burn the house."

The Broken Arrows had their recruits. But they had not won the people's hearts. Only their fear.

CHAPTER TWENTY-THREE

"Red 30 Rises"

As the morning sun crested the horizon, its golden glow shining brightly over the valley, Grant stood at the edge of his property with Logan. A thick column of black smoke twisted into the sky, a threatening signal against the dawn. This wasn't a small fire. This was probably something far worse.

"That's not good," Grant said, his eyes narrowing as he tracked the shifting plumes.

Logan, arms crossed, exhaled sharply. "That's not a campfire. Possibly even more several homes or buildings."

Grant let out a slow breath before shifting his gaze to Logan. "I appreciate you and your team stepping up. Or should I say the Red 30 gang?" He smirked. "How did you guys even come up with that name?"

Logan's lips curled into a smile, the question pulling him momentarily from the reality surrounding them. It was a brief escape, back to a time when the worst they had to worry about was losing a few dollars at the gambling tables.

"We weren't doing too well one night at a Vegas casino," Logan began, his eyes distant, seeing not the valley but the flashing lights and felt-covered tables of the past. "Owen was almost out of chips. He and Mace were playing roulette." The faint echo of rattling chips and the dull murmur of gamblers played in his mind as he allowed himself to go back.

Grant chuckled. "I think I see where this is going."

Logan nodded. "Yeah. Owen put everything he had left on Red 30. It hit, and they shouted like maniacs. From then on, 'Bet on Red 30' became our thing. Eventually, it just stuck."

Grant grinned. "Down on your luck, then suddenly, the universe deals you a winning hand. I like it."

"Mace even got it tattooed on his arm," Logan said with a laugh. "He'd bet on anything, how long it takes a leaf to hit the ground, whether it rains before noon. Gambling's in his blood."

Grant turned fully to Logan, his expression serious now. "Maybe lady luck is smiling down on me too, bringing you and the Red 30 gang into our lives. We're going to make it through this, Logan. It may not be easy, but we're gonna' come out of it."

Before Logan could respond, Grant's radio crackled to life, cutting through the morning stillness.

"Grant, it's Crackhead. You copy?" The urgency in his voice sent a jolt of adrenaline through Grant's veins.

Grant unclipped the radio from his belt as he and Logan moved toward the ATV. "I'm here. What's going on?"

"Samuel sent scouts over. They've got news you're gonna want to hear."

Logan was already gunning the engine, kicking up a cloud of dust and gravel as Grant pressed the mic again. "We're en route. Hang tight."

Behind the barn, Ty paced between the rows of vegetables, barely registering the greenery. His mind was stuck on his last phone call with his brother, Ethan. The base had been under attack. Real war, not just skirmishes, not just raids, but full-scale destruction. And Ethan had been right in the middle of it.

Ty had wanted one more minute, one more word with him. Something, anything to hold on to before the line went dead. But all he had now was silence, a void that stretched endlessly in his chest.

"Be safe, brother. I'll keep trying," Ty muttered, his gaze lifting to the tall antennas of the communications room.

Inside the communications room, Daryl was hunched over a radio setup, adjusting dials and scanning frequencies. He was continuing regular searches for any trace of Ethan or the westward military lines. He wanted to find Ty something that offered hope, something he could hold onto.

On the perimeter, underneath the invisible radio frequencies bouncing about, Mace and Owen moved methodically. They checked for weak points in the terrain, but also listened to nature. Owen knew Mace needed the distraction, and he watched as Mace stopped, listening to a bird chirping softly. Mace began talking casually, but Owen could hear the weight behind his words. The grief. The ghosts.

"Dylan and Caleb," Mace murmured, mostly to himself. "We used to hit the golf course on Sundays. Now... I don't even know how I'll tell their families, if they're still out there."

Owen swallowed hard. He knew that feeling all too well. The gnawing uncertainty. The realization that people he once called friends, people in cities that had been hit, were likely gone. No way to check, no way to know. Just silence where their voices and smiles should be.

Mace suddenly stopped. His expression darkened as he looked at Owen. "I think Jordan's gonna bail."

Owen frowned. "What makes you say that?"

"He keeps talking about how he's not a soldier. That he doesn't belong in this fight."

Owen sighed. "None of us belong in this fight. But here we are."

Mace's jaw tightened. "That's my concern. If things go south, can we count on him? Or is he gonna freeze up when bullets start flying?"

Owen scanned the treeline, weighing the risk. "We need to sit him down. Make sure he understands. There's no room for hesitation, no second guessing, no fear."

Mace smirked, tapping Owen on the shoulder. "Red 30, Uncle Owen. We stick together, no matter what."

Owen chuckled. "That's right, Mace. Red 30 for life. We're like the NWO, we're coming for you, brother!" he added, giving his best Hulk Hogan impression.

Mace let out a booming laugh, the sound cutting through the morning tension like a blade. Not far from their position, down through the trees at the main gate, Logan and Grant pulled up beside Crackhead and the scouts Samuel had sent. Grant wasted no time, his words direct.

"I'm Grant. This is Logan. What's the news?"

One of the scouts, his face tight with tension, got straight to the point in response. "Wolf and the Broken Arrows are tearing through neighborhoods. Anyone who resists is executed. Their homes? Torched. That smoke you see?" He gestured toward the black plumes in the distance. "That's what's left of them."

Grant clenched his jaw, his hands balling into fists. "Any idea when they'll come for the casino?" He hesitated, then asked a question he hadn't fully considered until now. "Or... have you thought about letting Wolf have it? It's just a building. It's not like it's operating anymore."

The second scout, a hardened man with deep-set eyes, shook his head. "The casino isn't just a building. It was built to help our people, to make this land prosperous. We can't let it fall into their hands." He exhaled sharply. "Losing it would mean losing everything. We have to fight."

Logan's gaze flickered to the truck parked nearby. His eyes locked onto a man in the backseat, someone different from the rest. His clothes were worn but practical. His posture wasn't tense like the others. It was composed. Calculated.

Logan's voice was sharp. "You're not with these guys. Who are you?"

The truck door opened slowly. The man stepped out, extending a weathered hand. "Eli Mercer."

Grant's expression shifted. Recognition. "You're the one they call the Ghost."

Eli nodded once. He was in his early fifties, a former Army soldier, then game warden, with an unmatched knowledge of the Smoky Mountain region. His rugged clothes bore the stains of weeks in the wild. His thick beard and messy hair gave him the look of a man who had seen survival at its worst, and mastered it.

"What's your stake in this?" Logan asked, his voice measured.

Eli glanced at the scouts, who gave him a silent nod before speaking. "I've been helping people escape. There are trails, dangerous ones, but I've been getting families out past the Broken Arrows' checkpoints."

Logan let out a dry chuckle. "Where were you on day one? I was ready to get the hell out of here." His expression darkened. "Now? Now I'm in too deep."

The scout interrupted. "Samuel said to bring Eli to you. He's at your disposal, will help as you need."

Logan exchanged a glance with Grant, who gave a small shrug. "We could use him."

Eli nodded, "Let's be very clear. I believe in what you are doing, it is for the greater good. But I work for no man."

Logan and Grant smiled slightly, then motioned Eli to the ATV. The Ghost climbed in, tossing his lone duffle bag beside him. As they rode back, a grim determination settled over them. The fight wasn't just about survival anymore. It was about stopping the Broken Arrows before there was nothing left to save.

Upon their return, they quickly gathered in the barn, the scent of hay mixing with the faint trace of gun oil and sweat. The Red 30 gang stood in a rough semicircle, joined by Grant, Crackhead, Brian, and The Ghost. There was an unspoken heaviness in the air, one of preparation, of war.

Logan introduced Eli, his voice steady. The older man met their gazes, his presence calm yet commanding. "The important thing is that I'm here to help," he said. "This land cannot, will not, fall to the Broken Arrows."

A heavy silence followed, the weight of his words pressing into each of them.

Then Ty stepped forward, his movements deliberate, his gaze unwavering. "We can't allow them to keep killing innocent people. It's time we take the fight to them."

He paced slowly, letting his words settle. They had all lost something, someone, to the chaos the Broken Arrows had unleashed. He could see it in their eyes, in the clenched jaws, the tightened fist, the quiet fury simmering beneath the surface.

"Wolf doesn't know our numbers," Ty continued. "And that's to our advantage. He outnumbers us, but that doesn't matter. We're going to use guerrilla warfare." He clenched his fist and pounded it into his palm. "Hit-and-run tactics. Psychological warfare. Sabotage. We make them feel like they're being hunted."

Logan stepped up, his tone sharp and deliberate. "We have to hit them hard and fast, before they have time to react. If we move right, they won't even know where the next attack is coming from. If they're on defense, they can't go on offense."

Owen, leaning forward with a wolfish grin, planted his boot on a nearby chair. "We're gonna break their confidence, make 'em question Wolf's ability to lead. The more we hit them, the more paranoid they'll get. We want fear to spread through their ranks like a damn wildfire."

Ty nodded. "We start small, target their patrols, their supply routes, their comms. We avoid direct engagement until we've weakened them. Mace has worked out the order of attack. If we do this right, we'll deal a crippling blow in a single night."

Mace, smirking as he crossed his arms, took a step forward. "You can call me the shit show supervisor." A few chuckles broke the tension, but Mace's tone sharpened. "Doesn't matter how good our plan is, if someone screws up, the whole thing goes to hell in a hurry. Stick to your roles. Execute without hesitation."

Logan unfolded a map and placed it on a nearby crate. "The Ghost and Mace will be scouting the patrols," he said, tapping a series of marks along the map. "We've mapped their rotation times closely, Mace will finalize them. We'll hit them at a choke point where we can eliminate them fast and slip away without detection. That will be phase one."

Eli, arms crossed, nodded. "We also identify extraction points in case things go south." His tone was calm, but his eyes carried the weight of experience. "If we get pinned down, we need to know where to disappear into the woods."

With a deep breath, Grant spoke up. "Iron Hawk and Running Bear will be notified. They need to be ready, because once we start this, it won't take long for Wolf to retaliate."

A heavy silence settled over them again. This was going to be the first step in a hard, bloody war.

Owen exhaled through his nose, shaking his head with a grin. "We're about to stir a hornet's nest."

Logan smirked, cracking his knuckles. "Yeah. Let's just hope we're not the ones getting stung."

CHAPTER TWENTY-FOUR

"Red 30 - First Strike"

The Red 30 gang sat together in tense silence, each man methodically checking his gear, tightening boot laces, loading extra magazines, and ensuring their weapons were in working order. No one spoke. There was no need. Every man understood his objective. This was the first strike, the first real test of their grit. Once they began, survival would come at the cost of blood.

Logan finally broke the silence, his voice low but firm. "We ready?" His gaze swept over them as they continued their final checks. Without waiting for a response, he added, "We could lay low, try to survive a little longer... or we go kick some ass now and move on to the next task."

Ty clenched his fists, eyes flashing with determination. "Red 30!" he shouted, rallying the group. "We all fight as one, one fights as all!"

The sun dipped toward the horizon, bleeding red against the sky. The gang mounted their ATVs, engines humming low as they prepared to move out. The first stage of their plan was to eliminate the Broken Arrows' patrol, a routine sweep that passed through the area once every hour. They had chosen Whitewater Drive as the ambush site, a secluded stretch of road nestled between thick trees and the rushing Oconaluftee River. It was the perfect kill zone, isolated, silent, and out of sight from the main camp.

They rode in formation, keeping their lights off as they left Grant's property, winding through Seven Clans Lane before reaching Whitewater Drive. Once there, they set up their trap.

Mace and Owen set out a secondary trap if needed, unrolling a spike strip, carefully positioning it across the asphalt. In the low light, it was practically invisible. Ty climbed a nearby tree, settling into a sniper's nest with a clear line of sight to the road below. The Broken Arrows had been running two vehicles, a flatbed truck with a mounted machine gun and a standard pickup escorting it.

Logan and Grant, positioned near the river, built a small fire in the parking lot. They scattered a few chairs and set a cooler beside them, making it look like a fishing spot. Something they knew the Broken Arrows would investigate. The glow of the fire flickered against the water. It was an irresistible lure, one that would pull the patrol right into their hands.

Then, they waited patiently for their prey.

The deep growl of an engine broke the night's stillness. The flatbed deuce-and-a-half truck appeared first, its headlights illuminating the trees as it rumbled toward them. The pickup followed close behind. As expected, the convoy slowed near the fire before veering off into the lot.

Doors creaked open, and four men stepped out, two from the flatbed, two from the pickup. Their boots crunched against the gravel as they ambled toward the fire. Their postures were relaxed, weapons slung loosely over their shoulders.

"They ain't scared of shit," Mace whispered from the shadows.

"They should be," Owen whispered back.

The guards laughed among themselves, tossing casual glances at the staged camp. They had grown comfortable in their dominance, unaware they were already dead men walking.

They walked down near the river, calling out for those fishing in their waters. Then, something changed. One of them hesitated, his face twisting with suspicion.

"This don't feel right," he grumbled.

Another turned, frowning. "Yeah... contact Elijah. Something's off."

The men returned from the river, one shining his flashlight toward the gunner on the truck. They found him slumped over, blood seeping into his gray T-shirt. His throat had been silently slit while they had been distracted at the river.

"Trap!" one of them shouted. "Who's out there?"

Panic surged through the remaining guards as they yanked their rifles up, spinning wildly to locate their unseen enemy. They stumbled backward toward the pickup, their nerves fraying. One reached for the radio inside the cab. As soon as he opened the door, Crack!

A single suppressed shot rang out, and the man collapsed against the truck, his head snapping back as a mist of blood sprayed across the windshield. Mace, hiding inside the cab, had fired point-blank, ensuring a clean kill.

The remaining three men froze. The silence was unbearable, the weight of death pressing in from all sides.

Then, another shot. A high-powered rifle cracked through the night, and their leader's skull exploded in a spray of bone and brain matter. Ty's sniper round had found its mark. The last two men dropped their weapons instantly, arms shooting up in surrender.

Before they could beg for their lives, The Ghost and Owen emerged from the darkness, knives flashing in the moonlight. Each man seized a captive, and with a swift, precise slice, their blades carved through flesh and artery. Blood gushed in rhythmic bursts before their bodies crumpled to the dirt.

The ambush was over, it had worked as planned, smooth, quick and to perfection. Without wasting time, they stripped the trucks of weapons, loading the mounted machine gun, spare ammo, and radios onto their ATVs. The bodies were tossed back into the vehicles before Logan struck a match, tossing it onto the gas-soaked upholstery. Flames erupted, engulfing the trucks in an inferno that would send a message to Wolf himself. This was only the beginning.

As Jordan drove the ATV back to unload their haul, Mace took a final moment, shaking up a can of red spray paint before scrawling across a large boulder: RED 30. No more hiding. No more running. Wolf was the hunted now.

The second stage of the mission was even riskier, they were about to enter the Wolf's Den itself. The Ghost led them to a narrow, overgrown trail, one that veered off the dirt road leading up the mountain. They rode their ATVs as far as possible before ditching them, proceeding on foot through the darkness.

The base camp lay ahead, barely illuminated by scattered dim floodlights. Trucks rumbled down the mountain road, likely reinforcements responding to the burning vehicles from the patrol. It was the perfect opening, and Red 30 was ready.

Logan and Ty moved first, creeping toward two smoking guards near the camp's perimeter.

"I dunno," one grumbled, exhaling smoke. "All I heard was two of our trucks went up in flames. Men are missing."

"Someone's got a death wish," the other scoffed. "Nobody's stupid enough to take on Wolf."

As their cigarettes burned low, Logan and Ty struck. Blades flashed, slicing deep into the guards throats. Blood sprayed as the guards were yanked backward into the brush, their bodies silenced before they could make a sound.

Meanwhile, Owen and Crackhead approached a canvas tent, its interior lit by a flickering lantern. Owen peeked through the back flap, spotting an elderly man hunched over a rifle. He looked to be in his seventies, far too old to be running with a gang of killers, but he wasn't discriminating on age.

Owen frowned. "Why the hell's an old man in here?"

Crackhead cracked his knuckles. "I got this one. He ain't outrunning me." He pushed into the tent, and immediately tripped over a wooden crate, sprawling onto the dirt floor. The old man jolted upright, startled.

"Jesus, Crackhead," Owen said, his gun now trained on the elder. "Who the hell are you? You Wolf?"

The old man raised his hands, his voice shaking. "They call me Gramps. They took me and my grandson, forced us to work for them. I swear, we ain't with them. You good guys?"

Owen's stomach tightened. Not everyone in this camp was a monster. And some of them mere prisoners.

The Ghost led Mace under the cover of darkness, weaving through the shadows toward the helicopter. Logan and Owen moved separately, making their way to the garage. Ty remained in position, providing cover in case things turned south.

The Ghost and Mace crouched low, their bodies hidden beneath the towering silhouette of the Broken Arrows' helicopter. The metal fuselage gleamed dully under the dim security lights, its rotor blades still and waiting. Voices murmured from nearby tents, but no one was paying attention to the aircraft. They had minutes, maybe less, before someone wandered too close.

The Ghost pulled two pipe bombs from his pack, each no longer than Mace's forearm. Their ends were capped, a small dial protruding from the side, simple mechanical timers, ready to begin ticking softly.

"Listen close," The Ghost whispered, his voice barely more than a breath in the night air. "These are simple but deadly. Black powder and shrapnel packed tight. The second that timer hits zero, a striker pin slams forward, igniting the powder. Boom. No more helicopter." He handed one carefully to Mace. "Seven-minute timer. Once we set it, we haul ass. No second chances."

Mace swallowed hard and nodded, gripping the device tightly. "Where do we place them?"

The Ghost's eyes swept over the aircraft like a predator sizing up prey. He pointed to the rotor gearbox beneath the main rotor assembly. "Right there. That's the heart of the machine, where the power from the engine transfers to the blades. Take that out, and it either shears the rotors off or destroys the transmission. Either way, this bird isn't flying."

Mace moved with calculated precision, pressing his back against the cold underbelly of the helicopter. His heart pounded as he secured the bomb against the gearbox housing with industrial tape. The timer clicked as he twisted it to begin.

"Done," he whispered.

The Ghost gave a sharp nod. "Now for the fail-safe." He handed Mace a second, slightly smaller pipe bomb and pointed to the fuel tank line running along the underside of the fuselage. "If the first one doesn't kill it, this will. Fuel goes up, the whole thing burns."

Mace crouched, affixing the charge to the fuel feed pipe with nervous, shaky movements. Another timer. Another countdown to destruction.

With the final strip of tape secured, The Ghost patted Mace's shoulder. "We're both ghosts now. Silent and gone." With one last glance at the deadly devices now ticking down, they melted into the night.

Inside the garage, Owen approached a young man hunched over the engine of a truck. "Joseph," Owen whispered.

The man's head snapped up, searching for the voice.

"I'm friends with Gramps," Owen added quickly, holding a finger near his nose, signaling him to keep quiet.

Joseph's eyes darted toward the rear of the garage. He held up two fingers. "Two guards in the back," he whispered.

Logan didn't hesitate, moving toward the rear where he ducked behind a row of oil drums.

"Stay here," Owen instructed Joseph before following his brother.

They crept around the side of another truck, hearing the guards talking and laughing near the back. "Wolf wants to wait until the casino generators run dry. Two or three more days, tops," one of them said. "He plans to block their fuel supply."

"I can't wait to see what's inside that vault," the other chuckled. "I wanna roll in the money."

Logan and Owen exchanged a glance beneath the truck. With a silent nod, they moved, swift, lethal, and precise. Blades flashed in the darkness. Owen did it just as Logan had taught him, one hand clamping over the guard's mouth, the other driving the knife upward into his chest, straight into the heart. The men collapsed without a sound.

Then a door for the garage opened, the metal hinges creaking loudly in the silence. "Who's ready to be relieved?" a voice called, friendly and unsuspecting.

The new guard barely had time to register Joseph before suspicion crept into his eyes. "Why you looking at me like that, boy?" he asked, stepping forward.

Joseph shook his head quickly. "No, sir. I'm not looking. I'm working, sir," he stammered.

The guard kept advancing. Joseph's fingers clenched around a screwdriver, his knuckles white.

"What you planning to do with that, boy?" The guard let out a low, growling chuckle.

Joseph swallowed. "Stay away from me."

The guard laughed. Then his arm shot out, backhanding Joseph hard across the face. The screwdriver clattered to the floor as Joseph rubbed his hand across his split lip.

"That's what I thought," the guard sneered. "You ain't gonna do nothing, you little piss ant."

Joseph trembled, anger and fear mixing inside him, his fists clenching. "I may be a piss ant," he mumbled, glancing over the guard's shoulder, "but that guy's not."

The guard turned sharply, too late. Logan was already there. His grip clamped around the man's throat like a steel vice, lifting him off his feet. The guard kicked, gasping for air, but Logan held him firm. With a brutal slam, he drove the man into the concrete floor. A sickening crack echoed through the garage. Logan pulled his knife, plunging it deep into the man's chest, ending him quickly in one swift motion.

Logan wiped the blade and looked up at Joseph. "Don't let anyone intimidate you. Act first. Act fast. I need to set this, Ghost gave it to me. Then we move."

Owen stepped in. "You need to get to your grandfather, Joseph. Follow the path past the helicopter. When you reach him, get off this mountain. Time is literally ticking. You've got less than five minutes." Joseph gave a firm nod.

The team all regrouped at their extraction point, joined by Crackhead, Joseph, and Gramps who waited. The only ones missing were Grant and Ty. "Take your gramps and go. Stay out of sight," Logan ordered.

Gramps hesitated, then turned to them. "Thank you for your help." With that, he disappeared into the darkness.

The radios crackled to life. A voice from Wolf's cabin came through, urgent. "Wolf, Elijah, come in. We've got a problem. A big one."

A deep, gravelly voice answered. "This is Wolf. What's the problem?"

"We found the patrol. All the men are dead."

Throughout the camp, guards stirred from their tents, emerging in confusion and alarm. Near Wolf's cabin, Grant crouched by a window, preparing to climb onto the back porch when a firm hand yanked him down.

"Shhhh," Ty hissed, clamping a hand over Grant's mouth. "It's too late for this. They're moving everywhere now. We need to go. Wolf is too guarded."

Grant turned, eyes wide. Ty had found him, stopping him before he did something reckless. Blood coated Grant's hands and sleeves, fresh, still warm.

"The Reaper, right?" Ty whispered.

Grant froze. "It's only a name?"

Ty smirked as he nodded toward the camp. "I saw you slipping in and out of those tents. I knew the Reaper was at work."

Grant exhaled slowly. "I thought I buried that side of myself long ago."

Ty nodded. "This is a good time to bring it back. Now let's move before the fireworks start."

A voice cut through the night. "We got men dead, murdered in their bunks!"

Then the explosion hit. The first bomb detonated, ripping through the helicopter. The fuel ignited, and the blast lifted the aircraft before slamming it back down in a fiery wreck.

In the garage, Logan's planted bomb erupted, igniting gasoline and oil. The fire spread to the vehicles, sending them up in a chain reaction of destruction.

"Search the camp!" Elijah bellowed. "Find them!"

A voice over the radio crackled, "Red 30, it's painted here where the patrol was killed. Red 30."

Wolf's expression darkened. "The men helping Grant?" He looked across to the helicopter, burning rubble now.

More reports came in. "Sir, we're not finding anyone, but we have nine dead. Maybe more."

Wolf's voice was a growl. "Find me someone! They will pay for this!"

Another voice hesitated. "Sir... Someone's painted 'Red 30' on the tents and buildings."

Wolf's eyes narrowed, the weight of realization sinking in. He didn't know who the Red 30 were, but he knew what he wanted done to them.

CHAPTER TWENTY-FIVE
"Hellfire Rising"

Elijah stood beside Wolf in the center of the base camp, his hands clenched into fists at his sides. The morning light crept through the smoke-filled sky, revealing the full extent of the devastation.

Wolf's jaw tightened as his sharp eyes swept across the wreckage. "Elijah," he said, his voice low but brimming with restrained fury. "The Reaper is back. But he didn't do this alone. I want these Red 30 soldiers helping him."

"We've had men scouring the mountain all night, they found the path they used to sneak in," Elijah said.

Wolf didn't respond as he moved to the door, his eyes scanning the damage.

The garage was nothing more than a heap of smoldering rubble, its metal frame twisted and charred. The remains of three of Wolf's trucks lay buried beneath the collapse, little more than blackened husks. His gaze shifted to the helicopter, its broken, burned-out shell a cruel reminder of how easily the enemy had slipped in under the cover of darkness, struck with precision, and vanished before the Broken Arrows had even grasped what was happening.

Elijah hesitated before speaking, knowing Wolf's patience was thin. "The Reaper was definitely involved. The bodies in those tents... it's his work." His voice was grim as he gestured toward the row of body bags being dragged from the tattered remains of the soldiers' quarters.

A crude, hastily painted '*Red 30*' symbol adorned the flaps of one of the tents, its bold crimson strokes flapping mockingly in the breeze. Each snap of the fabric was a slap in the face.

Wolf's demeanor darkened. "Cover that up. I don't care how. Just make it disappear."

Elijah gave a short nod, then rattled off the list of their losses. "We lost the deuce-and-a-half truck and the machine gun in the ambush on the patrol. One of the pickups too. Then the garage fire took out two more trucks and a Jeep. The helicopter's destroyed, but we managed to save the ammunition."

Wolf didn't respond immediately. His eyes moved over the scattered remnants of his once-dominant force. The Broken Arrows had been untouchable, until now. He exhaled sharply through his nose. "Let's go to the gunsmith's tent."

They moved through the camp, the ground beneath Wolf's boots smushing as his tracks left prints in the mud. The wet earth was littered with boot prints, blood stains, and fragments of burned wood from the attack. The closer they got to the gunsmith's tent, the more evidence of hasty repairs they saw, militants hammering at truck fenders, checking magazines, arguing over damaged weapons.

The tent itself was a dull, weathered beige, stained from years of use. A stack of wooden crates was piled outside, each marked with faded military surplus codes. Some were pried open, revealing stacks of rifle magazines, disassembled gun parts, stocks and barrels. The flap of the tent hung loosely, swaying slightly in the breeze as Wolf yanked it open.

Inside, the smell of gun oil and metal filled the air. A wooden workbench ran along the back wall, cluttered with half-assembled rifles, gun cleaning kits, and neatly arranged repair tools. A metal rack to the right held a row of broken-down

174

firearms, some tagged with scraps of paper detailing their issues.

Wolf's eyes swept the tent, his brow furrowing.

"Where is the old man?" he asked, his voice quiet but demanding. "We need him inspecting all weapons."

Wolf turned back to the chaos of the camp, inhaling deeply before exhaling slowly. His men were watching him, waiting for orders. Their fear wasn't of battle, it was of losing control. Wolf simply could not allow that.

"We need him to check all our weapons for malfunctions," Elijah added, already motioning to several nearby soldiers. "Find his grandson, the mechanic. If he's not here, start digging through that rubble. I want to know whose bodies are in there."

Though unspoken, both men had the same suspicion, was this attack a cover for a rescue mission? Had this gang calling themselves Red 30 come for Gramps and his grandson?

Wolf exhaled sharply, shaking his head. "We're supposed to be the ones on the attack. We're supposed to be striking fear into the community, not scrambling to recover from a hit." He turned to Elijah, his voice cold and decisive. "It's time...."

The low hum of an engine echoed up the dirt trail, cutting him off. Heads snapped toward the camp entrance as a battered truck rumbled into view, coming to a stop near Wolf. Two men jumped out, their expressions tense.

"Wolf. Elijah." The driver gave a curt nod. "The base camp wasn't the only thing they hit."

"Yeah, we know," Elijah interrupted. "We lost a patrol too."

The man nodded grimly. "That, and two checkpoints. One on Route 441 at 74. The other on 19."

Wolf's face darkened further, his skin turning a shade redder, like a thermostat about to explode. "What did we lose?"

The soldier swallowed hard and looked at the ground before forcing himself to meet Wolf's gaze. "They killed everyone. Four men at the 441 checkpoint. Two more at 19. They took out three vehicles. Stole the weapons and ammunition."

Wolf closed his eyes, inhaling deeply, forcing himself to stay measured. "Did they leave a mark?"

"Yes, sir," the soldier confirmed. "Red 30. Painted at both sites."

Elijah gave the man a sharp nod, silently dismissing him. As the soldiers hurried away, he turned back to Wolf. "We have to act. But, we're spread too thin right now."

Wolf's expression was set like stone. "The casino," he said. "We need to call in our troops. Get everyone back here by tonight. We fortify the camp, if they come back, we'll be ready. And by tomorrow night..." He turned toward his cabin but stopped just before stepping onto the porch. "We take the casino. Then we take out these Red 30 troublemakers."

Elijah turned toward the gathered soldiers, raising a megaphone to his mouth.

"Brothers! Look around you, look at what they've done! The fires still burn, the wreckage still smokes, and the blood of our fallen stains this ground! They thought they could break us. They thought they could take us by surprise. But they made one fatal mistake..."

He stepped forward, his voice a venomous growl. *"They trusted a traitor."* He waved his hand around the group of soldiers.

"Grant Whitlock, a man who ate with us, drank with us, fought beside us, then betrayed us! He led the Red 30 bastards straight to our camp! He sold us out, then spilled our blood! For what? To save the weak, pathetic scum in that casino?!"

Elijah slammed his fist into his palm.

"And the Red 30? They think they've won something. They think we're beaten, that we're licking our wounds like dogs. But we are NOT beaten! We are NOT weak! We are Broken Arrows! And when someone strikes us, we strike back TEN TIMES HARDER!"

"The casino sits there, fat and full, stuffed with supplies that should be ours! They think their walls will keep them safe! But we will rip down those gates, gut anyone who stands in our way, and take what belongs to us!"

"Wolf leads this unit! He has given us strength, given us purpose, and now, he gives us war! Tomorrow, we burn them to the ground!"

"ARE YOU WITH ME? LET ME HEAR YOUR HOWL!"

A thunderous roar erupted from the soldiers.

"ALL HAIL WOLF!" they shouted.

Wolf stepped forward, only motioning for them to carry on, his fury was blazing like a furnace inside himself.

Inside Wolf's cabin, he and Elijah pored over the battle plans, their agreement solid, no prisoners, no mercy.

A knock at the door interrupted them. A guard entered, his face pale. It was Big Wes, a large man with bulging arms and lots of tattoos. "Sir, we dug through the garage. Three bodies. All ours. We recognized the weapons, though they were badly burned."

Elijah's eyes sharpened. "And the mechanic?"

Big Wes hesitated. "No sign of him. Gramps is missing too."

Elijah turned to Wolf, his voice low and cold. "They're gone."

Wolf's expression didn't change.

"Take a patrol back to the old man's house," Elijah ordered. "If they're there, kill them. Right in the street. Take a dozen men. Everyone stays on high alert."

Big Wes nodded, spun quickly and left the room.

Big Wes did as ordered, leading the convoy of trucks down the cracked and debris-littered street, their engines snarling as they rolled toward Gramps' house. Flames still flickered in the hollowed-out shells of nearby homes, structures reduced to blackened skeletons by the Broken Arrows' previous raids. The choking scent of charred wood and old death clung to the air, thick and suffocating.

Big Wes sat in the lead truck, his thick fingers drumming against his knee, his expression hard as stone. He was a mountain of a man, his torn sleeves exposing tree-trunk arms inked with faded tattoos. His men rode in silence, rifles resting across their laps, tension thick enough to snap like wire.

As the trucks screeched to a halt in front of Gramps' house, the soldiers leaped from the cabs and beds, boots crunching against the loose gravel. Wes stepped down heavily, surveying the home. It stood intact, untouched, too untouched. Just stillness. The front door sat slightly ajar, creaking faintly in the breeze.

Wes scowled, rolling his thick shoulders. "Fan out. Surround the house, find the old man," he ordered.

The guards obeyed, moving quickly into position. Inside the trucks, other men readied their weapons, scanning the street for any sign of an ambush.

Wes stepped forward, lifting his megaphone. "You can't hide from us, old man! Come out now, and we'll take you back to camp nice and easy. Don't make this harder than it needs to be!"

Silence. His scowl deepened. "One, two, three..." he signaled, and his men stormed the house.

The screen door banged against the siding as the first guard kicked in the interior door. Darkness swallowed them as they rushed inside. Flashlights flicked across empty furniture, dust swirling in the beams. A battered couch sat untouched, a few dishes rested on the table. A rifle rack stood empty against the far wall, no weapons left behind. The place wasn't just abandoned, it was staged. It was a trap.

Outside, Brian and Crackhead crouched in the trees, rifles raised, watching the scene unfold through their scopes. They had picked their targets. Two guards lingered by the trucks, scanning the area. Brian steadied his breathing, lining up the shot. Crackhead did the same.

Two sharp cracks cut through the air. The guards dropped instantly, one crumpling against the truck, the other collapsing onto the street, blood pooling beneath his head.

Big Wes whirled, ducking instinctively. His hand shot to his pistol, his gaze snapping toward the trees. And that's when he saw him. The Ghost.

Stepping from the shadows, half-shrouded by the tree line, the figure lifted a hand in a casual wave. The movement was slow, mocking. In his other hand, he held something small, too small to see clearly from this distance. But Wes knew.

His breath hitched. "Shit."

The Ghost pressed his thumb down and the world erupted in fire. A deafening boom split the air as the house detonated, a monstrous fireball bursting through the windows and door. The shockwave slammed outward, shattering glass, rattling the trucks, and sending a blast of heat washing over the street.

Wes was thrown backward, hitting the pavement hard. Splinters and flaming debris rained down, smoke billowing into the sky like a raging firestorm. Inside the inferno, his men screamed, a brief, agonized chorus before being swallowed by the blaze, their cries going silent.

Gritting his teeth, Wes rolled onto his side, ears ringing, his vision swimming. His pistol was still clenched in his fist, shaking as he forced himself to his knees. He snapped his head toward the trees, The Ghost was gone.

Wes sucked in a sharp breath, lungs burning. His fingers fumbled for the radio clipped to his belt, bringing it to his lips with a trembling grip.

"Elijah, come in," he growled. "It's Big Wes."

Static. Then a crackling response. "Go ahead, Wes, I'm here."

Wes wiped a hand over his sweaty face, his muscles trembling from the adrenaline dump. He stared at the burning ruins of the house, his voice raw with fury.

"It was an ambush. My team is dead. All of them."

Silence followed. Then Elijah's voice, cold as ice. "Explain."

Wes clenched his jaw, watching the flames twist and coil, the heat scorching the pavement.

"The house was rigged to blow. The second my men went in, it was over."

Back at the Broken Arrows' base camp, Wolf slowly turned from the radio, his face unreadable. He walked to the table, picked up a bottle of bourbon, and pulled the cap off. Lifting it to his lips, he took a slow, deep swig before resetting the cap. Then, without warning, he hurled it across the cabin. The bottle shattered against the wall, glass exploding in all directions, amber liquid streaking down the wood like blood.

Elijah lowered his head slightly, gripping the radio tighter.

"Wes," he said, his voice like distant thunder, "get back to camp."

Wes didn't respond. He just stared at the fire, jaw clenched, heart hammering.

This wasn't just a setback. This was another strike in this new war with the Red 30 gang, a war they seemed to be loosing. However, the Broken Arrows weren't going to take it lying down.

CHAPTER TWENTY-SIX

"The Final Hole"

The radio crackled in Logan's hand, the static clearing just enough for Crackhead's voice to break through, laced with satisfaction and dark amusement. "Eleven more down at Gramps' house. The plan worked like a charm."

Logan exhaled slowly, his fingers tightening around the radio as he lifted his gaze to Running Bear and Iron Hawk. Their expressions remained unreadable, but there was something in their eyes, a glint of approval, an unspoken acknowledgment that this war was turning in their favor, inch by bloody inch.

He pressed the mic, his voice steady. "Nice job. We're with Iron Hawk now. See you at base camp shortly."

As the words left his mouth, he lowered the radio to his lap, letting the weight of the moment settle on his shoulders. The reality of what they were doing, killing, dismantling, sending a message, wasn't lost on him. They weren't just fighting a gang; they were carving fear into the bones of the Broken Arrows, forcing them to question every step they took.

Iron Hawk and Running Bear exchanged a glance before Iron Hawk nodded, a slow, measured smile pulling at the corners of his lips. "Continue," he said, his voice calm but carrying the quiet fire of a warrior who had seen more battles than most men could stomach.

Logan's eyes glanced to Grant before turning back to them. "We hit their base camp last night. Took out their helicopter, would've been a real problem for us if we hadn't. We also destroyed more vehicles and took down at least fifteen, maybe twenty of their men."

Iron Hawk's face split into a grin, his enthusiasm finally breaking through. He clapped his hands together, the sound sharp in the heavy air. "That is great news." His excitement was visible as he smacked the table hard enough to rattle the cups sitting on its surface. "Eleven more now," he continued, his tone shifting into something darker, more calculating. "That puts us near forty already." He leaned forward, his sharp gaze sweeping over them. "They still have numbers, but this... this will put fear in the rest."

Logan knew what he meant. It wasn't just about the body count, it was about the message. The fear. The doubt.

Running Bear sat up straighter, his movements fluid yet purposeful. Even in a moment like this, his presence radiated authority, a man who had spent a lifetime preparing for war, not just surviving it, even if it was in a boardroom.

"Wolf must be questioning himself right now," he said, his voice calm but certain. "Every step he takes from this moment on is a test. If he hesitates, if he falters, his men will feel it. Tonight, he has no choice. He will come. Taking the casino is the only way he holds the Broken Arrows together. Without it, without a victory, they'll lose faith in him."

The room was silent for a moment, the weight of his words pressing down like an invisible hand. Logan inhaled sharply, nodding. "We're heading back to Grant's now." He pushed back from the table, his chair scraping against the floor. "You know what needs to be done. Anyone who stayed behind today, better be ready to fight tonight."

No one needed to say anything more. Without another word, they turned and walked out, the unspoken understanding settling in like the calm before a storm. A storm they would be standing in the center of before the night was over.

Upon his return, the smell of hay and old leather filled Logan's lungs as he stepped into the barn at Grant's property. Dust motes drifted lazily in the afternoon light, the quiet hum of the world outside momentarily dulling the weight on his shoulders.

His eyes landed on the golf bag propped against the wall near the door, an odd relic of a life that felt distant, almost foreign. He barely had time to process the thought before a voice rang out behind him.

"Get your clothes on, old man, we're going golfing."

Logan turned to see Mace standing in the doorway, grinning like a kid who had just pulled off a perfect con. He looked absurdly out of place in his pristine golf outfit, as if the past ten days hadn't been a relentless storm of blood, fire, and death.

Beside him, Ty stood with his arms crossed, dressed just as sharp. His usual smirk tugged at his lips, but there was something behind it, something unsaid.

Owen threw his arms out dramatically and spun in place, his shoes kicking up bits of hay. "I've been waiting three years to wear this! Three! We got rained out twice, then we got attacked, and I'll be damned if I don't wear this at least once before I die."

Logan huffed a short laugh, shaking his head. "What the hell is going on?"

Mace's grin softened, but it didn't fade. "We figured it like this, Dad, tonight could go either way. So, we're gonna play some holes on the back nine, stay out of sight, and do what we came here to do to begin with."

His voice trailed off, but Logan heard the weight behind it. He could feel the emotional need that each of them felt.

Ty stepped forward, extending his hand. "One more time, just in case, brother."

Logan grasped it firmly, the calluses on their hands rough against each other, men who had held both clubs and rifles, who had fought wars on greens and battlefields alike.

Owen held Logan's shoulder, his grip strong. "Red 30, brother." He smirked, but his eyes deceived him, glistening with something heavier than humor. "We ride or die, but first, we play." He gave Logan's shoulder one more squeeze before stepping back. "Now get ready, Cinderella. We're teeing off."

Logan chuckled, shaking his head as he moved toward his suitcase. He unzipped it, fingers brushing over the neatly folded slacks and polo shirts. For a moment, he hesitated, the fabric feeling strange beneath his touch, like something belonging to another man, another life.

It had only been ten days, but it felt like years. Still, as he changed, something inside him settled. For the next few hours, war could wait. This was their moment, and they would have it.

As Logan joined the others by the door, his smile faltered. "Where's Jordan?"

Mace's grin faded. His shoulders slumped slightly, and for a moment, he just stood there, as if searching for the right words. "He left, Dad." His voice was quieter now, stripped of its usual confidence. "He said he couldn't do this. He wanted to take his chances going home." He exhaled, shaking his head. "He took Ty's rental. Since we destroyed the checkpoint last night, he figured he had a shot at making it."

Logan's jaw tightened. He wasn't angry, just... disappointed. "Does he think it's the only bad guys and the only checkpoint he will run into?" He knew this fight wasn't for everyone. Hell, he couldn't blame the kid for wanting to run. But a part of him had hoped Jordan would stay, that he'd find something worth fighting for alongside them.

The silence stretched a bit too long.

Logan inhaled sharply, forcing the heaviness from his chest. Then he clapped his hands together, breaking the moment before it could linger. "Well, as much as I hate to hear that, it looks like I got three asses to go whip on the course."

Laughter erupted, the tension peeling away like a layer of old skin. They piled into Owen's truck, the air inside lighter now, if only for a little while. Just as Owen shifted the truck into gear, a voice called out behind them.

"Hey, Ty! Wait up!" Daryl jogged toward them, breathless but urgent, clutching a folded piece of paper in his hand. Ty rolled down the window, his brows knitting together as Daryl leaned in.

"Take this." Daryl pressed the note into Ty's palm, his grip lingering just a second longer than necessary. "You guys be safe. We need you back here."

Ty hesitated, staring down at the folded paper as if it might burn him. The others exchanged glances, their earlier excitement dimming.

Owen's hands tightened around the wheel, his jaw flexing. "Ty... you wanna go back inside to read it?"

Ty swallowed, rolling the note between his fingers before exhaling sharply. He shook his head. "I got my other brothers here with me. No better time than now."

The truck went silent. No one spoke, but no one looked away either. As much as they tried to act casual, their gazes were locked on Ty's hands as he carefully unfolded the note. His eyes scanned the words, and for a long, excruciating moment, he didn't move. Then, his lips parted slightly. They saw it, the way his breath hitched, the way his eyes shone just a little too much under the afternoon light.

"Ty?" Logan's voice was gentle.

Ty looked up, his voice unsteady, barely above a whisper. "He's alive." He exhaled, almost in disbelief. "Ethan's alive."

The truck was silent. Then, Mace snatched the note, his voice urgent as he read aloud: "Tell my brother, Ty, I've made it. We survived the attack on the base. We're living here right now.

185

Things are really bad. Don't travel. We're going to survive, but it's going to take a long time to recover. Tell him to reach out tomorrow, I'll be waiting by the radio."

A slow grin stretched across Mace's face. He turned to Ty and smacked his hand in a high-five.

Logan let out a breath he hadn't realized he was holding. "Hell yeah, brother!" He reached back, gripping Ty's hand firmly.

Ty turned away for a second, rubbing his face. He had spent days convincing himself Ethan was gone, that there was no chance he had made it. But now... now he could breathe again.

Finally, he let out a sharp exhale and turned back to them, a renewed fire in his eyes. "Let's go play golf!" he shouted.

The truck roared to life, rolling toward the course. For a little while, they could forget the war waiting for them on the other side of the sunset. The sun hung low, its bright rays warming the men as they laughed like it was just another Saturday afternoon on the course. They walked toward the first tee, golf clubs slung over their shoulders like warriors preparing for battle.

"I hope Owen brought plenty of balls," Mace said, shooting a smirk at his uncle. "He doesn't get the luxury of a cart today. No more driving all over creation to find his shanks."

Owen scoffed, flipping Mace the bird. "I lose one damn ball, and suddenly I'm a liability?"

Mace grinned. "One? Try twenty. I quit counting before the back nine on our last round."

They stepped onto the tee box, surveying the course. The fairway stretched ahead, a rough, patchy mess, barely clinging to its former glory. Once a pristine green oasis, it was now a battlefield where nature had begun reclaiming its ground. Weeds shot up like defiant little soldiers, patches of grass clung desperately to the edges of bunkers, and the sand traps looked more like dried-out wastelands than hazards.

"Well, shit," Ty muttered, nudging a golf ball with his foot. "This place went downhill faster than Logan after a bottle of whiskey."

Logan, his belt barely containing the gut he'd earned from years of good beer and bad decisions, scoffed. "Screw you. I stayed upright for at least twenty minutes." He gave his stomach a pat and grinned.

Owen chuckled, tapping his driver against his palm. "Ain't that the truth? I've seen Logan take tumbles that'd make Olympic divers jealous."

"At least I get back up, unlike your golf game." Logan yanked his driver from his bag with exaggerated confidence.

Owen stepped onto the tee box first, twisting his neck like a pro. "Watch and learn, boys. This is how it's done."

The group gathered around, smirking as Owen planted his feet, waggled his club, and took a mighty swing. The ball rocketed off the tee... then hooked hard right, vanishing into the knee-high grass beyond the fairway.

Mace doubled over laughing. "Textbook slice! That ball's gone, man. You just made a donation to the local wildlife fund."

Owen squinted after it. "Nah, it's playable. Just gotta...."

"Gotta rent a machete to find it?" Ty cut in. "Face it, man. That thing's already in Florida."

Shaking his head, Owen stepped back as Ty took his turn. He squared up, took a breath, and swung, sending the ball skimming the ground like a flat stone skipping across a lake before it died fifty yards ahead. A silence fell over the group before Logan let out a slow whistle.

"Nice worm-burner," he said. "Real considerate of you to keep it under the wind."

Ty rolled his eyes. "Laugh it up. At least mine's still on the fairway."

Logan twirled his driver like a baseball bat. "Alright, amateurs, watch a master at work." He lined up, focused, and swung, only to completely miss the ball. The sheer force of the whiff spun him in a full circle, his club clattering to the ground as he stumbled.

For a second, no one said anything. Then the entire group exploded into laughter, Owen nearly doubling over while Mace wiped tears from his eyes. "Master at work, huh?" Ty gasped between chuckles. "What was that, an interpretive native dance you're mastering?"

Logan scowled, snatched up his ball, and shoved it into his pocket. "Forget this. Mulligan. I'm hitting from the fairway." He turned to walk off dramatically before stopping short and placing the ball back on the tee. "Fine. One more, I'm rusty."

He squared up again, inhaled deep, then swung with precision. The ball started left before curving back, settling beautifully in the center of the fairway. He grinned. "There's my swing."

Mace lined up next, wasting no time as his smooth, practiced swing launched the ball cleanly down the fairway. "There you go, baby! Get up there."

The group watched as the ball soared, only to hit an isolated clump of weeds, bouncing left and rolling straight into the rough. "You've gotta be kidding me!" Mace groaned.

The banter continued as they trudged down the uneven fairway, clubs slung over their backs, stepping through patches of wild grass, laughing and hurling insults at each other's miserable golf skills. The course was in rough shape, but none of them cared. It was still a game. And in a world that had gone to hell, that was enough.

As they reached the final green, the mood shifted. The laughter softened. The neglected putting surface stretched before them, the grass uneven and patchy, a poor imitation of what it had once been. Owen exhaled, shaking his head. "Five holes played, nine balls lost. I really hate this game."

The others chuckled, but the moment lingered, heavier than before. Mace bent down, setting up his final putt. He adjusted his stance, gripping the club, but then hesitated. He straightened, looking around at the others, his usual smirk fading as he softly tapped his putter on the grass.

"You know..." he said, resting the club against his shoulder, "once I hit this, the fun's over." His gaze drifted past the fairway, past the abandoned course, to the world beyond. "Then it's back to the real shit. The kind where bad shots don't just cost you a stroke, they can cost you everything."

The air around them changed. The weight of what lay ahead pressed down, unspoken but understood. The battle with the Broken Arrows wasn't just another fight. It was going to be brutal. Some of them might not make it through the night. The thought of one day being back here without all four was a real possibility, although they tried to push that thought away.

Logan stepped forward, tapping Mace's shoulder. "Yeah... but we'll be back." He forced a small grin. "One day, we'll stand right here again, talking shit, hacking up this course, and drinking cold beer." He nodded toward the ball. "So go ahead. Sink the putt. We'll be back."

Mace exhaled, gave a slow nod, then bent over and tapped the ball. It rolled unevenly across the green, bouncing slightly before disappearing into the cup with a soft rattle. No cheers. No fist pumps. Just a quiet moment of understanding.

Logan turned away, gripping his club tightly as he walked off the green. He wanted to believe what he'd just told Mace. He needed to believe it. But as he glanced up at the darkening sky, he felt the cold fingers of doubt creeping in. "I just hope it's in this life that we come back here."

CHAPTER TWENTY-SEVEN

"Red 30's Last Bet"

The moment the dust cloud rose in the distance, Crackhead leaned against his rifle and let out a loud whistle. "Here comes Jack Nicholson and the gang!" he called out with a big grin, waving as the vehicle approached the gate. The humor in his voice was there, but exhaustion clung to him like a second skin. "Who won?"

Owen smirked as he hung his head out the side window, offering Crackhead a fist bump. His knuckles met the other man's hardened hand with a solid thunk. "I can tell you who didn't win. That would be me." He chuckled, shaking his head. "Everything been quiet here?"

Crackhead nodded, wiping sweat from his brow. "All good so far. Julia's in the kitchen, fixing us a meal. Should be about ready. She said we needed to eat well before we head into battle." He forced a grin and patted his stomach, but his eyes carried the weight of sleepless nights and too many close calls.

Ty climbed out of the truck, adjusting the strap of his rifle as he strode over. "Crackhead, I'm taking over watch. Get your ass in the truck, go eat, and get some sleep. You're gonna need it." He jerked his thumb toward the house. "Send me down a replacement when someone's done eating."

Crackhead exhaled and stretched, his joints popping as he climbed into the truck bed. "Be careful, man. Don't wanna be explaining why you got shot on my shift."

Inside the house, the scent of garlic and tomato sauce clung to the warm air. Laughter echoed against the wooden walls, but beneath the forced smiles and teasing, tension simmered. They all felt it, the weight of the unknown. Would Wolf attack tonight? Tomorrow? They had no choice but to be ready.

Julia moved through the room, setting down fresh-baked bread as Logan practically buried his plate under a mound of spaghetti. "Julia, this looks amazing," he said, twirling his fork through the noodles. "Didn't think I'd be seeing spaghetti anytime soon."

Julia smirked, wiping her hands on her apron. "Easy enough when you've got the sauce already jarred. Just had to cook the pasta." She dropped a slice of bread onto his plate before glancing at the others. "Eat up. No one's going out there on an empty stomach."

The warmth of the meal settled over them, but it didn't last. Brian tapped his glass lightly, the soft clink cutting through the low buzz of voices. The room fell silent as all eyes turned toward him.

"I just want to say something," he began, his voice steady but carrying the weight of years unspoken. "I appreciate every one of you here today. Emily and I... we weren't fortunate enough to have a family of our own." His eyes shifted to his wife. Emily's lips curled into a loving smile, but the sadness in her eyes was unmistakable.

"But despite that, Grant and Julia became our family long ago, and we've been blessed to meet all of you," Brian continued, his voice thick with emotion. Emily smiled at him, though her eyes glistened, the mention of what they never had twisting like a silent knife.

Brian lifted his glass higher. "We're going to win this fight. And Julia...." he turned toward her with a grin "...you're gonna owe us a celebration meal afterward."

Julia laughed, shaking her head. "Fine by me. Y'all can pick the menu."

Crackhead raised his glass, his grin stretching wide, but Julia's sharp glare stopped him mid-motion. "Hold on there, big boy," she warned, pointing a finger at him. "Don't you dare clink that glass with that knife, you do remember last time?"

The big man's face flushed red as laughter broke out. "I forgot about that," he admitted, setting the knife down. "I better not try it again." He rubbed the back of his head sheepishly. "I just want to say...thank you, Grant and Julia. You took me in when I had nowhere to go. I'm grateful to stand with The Reaper and the Red 30 gang."

Julia wrapped an arm around his thick neck from behind, squeezing him in a quick, affectionate hug. "Last time he did that, he broke my damn glass."

Silence fell like a hammer. Grant's jaw tensed, his fingers tightening around his fork. That name, the Reaper, was a ghost he thought he had buried long ago. But the Broken Arrows had dug it up, dragged it back into the light. Tonight, he would have to embrace it once more, more threatening than ever before.

Clearing his throat, he shifted the conversation. "Samuel was sending out scouts after we left, asking for volunteers to help us tonight."

The men nodded, the momentary lightheartedness gone. Forks scraped against plates, the sound filling the room as they focused on the meal, eating like it might be their last.

Daryl wiped his mouth with the back of his hand and pushed back from the table. "I'm gonna relieve Ty. Thanks, Julia. Greatly appreciated."

Before he could step outside, Ty's voice crackled over the radio. "Hey, guys. I got a big truck rolled up with an older man inside. Name's Marty."

Owen's head snapped up. He exchanged glances with Logan. "I met a Marty at the Army surplus store before the attack."

"What's he want?" Logan asked.

"Says he's got supplies for us. Met Owen before," Ty replied.

Owen nodded. "That's him."

Logan turned toward the others. "Send him up."

They moved outside, positioning themselves strategically, just in case. Mace and Owen took defensive spots, rifles at the ready, as the rumble of the big truck engine grew louder. The heavy truck groaned under its own weight, rounding the last bend before coming into view.

An M35 Deuce and a Half. A beast of a military vehicle. Six wheels, a massive steel frame, and a covered cargo bed.

Owen and Mace flanked the truck as it rolled to a stop. With smooth movements, they climbed into the cargo area, sweeping it for uninvited passengers.

"All clear," Mace called as they jumped back down.

Marty climbed out, the old man's boots hitting the dirt with a thud. He grinned at Owen, extending a rough, calloused hand. "Well, look at you, son. This came quicker than expected."

Owen shook his hand firmly. "Wasn't expecting it, but damn, I am glad to see you."

Marty glanced around at the watchful faces. "I like what y'all are doing here. Been hearing rumors about a group fightin' back, but I couldn't get through till that checkpoint went down."

"How'd you know we were here?" Owen asked.

Marty chuckled, rubbing his jaw. "You mentioned your crew had a name. Red 30. Ain't exactly a common one in these parts to hear. And word's been goin' 'round that Red 30's been giving the Broken Arrows hell."

He moved to the back of the truck and unlatched the tailgate, letting it drop with a metallic clang. "I can't fight anymore, but I brought some goodies you might find useful."

Grant stepped forward, wary. "We appreciate it, but we can't pay you right now."

Marty waved him off. "Ain't about money. What you're doing helps all of us. This is the least I can do."

Mace's eyes locked onto a box near the front. The label read *Dark Sight NV-22*. His lips curled into a grin. "Night vision goggles?"

Marty nodded. "Yep. Also got battery-powered strobe lights, remote-controlled sirens, laser tripwire alarms for perimeter defense, Kevlar vests, helmets, smoke grenades, tactical gloves, boots, hell, even flare guns."

The men wasted no time unloading, their movements quick and efficient.

As they worked, Marty folded his arms. "The Broken Arrows still got close to two hundred men. And they ain't just coming to take over. They're coming to kill anyone standin' in their way. You boys really need to be careful."

Silence fell. They all knew what was at stake.

"If you wanna stop 'em," Marty said, looking Grant dead in the eye, "you gotta hit 'em hard. And if you don't take out Wolf and Elijah, they won't ever go away."

"I came to Cherokee to play golf and gamble. If this is my last night, then I'm going out with a bang," Mace said, his usual smile back. "We're going to survive this, we're going to win this, that is my last bet."

CHAPTER TWENTY-EIGHT
"The War Cry"

Grant rode in the last truck down the winding trail, his grip tight on the rifle across his lap. He had insisted on being the last to leave, wanting to lock the main gate himself, a final act of protection before he left those he loved behind. His wife, Julia, and several others were staying behind at the armory, the safest structure on the property. Its thick concrete walls could withstand bullets, shielding those within. Still, leaving them behind weighed heavily on him.

Daryl had looked him in the eye before they departed, his voice firm with conviction. "I swear, Grant, I'll die before I let anything happen to them."

Now, as Grant pulled the thick steel chain through the iron bars of the gate, he wrapped it several times before securing the heavy padlock with a definite clank. The weight in his chest settled like a stone. Even with a guard stationed here, tonight carried too many unknowns. He hesitated for a brief moment, staring back up the trail beyond the gate, before finally pulling open the passenger door and climbing inside the truck.

The convoy rolled forward, single file, their headlights cutting through the evening air. The feeling in the truck wasn't as tense as expected, the guys making small talk and chuckling softly. Their minds still focused on what was to come.

As they neared the town, Ty pointed toward the old hotel parking lot up ahead, his jaw tightening. A truck sat there, unmistakable in the dim light, the Broken Arrows logo was emblazoned across its side, stark and menacing. Two guards stood beside it, their silhouettes stiffening as they turned toward the approaching convoy.

Ty patted the dashboard impatiently. "Those guys are gonna come for us sooner or later. Let's take them out now."

Owen didn't hesitate. He jerked the wheel, sending the truck veering sharply into the lot. The tires screeched against the pavement before they came to a lurching stop beside the enemy's vehicle.

The two Broken Arrows guards reacted slowly, almost confused by the sudden new guests, their hands flying to their weapons as they recognized who was inside, or better yet, didn't recognize which was worse. But they weren't fast enough.

Ty fired first. Two rapid shots struck the nearest man square in the chest, sending him crumpling to the ground before he could even get his rifle up. The second man managed to lift his weapon, his face twisted in shock, but Ty shifted his aim without pause. Another two shots rang out. The man staggered, then collapsed in a lifeless heap.

"It's on now," Logan said from the back seat, his voice low and edged with steel. "Act first, act fast."

Ty nodded hard, "my shot is back."

Owen slammed the gas pedal, the truck's tires squealing as he wrenched the wheel, skidding back onto the road. Ahead, Crackhead and Grant were waiting, their vehicles already moving. Brian and Emily followed close behind. Without slowing, they all sped toward the casino, the adrenaline humming in their veins.

They barreled down the hill, blowing through the intersection, crossing the bridge, and tearing into the parking lot. The night felt heavier now, darker, as though the very air was bracing itself for the violence to come.

The convoy disappeared behind the casino, parking out of sight. As the men climbed out, Samuel emerged from the rear entrance, his expression tight with unease. "I was getting nervous," he admitted, shaking each of their hands firmly.

Logan wasted no time. "Any word? Is everything we discussed in place?"

Samuel gave a sharp nod. "Everything except Casino Trail. We were waiting on you. My guys are on it now, it'll be ready in a few minutes."

Logan scanned the dimly lit parking lot, his mind racing through their battle plan. "That's a critical point," he said. "We need to choke their vehicles out, force them to approach on foot. Ambushes, sniper positions, guerrilla tactics, every advantage we can get."

Samuel gestured toward the side streets. "We've got concrete barricades, vehicles blocking the routes, brought in some school buses too. They won't be driving in."

Logan nodded approvingly. "And the spike strips? The trees?"

Samuel's smirk was grim. "Both in place. The spike strips are first, those tires'll be shredded before they know what hit them. Then, they'll hit the trees. They'll waste time cutting those apart, and by the time they reach the barriers, they'll be pissed."

Logan turned his gaze toward Casino Trail. A large pump truck was spraying used cooking oil down the hill, a slick, nasty mess that would turn the pavement into an ice rink. If the Broken Arrows made it that far, whether on foot or by vehicle, they were in for a brutal surprise.

Samuel continued, "We've got pits dug out too, hidden with loose boards. If they try to rush across, they'll fall right in."

Logan turned to The Ghost, nodding toward the road. "Get the charges set. Mace, you're with him."

The Ghost, a silent shadow as always, gave a short nod before heading off. Mace followed, his excitement barely contained, he had been training under The Ghost these past few days, learning the art of stealth, and he was eating it up.

The Ghost dragged along two prisoners, remnants from the helicopter raid. He smirked coldly. "Still planning on using these two?"

"That's right," Logan confirmed. "Set them up how ever you want."

Owen watched as casino troops strung barbed wire across the entrances, reinforcing their defenses. He turned to Samuel, frowning. "Why didn't you have all this in place before now? You could've been fortifying the whole time."

Samuel exhaled sharply. "You think we didn't want to? Stress does things to you. You forget the basics."

Grant's gaze drifted upward to the casino rooftop. "You got the Molotovs set up?"

Samuel nodded. "Done. Three sniper positions too." His eyes landed on Ty, who was already carrying his rifle case. "We've got spots ready for you."

Ty grinned. "Someone show me the way, and I'll get to work."

Samuel motioned to one of his guards. "Take him up. Show him both exits. We'll have some extra men up there."

Logan's chest swelled with satisfaction. Samuel had pulled through, following every recommendation. They were vastly outnumbered, four to one, maybe even five, but if they played this right, they stood a damn good chance.

"Act first, act fast," Owen said loudly, sharing a quick fist bump with Crackhead.

The casino guards worked tirelessly, maneuvering two massive school buses into position to block the entrance across Soco Creek. They moved with urgency, each man following orders like worker ants, precise, efficient, determined.

Inside, Logan met with Running Bear. The old warrior grasped his hand firmly. "Mr. Logan, we are grateful for your help. Should we be victorious, we will see that you are rewarded handsomely.a"

Logan returned the handshake, his voice steady. "This isn't just about us. It's Grant and his team too." He paused, his gaze unwavering. "The supplies we asked for aren't just for us, they'll be spread out to those who need them."

Running Bear studied him for a long moment before nodding. He saw it, the rare, unwavering honesty in Logan's eyes.

"This isn't just about the casino," Logan continued. "It isn't just about us. The people here deserve a future. The Broken Arrows can't be allowed to rule this land, not while we can still fight."

Iron Hawk approached, his expression unreadable. "We have everyone in position. Now, we wait."

Logan's stomach tightened. He knew Wolf wouldn't charge in recklessly, but he'd be there, lurking, watching from the shadows.

Logan lifted his radio. "All stations, check in."

One by one, voices crackled through the speaker.

"Red One, check."

"Red Two, check."

"Red Three, check."

All accounted for. The minutes crawled by. The night was unnervingly still, thick with an unnatural silence. Logan paced, checking the perimeter, anything to keep his mind from dwelling on what was to come.

Owen ripped into a piece of jerky, chewing thoughtfully before passing the bag around. The tension was a living thing, pressing down on them as they stood in the quiet darkness. Waiting, the storm was coming.

The radios crackled to life, Logan's voice flowing through the speakers, calm but firm.

"To my Red 30 team, to the Reaper and his men, to The Ghost, Iron Hawk, and all those defending the casino..."

A pause briefly followed, the silence stretched, heavy and deliberate, settling into their bones. It was the kind of silence that came before the storm, before steel clashed and blood was spilled. Then, Logan's voice returned, steady, controlled, laced with something deeper. Conviction.

"I know what you're all feeling. We've fought before. We've had close calls, scraped by, survived. But tonight... tonight is different."

Outside, the night pressed in, thick and unrelenting. The wind carried a biting chill, whispering through the buildings and trees like a ghost foretelling what was to come.

"The Broken Arrows aren't just coming to fight. They're coming to wipe us out. To erase every damn thing you've built here, everything you've sacrificed to protect."

His hand curled into a tight fist at his side. He paced, slow and deliberate, his words sinking into the hearts of the men listening.

"But we are not just scattered gangs. We are not just survivors clinging to scraps. We are more than that. We are warriors. And this isn't just about you or me. It's about every man, woman, and child who calls this place home. It's about the people who have no choice but to trust that we will hold the line. It's about the future, the generations who will walk these streets long after we are gone."

His voice rose, a fire building in his chest.

"We are the only thing standing between them and chaos! If we fall, they take everything. They don't care about your families. They don't care about mercy. They don't care about the future. But we do. And that is why we fight, not for ourselves, but for something bigger than any one man here. We fight because this land is the peoples, and we will not let them take it!"

A murmur of agreement rippled through the men. Fingers tightened around weapons. Breaths grew deeper, steadier. Some cracked their knuckles, others exchanged silent nods.

"They think we'll scatter. That we'll break. That's their mistake. Because we stand together. They can send a hundred men, two hundred, it won't matter. Because they fight for greed. We fight for something real. And that is why we will win."

The tension in the casino was electric, an unspoken understanding binding them all together.

"They have numbers. More men. More firepower. More bodies to throw at us. But they lack the one thing that makes all the difference, we have each other. They are just an army of killers. But we? We are a brotherhood. We are family."

The weight of it settled over them like armor, solid and unbreakable. They felt a can't lose mentality building in them.

"I don't want men who fight for themselves tonight. I want men who fight for the one standing beside them. Because that's what will get us through this. Not our guns, not our traps, but our unity. We fight as one. We bleed as one. We survive as one."

A hush followed, thick with unspoken promises.

"The Broken Arrows think they're coming to finish us off. But what they don't know is we are waiting for them. Ready for them. And by the time the sun rises, they will know what it means to fight men who have something worth dying for."

Logan exhaled slowly, steadying his heartbeat. He turned his gaze to the large windows, where the night stretched endlessly into the darkness. Somewhere out there, Wolf and his men were coming. He knew it, and he needed his team to know.

"Stand strong. Stand together. And don't give them a single damn inch. Tonight, we are all Red 30!"

The response was immediate. A roar erupted from the men, fists pumping into the air, hands slapping backs, weapons lifted in silent oaths. They were not just ready. They were unbreakable.

Then, without warning, Running Bear rose to his feet. His chest rose and fell with deep, steady breaths. Something ancient stirred in his blood, something primal. His heartbeat pounded, not with fear, but with fire. A warrior's fire, and he could no longer contain it.

Throwing back his head, he let out a thunderous war cry, the sound bursting from his lungs like a battle drum pounding through the air. It was raw, powerful, an echo from the past, a call of warriors long gone.

The men around him tensed at first, startled by the sudden cry. But then they felt it, the power, the energy, the strength behind it. Beside him, Iron Hawk rose. The fire in Running Bear's eyes ignited something in his own chest. He joined in, his deep, gruff voice rising alongside his brother's.

The chant filled the casino, a primal, ancient force shaking the very walls. It was not just a chant. It was a declaration. A shiver ran through the gathered men. Their grips tightened on their weapons. This was no longer just a battle. This was a reckoning.

As the final echoes of their war cries faded, Running Bear stood, his breath heavy but his spirit blazing. He turned to Iron Hawk, his old friend, his brother in arms, and saw the same fire reflected back at him.

Iron Hawk nodded, his voice unwavering. "Logan is more than just a leader. He is a man of a higher calling. He carries the burden of those who lead men into battle, and yet he does not waver. He stands strong, refusing to break."

Running Bear exhaled sharply, nodding in agreement. Iron Hawk placed a firm hand on his shoulder, his grip strong. "We cannot be defeated, Running Bear. Not with men like this. Not with men who fight with their souls, not just their weapons. This is our stand."

A grin spread across Running Bear's face, a wild, fearless smile that belonged to a warrior who had already accepted his fate. "Then let's make it one for the ages."

Around them, the fighters stood taller, their spines straightening, their blood burning hot in their veins. They weren't just going to fight. They were going to make history.

Nearby, another army was building. The clash was coming, and no man was safe from its fury. The distant hum of insects filled the silence, blending with the low sound of nearly two hundred men gathered in a loose semicircle throughout the large parking lot. Some leaned against their trucks, others adjusted the straps of their rifles, shifting impatiently. But every set of eyes, hardened, hungry, was locked onto the man standing atop a large military truck. Wolf.

Dressed in dark tactical gear, he stood tall, his presence alone commanding attention. The glow of headlights cast shadows over his cold, calculating eyes, which swept over the gathered soldiers like a predator assessing its pack. His lips curled into a knowing smirk.

These men weren't here for honor. They weren't here for justice. They were here for blood, power, and wealth. Wolf knew exactly how to feed their hunger. He raised a gloved hand. Instantly, the voices died down. The air stilled, as if the night itself was holding its breath.

"Look around you." His voice, calm but sharp as a blade, cut through the silence. "This is the last night we will be on the outside looking in at the casino. Right now, they sit inside, thinking they have a chance. Thinking they've got what it takes to stand against us." A dark chuckle rumbled from his throat.

"But they don't. They're nothing but people past their primes. Weak. Fragile. Expired. They have outlived their worth." His smirk deepened, voice dripping with disdain. "They're being helped by a pack of gamblers and wannabe warriors. A few lucky shots, a few dead men, and they think they matter?" He shook his head. "They've been playing games."

The smirk vanished. His tone hardened, dropping into something rough and jagged, like gravel grinding against steel. "But tonight? Tonight, their luck runs out. And we're bringing the demons from the dark."

A few men shifted, the weight of his words sinking in. Others grinned, eyes gleaming with something feral. Wolf's voice grew sharper, more dangerous. "Tonight, we take what's ours. That casino? That territory? It belongs to us. And when the sun rises, every last one of those Red 30 dogs and their elderly cowards will be either dead or kneeling at our feet, begging for mercy they ain't gonna get."

A ripple of cruel laughter spread through the crowd. Some spat on the ground. Others rolled their shoulders, itching for violence. But Wolf wasn't finished. His expression darkened, his voice dropping to a lethal whisper.

"You want riches? You want power? You want to live like kings?" He let the words hang in the air, watching as the greed ignited in their eyes, as fists clenched, as jaws tightened.

"Then earn it. Any man who kills a member of Red 30 will be rewarded." A few heads snapped up.

"You bring me the head of that bastard, Logan?" He let the pause stretch, eyes gleaming. "You'll be drinking whiskey from a golden cup for the rest of your damn life."

Someone let out a low whistle. A mutter of approval spread through the ranks. Wolf continued, voice like a viper.

"You take out his men? You'll be eating better than you ever have before. And Grant?" His sneer deepened. "The Reaper?" Silence followed. The tension tightened, thickened.

"Whoever kills that son of a bitch will be treated like a damn legend forever more."

The reaction was instant. A roar erupted, cheers, shouts, men slamming fists against truck hoods, the deep metallic thuds turning the parking lot into a war drum. Some smacked each other on the back, others let out low, hungry growls. The energy crackled like wildfire, spreading fast, consuming everything.

Wolf's smirk returned. He had them. "So go in there and take what's yours. No hesitation. No second thoughts. Burn them out, drag them into the streets, and show these people what happens when you cross the Broken Arrows."

He lifted his radio, pressing the button.

"Prepare to move in. Kill them all."

Engines roared to life. Boots slammed against asphalt. Weapons were locked and loaded. The hunt was beginning.

CHAPTER TWENTY-NINE

"The Kill Zone"

"They're here," Ty announced over the radio. Lying atop the casino's roof, nestled into a makeshift sniper's nest. His rifle, a .308 Remington he'd gotten from Grant, rested comfortably against his cheek as he peered through the scope. The barrel remained steady, his heartbeat syncing with his breath as he scanned the approaching threat.

The twisted and jagged remains of the collapsed parking garage extended from the earth, a monument to destruction. Twisted steel beams and shattered concrete slabs lay in a tangled heap, the remnants of the fire and destruction from the first night now serving a new purpose. Red 30 had turned the wreckage into a fiery beacon, a gateway to hell itself.

They had scavenged whatever they could find to fuel the inferno. Splintered hotel furniture, broken wooden doors, shattered vending machines, and even fallen trees dragged in from the surrounding ruins were piled high atop the rubble. Gasoline, siphoned from abandoned cars, was poured over the mound, soaking deep into the debris. With a single spark, the night was set ablaze. It was an idea Owen had gotten from an old Clint Eastwood movie where he painted a town red.

Flames roared to life, devouring the offering, climbing skyward in wriggling branches of orange and red. The heat pulsed outward, baking the air, heating the metal remains of the garage until they groaned like tortured spirits. Smoke billowed in thick, black columns, rising like a signal to the damned. The firelight danced across the faces of the Red 30 fighters, their eyes gleaming with a mix of anticipation and fury. The message was clear. There was no retreat, no mercy. The Broken Arrows would march toward the casino, and when they did, they would walk straight into the gates of hell.

Across the intersection, two headlights crested the hill, glowing like the eyes of a venomous snake poised to strike. Another pair joined them, then another. Within moments, five trucks stood in formation, their arrangement like a pack of wolves encircling wounded prey, ready for the kill.

Ty swallowed hard, his muscles tensing as men began to emerge, forming ranks near the vehicles. They stood silhouetted against the headlights, dark figures moving with practiced coordination. This wasn't a scouting party. This was a full-scale assault. The reality of the situation settled heavy in his chest.

"Logan, I've got at least thirty men across the intersection, top of the hill," Ty reported, his finger resting lightly along the rifle's trigger guard.

"Stay calm, everyone," Logan's voice came steady, but firm over the radio. He moved along the second-floor hallway of the casino, peering out the large windows. "Don't shoot until Mace lights up the area." He could see the enemy assembling, trucks lined up like workhorses, their engines idling in the dark.

One of the scouts clicked his radio. "They've entered the Tsalagi "CHA-lah-gee" Road traps. We have eyes on them. They're cutting trees out of the way now."

Beyond the barricades, the Broken Arrows' trucks began rolling forward. The night air was thick with tension as the Red 30 scout team crouched low, moving under the cover of darkness. Just ahead of the casino, the roads leading into their territory had been carefully prepared. A near-invisible layer of cooking oil had been slicked across the pavement, thick, uneven, pooling in cracks and dips like a patient predator waiting to strike at its next meal.

At the barricades, Mace stood ready, gripping a Molotov cocktail. The cloth wick was soaked in gasoline, his knuckles white around the glass bottle. His breath was slow, controlled. He watched the trucks approach, knowing the plan was simple: let them charge in, let them feel confident in their numbers, then light the whole damn thing up.

Engines rumbled louder as the first convoy rolled toward the kill zone. Headlights cut through the darkness, illuminating the road ahead. The lead truck rolled through the oil, at first, nothing happened. Then as the driver pressed on the brakes down the slope, the trap was triggered

The first vehicle skidded, the driver now slamming the brakes hard. The truck lost traction, its back end swung around and slammed into another truck. A third tried to correct but slid out of control, crashing into a concrete barrier.

The soldiers on foot fared no better. Their boots soaked up the slick oil within seconds, and those who tried stopping only found themselves on their backs, sliding helplessly down the hill. The incline worked against them, and once they started descending, there was no climbing back up, the oil wouldn't let them. The hill, once just an obstacle, had become an inescapable chute leading them straight into the heart of the ambush. At the bottom, they scrambled to their feet, weapons clutched in slick hands, only to realize their boots were now caked in thick black tar spread deeper in the kill zone.

Then, Mace lit and threw the Molotov. The bottle's flame flickered in the night before it shattered on impact. In an instant, flames raced across the surface like a living thing. The oil ignited, slithering up tires, undercarriages, and boots.

The next part of phase one was ready and the tar caught fire. Unlike the quick-burning oil, the tar burned slow. Thick, relentless, unforgiving. The sticky, molten substance clung to everything, boots, bodies, hands. Soldiers screamed as the molten substance latched onto them, their frantic attempts to strip off burning clothing proving futile.

One man collapsed, flailing as the fire devoured him. Another tried running but found his boots stuck fast in the melting tar, his fate sealed as the inferno swallowed him whole. His screams twisted before he vanished into the underworld.

From his vantage point, Logan watched impassively. His rifle was slung over his back now, arms crossed as the Broken Arrows burned in their own greed-driven charge. He exhaled slowly, his voice cold. "They should've known better."

The ambush had only just begun. The radio crackled again. "They made it past the trees, but their tires are shredded on the spike strips." One scout announced.

Logan raised his mic. "Let them enter the tar. Then light up the rest of it."

Up along the key chokepoints, more roofing tar had been poured in wide, jagged streaks, just like at the intersection near the casino. The thick, black sludge clung to anything it touched, slowing movement, stealing traction.

Ty tilted his head, hearing the distant screams. "More traps triggered," he muttered. He adjusted his scope, his eyes narrowing as the first figures tried desperately to push through the burning wreckage. The distant screams of the trapped and dying echoed through the night.

The radio clicked again. "All tar is burning as planned." The Broken Arrows' agony-filled screams rose into the night, until their own men did what desperate men do and ended their suffering. They turned their weapons on their own, firing round after round to put them down. Gunfire cracked through the flames as they shot their comrades, sparing them from prolonged suffering. Their lifeless bodies slumped into the fire, consumed by the very charge they had been so eager to make.

Then, a new voice cut through the chaos. Over the Broken Arrows' radio, his voice broke the static, Wolf. His tone was steady but had a snarl that rang through the darkness. "Stay off the roads! Move through the creek!"

From the safety of his truck, Wolf watched the carnage unfold. Elijah, seated beside him, turned sharply. "We need to fall back, Wolf. Regroup. This is a suicide mission now. They're well prepared and know what they're doing."

Wolf's eyes burned with rage as he snapped his gaze toward Elijah, his teeth grinding. "We're getting inside that building. They don't have enough men. That's why they're playing these games."

Logan's voice came steady over the radios. "Phase two."

At Soco Creek, the water churned as the Broken Arrow soldiers splashed through the shallow water, moving quickly. Their charge was frantic, driven by desperation. Gear rattled, breaths came heavy. Shouts echoed through the night, a recklessness to their movements. They thought they were closing in. They had no idea they were running straight into a death trap, running straight into hell.

Mace and The Ghost had rigged the creek. Explosives were buried in a deadly network beneath the soil and hidden along the banks. Each device packed with shrapnel and incendiary compounds. But at the very center? A single tripwire stretched across the water, nearly invisible under the moonlight.

The first soldier hit it at a full sprint. The moment the wire snapped, hell erupted. A chain of explosions tore through the creek, blinding fire and twisted steel ripping into the mass of soldiers. The shockwave sent bodies flying, limbs severed, torsos shredded by the force of the blast. Some never even had a chance to scream, the concussion of the explosion ending them before their minds could register what had happened.

Flames licked up the banks, scorching trees, igniting dry brush. Men, engulfed in fire, stumbled out of the creek, screaming as the flames clung to their skin, their clothing fused to their flesh. The water, once clear, turned dark with blood and debris, the broken remains of what had once been a wave of soldiers now reduced to charred, dismembered bodies.

Mace, crouched behind cover, watching as the flames reflected in the moving water as the carnage unfolded. His face was unreadable. He knew the job wasn't done. The ones who survived weren't running anymore; they were crawling. Dying slowly. Screaming for help that wouldn't come. The fight wasn't over. The next trap was already waiting.

"Wolf!" Elijah barked. "This is insanity!" He grabbed Wolf's arm roughly.

Wolf responded with a sharp slap across Elijah's face. "Get yourself under control, soldier." His voice was rough, dangerous. "We're taking that building. Let's move." He lifted his radio. "They think they're winning. They're just delaying the inevitable. Move in!" He called out, clenching his fists, his face barely hiding the controlled rage he felt.

The Broken Arrows surged forward, their numbers thinned by fire and explosions, but their rage remaining. They weren't stopping. And Red 30 was ready for them.

"Let the bloodbath continue," Mace mumbled as he watched the next wave move closer.

The Broken Arrows surged forward, their ranks thinned by the fires on the road and the explosions at the creek. But they did not slow. Fear and bloodlust drove them, a desperate refusal to die without dragging someone down with them.

Ahead, the casino loomed, its once-vibrant signs now dark, like the fallen soldiers of the night. And just before it, a seemingly open path stretched forward, flanked by rows of casino buses, their dirty paint still promising jackpots and riches. It was the only way forward. But it was no salvation. It was a funnel. Another one of the Red 30's traps. It wasn't just a trap, it was a grave.

Perched atop the casino, Ty lay prone, his rifle steady against his shoulder. He watched the Broken Arrows come. One by one, reckless, desperate, blind to the truth of their situation. They were so close now they could taste the victory.

His breath slowed. His heartbeat steadied. The first soldier stepped into the kill zone. "Act first, act fast," Ty mumbled as he squeezed the trigger.

BANG! The bullet split through the man's forehead, sending him crumpling like a puppet with its strings cut. For a fraction of a second, there was silence. Then, hell erupted.

The moment Ty's shot rang out, the entire Red 30 force opened fire. From the rooftop, from barricades, from the shadows, gunfire thundered through the night, tearing into the trapped soldiers with ruthless precision. Brian held onto the machine gun they had stolen from the patrol, his arms vibrating vigorously as he held the trigger, its mighty rounds tearing through anything in its path, cars, buses, humans.

Snipers picked off targets, their bullets punching through skulls, the bodies hitting the ground. Semi-automatic rifles spat fire, barrels glowing red-hot as they cut men down in waves. Shotguns roared, tearing flesh apart with brutal force. Explosives rigged to the buses detonated in sequence, sending fire and shrapnel slicing through the panicked ranks of the Broken Arrows.

The Broken Arrow soldiers panicked. They tried to push forward, but the gunfire was relentless, mowing them down. They tried to turn back, but bullets tore them apart. They tried to find cover, but there was none. Blood splattered the pavement, streaking the bus exteriors, pooling in the dirt. The corridor became a slaughterhouse.

Men screamed. They clambered and clawed their way over the bodies of their own comrades, desperate to escape. But the weight of the dead piled up, forming walls of flesh that slowed them down.

The gunfire did not stop. The echoes of battle thundered through the valley, shaking it like the very first day of the attack shook the country. Smoke filled the air, mixing with the stench of burning flesh and gunpowder. The flashes of muzzle fire lit up the corridor kill zone like a violent strobe light in hell.

Wolf's men, his killers, his loyal dogs, were being torn apart, their numbers vanishing in seconds. Some tried to raise their hands in surrender. It didn't matter. They were cut down all the same. No mercy.

The Broken Arrows who had somehow survived stumbled backward, their faces twisted in horror. They saw it now, they had never stood a chance.

Logan radioed to Mace, "tell the Ghost," who stood ready with the detonator in his hand. With a single nod, the final trap was sprung. A deep BOOM! shook the ground as the remaining explosives ripped through the buses. The metal crumpled inward, crushing the dead and the dying beneath its weight. Smoke and fire spewed into the air. The walls of the kill zone collapsed in on itself, sealing the Broken Arrows inside.

For a long moment, only the crackling of flames and the distant moans of the dying remained. Then, silence. Was it over? It had to be, the Broken Arrows wouldn't dare continue this attack, not with the losses already incurred. They had yet to reach the building itself. But Wolf wasn't done, only angrier.

"We need another way, Wolf," Elijah yelled. "This is insanity I tell you!"

Wolf breathed deeply, exhaling slow, seething as he clicked the mic on his radio. "Men," he growled. "They've used what they had. It's our turn. On my signal, move in!"

The air was filled even in darkness with smoke and blood. The ground was littered with corpses. The once-mighty Broken Arrows force was crippled. But Wolf stood on a rocky hilltop across the street, his dark eyes burning.

He had lost soldiers before. But never like this. Never so mercilessly outplayed. He slung his rifle over his shoulder and dropped the tailgate of his truck. Reaching into a case, he lifted out an RPG. His one shot. His one chance to turn this massacre into a fight again.

With steady hands, he locked the warhead into place and hoisted the launcher onto his shoulder. He saw them, Red 30 fighters on the rooftop, reloading, regrouping, shouting orders. They thought they had a moment to breathe. They were wrong.

Wolf took in a deep breath and lined up his shot. He fired. The RPG streaked across the night sky, a spiraling tail of smoke behind it as it hurtled toward its target.

Ty barely had time to react. "GET DOWN!" He screamed as he threw himself aside just as the rocket slammed into the rooftop.

BOOM! The explosion ripped through the upper level of the hotel, a shockwave tearing apart concrete and steel. Flames erupted, hurling debris in all directions. The blast sent rooftop guards tumbling, some vaporized, others plunging off the edge.

Ty hit the rooftop hard, ears ringing, his world spinning. His vision was blurred, his body rattled. Shouts echoed around him, muffled and distant. The Red 30 team scrambled for cover, momentarily disoriented. It was exactly the opening Wolf wanted.

From the smoldering wreckage, the remaining Broken Arrows surged forward. Gunfire cracked through the smoke as they pushed up the street, some ducking behind wrecked vehicles, others sprinting through the chaos.

Wolf's lieutenants barked orders. "Push for the back entrance!"

The back doors were fortified, a barricade made from overturned tables, vending machines, and whatever else Red 30 had managed to stack in their rush to secure. But the Broken Arrows had the numbers and the rage. A group of them rushed the door, slamming into it with their full weight. The first attempt barely budged it. "Breach it now! Move, move!"

214

One of the soldiers pulled out a makeshift explosive charge, slapping it against the barricade. BOOM! The door splintered inward, the barricade blasting apart, sending wood and metal flying. The first wave of Broken Arrows stormed inside, rifles raised, boots thudding against the tiled floors of the hotel lobby.

"They've breached the doors, hold firm!" Iron Hawk called into the radio.

Gunfire erupted almost instantly as Red 30 fighters engaged from the hallway, but the breach had been made. The battle wasn't over. It was just moving inside.

On the roof and upper level, survivors used fire extinguishers to douse the fires the RPG had created upon it's explosion. The civilians who had been staying at the hotel, remaining behind because they had nowhere else to go after the attack, pitched in to help. Some were trained with guns, taking up arms while others worked behind the scenes. Logan and Ty had instructed them on several areas they could be useful.

The volunteers helped to keep doors barricaded and hallways blocked, to slow down the routes the Broken Arrows would be able to take. They had a medical room set up for triage, tending to the wounded with first aid in a safe area. They had runners who distributed supplies like ammo and extra guns.

But for many, the moment was too much. Some fled to their rooms, hiding. Others locked themselves in bathrooms, sobbing, shaking, the sounds of gunfire hitting like physical blows. Many others stood brave in the face of fear, willing to go down with the ship if that's what it took. They worked as scouts relaying enemy movements to Red 30 fighters and even acted as decoys, trying to distract the Broken Arrows, leading them into traps.

Logan and Ty's plans had worked well, but the battle wasn't over. Now, it had just moved inside the casino.

CHAPTER THIRTY
"Wolves at the Gate"

"**D**ad!" Mace called into his radio, pressing it closer to his ear. His voice was urgent, even a hint of panic. "Dad, can you hear me?"

Logan couldn't respond immediately. Positioned above the main lobby, he fired round after round into the chaos below. The Broken Arrows were spreading fast, peeling off into different areas of the casino and hotel, just as he'd anticipated.

Then, finally, Logan keyed his radio. "I got you, Mace. Go ahead."

"We lost sight of Wolf," Mace responded, his breath uneven. "They moved from the hill. I lost them after he fired the RPG."

Logan squeezed off a few more shots before ducking behind cover, glass shattering around him from return fire. "It's okay, Mace. Stay sharp. They're at the gate and moving in."

Ty dropped down beside him, swapping his .308 for an AR. "You're still breathing, I see. The bad news, Brian's wife, Emily. She's dead. Killed by that RPG."

Logan's jaw clenched tight. He exhaled through his nose, forcing himself to stay focused. "Damn it. What about Brian?"

"I lost him. I don't know where he is right now," Ty admitted.

The gunfire slowed, scattering into smaller bursts as the Broken Arrows split up, exactly what Logan had hoped for. But they had lost visual on Wolf and Elijah. That problem loomed over him, but there was no time to dwell on it now.

Then, the casino's sound system crackled to life with a short loud screech. A deep, eerie silence filled the air, but only for a moment. Then, the speakers began to whisper loudly, the singer of the song sounding like a ghostly voice slithering through the halls like a serpent.

"Let the bodies hit the floor... Let the bodies hit the floor..."

One of the Broken Arrow soldiers glanced at his partner, grinning. "Damn, this is badass. A little Drowning Pool while we kill, let's get it!"

The whispering chant built upon itself, layering in repetition, tightening the air with an unnatural tension. Then...

"LET THE BODIES HIT THE FLOOOOOOOOOR!" The song exploded loudly over the speakers.

The second soldier gave an approving nod. "As long as we're the ones doing the killing."

That was his last thought. His boot snagged on something, no, something snagged him. A metallic clink sent a slow-motion chill through his bones as he turned just in time to see the grenade pin sailing through the air.

BOOM! The hallway exploded in a blinding fireball. The force of the blast slammed their bodies into the walls, shrapnel cutting through their flesh and armor alike. The speakers roared in perfect timing over the screams, guitars wailing, drums pounding like war cries. The floor trembled beneath the force of the blast. It was psychological warfare.

The casino had become a bad dream itself, like a house of horrors. Throughout the various rooms and corridors, Broken Arrow soldiers staggered, clutching their ears, their equilibrium wrecked. The relentless music turned their surroundings into a sensory overloading nightmare. Orders were drowned in distortion, their movements becoming erratic, their coordination shattered. Their own gunfire became lost in the chaos. Some fired blindly into the shadows, convinced they were seeing Red 30 members everywhere.

For Red 30, it was fuel, an anthem of carnage and a declaration of dominance. A battle drum. A death march. And the killing had only begun. They had the advantage of being positioned where they wanted to guide the soldiers into, choking them into more kill zones. The Broken Arrows didn't quit, even though they believed the gates of hell had opened and the devil himself was waiting. They pushed deeper into the building when Iron Hawk powered up the gambling hall.

BZZZT! The lights flashed on in full force. The entire casino floor came to life, the slot machines lit up, their neon glow flickering wildly, clanging, ringing, a maddening loudness. Combined with the thundering music, it was pure disorientation.

Several Broken Arrow soldiers moved forward, moving cautiously, their senses under assault. Brian spotted them. His pulse spiked, and he moved to engage, only for Grant to yank him back into the shadows. "You're gonna get killed going in like that," Grant hissed. But as he looked at his friend's face, his stomach twisted. "Brian... what happened?"

Brian's breath hitched. His eyes filled with tears, overflowing before he could stop them. His voice came as a whisper, raw and broken. "They killed Emily. They killed my wife." His fists trembled. "They're gonna pay for it."

Grant's expression hardened. He grabbed Brian by the shoulder. "Stay here. I got this." And with that, he slipped away into the chaos, leaving Brian behind in one of the cashier cages.

Grant sprinted through the sportsbook section of the casino, his mind shifting into kill mode, instincts honed to a razor's edge. He moved with the efficiency of a hunter, his breathing steady, his grip firm on his blade.

Ahead, Broken Arrow soldiers crept cautiously, their weapons raised, eyes scanning the darkened areas, the rows of machines. They expected an ambush.

They just didn't expect him. Like a shadow in motion, The Reaper struck. His blade cut through the air, sinking deep into the exposed flesh just below the first soldier's neck. The man let out a strangled grunt, but the music swallowed his dying breath.

Before the second soldier could react, The Reaper was already upon him, driving another blade into his ribs, once, twice, quick, precise, deadly. Blood spattered across the dazzling casino carpet as the man crumpled.

The Reaper pressed forward, weaving through the rows of slot machines, his next victim crouched ahead. The soldier never had a chance. A hand yanked his head back violently, and in a single, swift motion, The Reaper's knife slit his throat.

The music suddenly cut out. A beat of silence. Then...

"Where the hell are they?" One of the two remaining Broken Arrow soldiers whispered.

His partner turned, his eyes darting over the rows of flashing machines. It took them a moment to realize they were three men short. Then, movement. "There!"

Gunfire erupted. CRACK! CRACK! CRACK! Muzzle flashes illuminated as bullets ripped through the slot machines, glass shattering, metal sparking. The Reaper ducked, rolling behind cover as lights burst in a frenzy of chaos.

He returned fire, just enough to keep them at bay, then melted into the shadows. The speakers roared back to life.

"Dead I am the one, exterminating son, slipping through the trees, strangling the breeze..." Rob Zombie's voice growled through the building, the bass vibrating the very foundation of the casino as the battle raged on.

"Let him go, stay the course, let's go to the upper level," one of the remaining guards shouted to the other.

At the back entrance, Wolf peered inside the doorway, his sharp eyes scanning for movement. The coast was clear. He stepped forward. Like a predator in the wild, he moved slowly, methodically. Precision was key. He knew exactly where he was going, down to the vault beneath the casino floor. That's where Running Bear would be, tucked away like a rat in a burrow.

The generators failed. The entire casino plunged into darkness once more. The machines flickered and died, their cheerful lights snuffed out in an instant. The music cut off mid-riff. Silence crashed over the casino, heavier than gunfire.

Wolf smirked. He moved like a phantom through the ruined halls, his footsteps muffled against the marble floor. The once-luxurious gambling den was now a battlefield, bullet-riddled slot machines, overturned tables, blood smeared across the walls. Faint echoes of distant gunfire trickled from above, but he barely registered them. His mind was focused.

Wolf passed through a shattered doorway leading to the poker room. And there, by the cashier's cage, two figures stood. Brian and The Reaper. Wolf halted. Brian's shoulders sagged, his grief a physical weight dragging him down. His hands clenched into fists, his voice cracking as he spoke.

"I can't live without her," he whispered, his words barely holding together between sobs. "She was everything, man. I don't...I don't know how to keep going."

Wolf smirked in the darkness. He raised his pistol as he stepped closer. "Then you don't have to."

BANG. Brian's head snapped forward, a perfect hole punched clean through his skull. Blood sprayed across the poker table as his body collapsed. The Reaper barely had time to react before Wolf leveled the gun at him next.

"You and I could've done great things together." Wolf's voice was almost... disappointed. "But you chose them. Tell me, who the hell is the Red 30?"

The Reaper's face hardened, his grief instantly replaced by cold fury. "What you're doing is wrong, Wolf. It's over. Walk away. The Red 30 is all of us, everything you'll never be!"

Wolf tilted his head, then let out a low chuckle as he pulled the trigger, click, the gun empty. "Okay." Then, without warning, he lunged.

The two men collided, fists flying, bodies crashing into tables and chairs. The Reaper struck first, a brutal punch to Wolf's ribs. Wolf grunted but retaliated with a savage elbow to the jaw, sending The Reaper staggering back. He recovered fast, driving Wolf backward, slamming him into the bar. Whiskey bottles toppled, shattering on the floor.

Wolf was quick, relentless. But The Reaper was stronger. He landed a vicious right hook into Wolf's gut, then followed it up with an uppercut that sent him sprawling onto a poker table. Chips scattered. Cards rained down like confetti.

Breathing heavy, The Reaper pulled his knife. The steel gleamed under the dim lights as he stepped forward. Wolf smirked, always one step ahead. His hand shot to his ankle holster.

BANG. BANG. BANG. Three bullets slammed into The Reaper's chest. He staggered but didn't fall. Wolf didn't stop.

BANG. BANG. BANG. Six rounds in total. The pistol clicked empty.

The Reaper stood for half a second longer, his breath hitching, his grip loosening on the knife.

Then, his knees buckled. His body hit the table, arms spread, eyes vacant. Blood seeped into the felt, staining it black.

Wolf exhaled as he holstered his empty gun. "That's a shame he chose the wrong side."

He stepped over Brian's corpse, then took one last look at The Reaper, before disappearing into the stairwell. Running Bear was waiting. And Wolf still had work to do.

CHAPTER THIRTY-ONE
"Hole in One"

"I'm heading towards the storefronts," Logan radioed, his voice steady despite the chaos around him.

On the level above, he moved carefully along the concourse, his boots scraping against the dust-coated tile. The once-bustling shopping district inside the casino was now a desolate graveyard of ransacked shelves and abandoned goods, designer clothes tossed carelessly onto the floor, mannequins missing limbs, their blank faces staring into the dark. The faint smell of cologne and perfume lingered in the air from the fragrance store.

Logan heard them before he saw them. The distinct shuffle of combat boots on the tile and oncoming muffled voices. He caught the movement in the dim lighting. Two Broken Arrow soldiers emerged at the far end of the corridor, their rifles snapping up the moment they spotted him.

"Shit!" Logan dove behind a row of overturned metal benches just as the first shots rang out. Bullets tore through the silence, sparking off the floor and chewing through storefront windows. Shattered glass rained down like a deadly mist.

He peeked over the bench, exhaled, and fired back, BANG, BANG, his shots precise. The first soldier jerked as two rounds slammed into his chest, sending him sprawling backward in a heap.

The second soldier moved fast, darting right to flank him. Logan barely had time to shift before a fresh burst of gunfire forced him behind a marble pillar. A large glass display sign beside him exploded in a spray of glass as shards rained down over him. He crouched, reloading, CLICK. Empty.

The second soldier grinned, sensing an opening, and rushed forward. Logan didn't hesitate. He rolled to the side, yanked his sidearm free, and fired rapidly, but only sending a couple shots, his pistol was also now empty. The bullet punched clean through the man's neck. A sickening gurgle escaped his throat as he collapsed, fingers twitching uselessly against the floor, his blood spreading in an uneven pool.

Logan barely had time to breathe before searing pain pierced through his left thigh. "Ah, hell—!" His leg nearly buckled as the bullet tore through muscle, a fresh wave of agony shooting up his side. He reached for his radio, only to find it was shattered, a bullet hole punched straight through its casing.

"Perfect," he moaned through gritted teeth.

Dragging his wounded limb, he stumbled into the nearest store. A golf shop with clubs lining the walls, signs promising 'Pro Gear for Pro Golfers!' Dust coated the merchandise, a stark reminder that luxury had no place in a war zone.

Logan grabbed a belt from a nearby display, yanking it free in one quick motion. He grunted as he looped it around his upper thigh, tightening it into a makeshift tourniquet. His breath came heavy as he slouched behind the wooden counter, pressing his back against it. The pain was sharp and unforgiving, but stopping wasn't an option.

"Little Red, where you at?" The voice froze him in place. Deep and cocky, thick with that familiar Southern drawl. Big Wes.

Across the hall, Logan heard the enforcer's heavy boots thudding against the tile, methodically moving past storefronts like a predator on the hunt.

Logan wiped the sweat from his brow, exhaling slowly. He risked a glance through the shattered display window. Wes was built like a brick wall, his bulked-up frame moving with

223

deceptive ease. His rifle was gripped loosely in one hand, but there was no mistaking the readiness in his posture.

"Oh... shit," Logan whispered. "That's a big dude."

His fingers brushed against a golf club resting in a stand beside him. He wrapped his hands around the grip, rolling his shoulders as he steadied himself. Wes entered the shop, his steps heavy and his hulking shadow stretching against the light.

The moment Wes stepped past the support pillar, Logan pivoted hard. "Fore!"

The seven iron whistled through the air, colliding with the side of Wes's skull with a sickening crack. The impact sent the rifle flying from his grip as he staggered, a groan rumbling from deep in his chest. He clutched his head, his breath coming in ragged bursts and blood began to seep from the gash.

Then he turned on Logan, eyes burning with rage. "You..." Wes growled, his voice dripping with malice. "You the leader of the dirty thirty?"

Before Logan could move away with his wounded leg, Wes's massive fist drove into his ribs. The force sent him crashing into a display shelf, knocking golf balls loose. They clattered onto the floor, rolling in every direction as Logan gasped, the air ripped from his lungs.

Pain flared through his side, but he barely had time to process it before Wes grabbed him by the vest, lifting him like he weighed nothing. With effortless strength, Wes hurled him straight through the storefront window. Glass exploded around him as Logan tumbled onto the cold tile. Jagged cuts burned along his arms, fresh blood seeping into his sleeve. He groaned, rolling onto his side, his vision swimming.

Through the haze, he saw Wes stepping to the shattered frame, eyes dark with murder. But Logan wasn't looking at Wes's face. His gaze locked onto the grenade strapped to the front of the enforcer's vest. His lips curled into a grin. Raising his hand, he revealed the grenade pin looped around his finger.

224

Wes's eyes turned down as realization hit. "Oh, you mother...."

BOOM! The explosion ripped through Wes's torso. His body jerked violently, the sheer force sending him backward. Smoke and debris engulfed the hall and golf shop as Logan shielded his face from the blast.

When the dust settled, he pushed himself up and hobbled forward, stepping over the remains of Big Wes. A gaping hole had replaced the enforcer's chest. His once-massive frame was now just another lifeless body on the battlefield.

Logan wiped blood from his lips, smirking. "That's a hole in one." He snickered at his own joke, bending down to pick up Wes's rifle. He yanked the charging handle, then hobbled toward the corridor using a golf club as a makeshift cane. He shook his head, laughing under his breath. "The guys would've liked that one... That was funny."

The occasional sound of gunfire echoed through the casino, distant and sporadic. The earlier chaos had died down, the bodies of most Broken Arrows now decorating the ruined building like grim reminders of their failed assault. Logan exhaled, rolling his jaw slowly as he struggled to walk ahead.

The Ghost and Mace had been running for what felt like miles, dodging bullets, cutting through corridors, slipping between wreckage and bodies like shadows. Their lungs burned, muscles screamed, but they didn't stop, not yet. The air was thick with the stench of gunpowder and blood, the distant echoes of gunfire rattling through the casino's ruined halls.

Now, crouched near one of the casino kitchens, the Ghost pressed his back against the wall, his chest heaving. Sweat slicked his forehead, mingling with the grime and smoke clinging to his skin. His usually steady hands trembled slightly, but his eyes, sharp as ever, never wavered. He turned to Mace, looking over the younger man like an appraiser sizing up his latest work.

"You've done really well, kid," the Ghost said, his voice low but firm. Despite the chaos around them, there was something almost amused in his tone. "I've enjoyed working with you." He exhaled, then smirked. "I think I'll call you Fuse."

Mace blinked at him. "Fuse?"

Before the Ghost could answer, an ear-splitting wail erupted down the hall, the shrill, unmistakable screech of a battery-powered motion sensor alarm. One of Marty's little gadgets he had given the Red 30 gang.

The Ghost's head snapped toward a small window in the door, his body tensing. He peered out, then gave a slow nod. "You're fast. Turning into a damn good detonator. And you can vanish in a flash." His smirk faded as his expression hardened. "I need you to be quick now. The Broken Arrows are heading this way. They'll be in the dining hall in seconds."

He reached into his pocket and pulled out a handful of small items, scraps of wire, a battery, and a makeshift trigger. Pressing them into Mace's hands, he nodded toward the kitchen. "Grab a pot. Pack it with whatever you can find, metal, broken glass, hell, even sugar will do. We're making a surprise for our guests."

Mace took the materials, his mind racing. He had seen the Ghost work before, had learned from him, but now it was his turn. His hands moved fast, instinct taking over as he pieced the bomb together. His heart pounded, but his fingers remained steady.

Then, something caught his eye, dark liquid pooling across the floor, seeping into the cracks of the tile. Blood. His stomach twisted. The Ghost was leaning against the wall more than before, his face paler now, his breath shallow. Mace's eyes darted downward, to the dark stain spreading beneath the Ghost's jacket, just below the ribs.

"You're hit," Mace whispered.

The Ghost smirked, waving him off. "I'm not dead yet. Focus, Fuse."

Mace swallowed hard and twisted the last wire into place. He knew there was no time to panic. He shoved the explosive into a pot, gripping it tightly.

"Now, listen close," the Ghost said, his voice dropping to a whisper. "I'm gonna throw this smoke grenade. You're gonna run out there, slide that pot across the floor. The second it blows, we open fire."

Mace gave a sharp nod, gripping the pot with white-knuckled hands. The Ghost yanked the pin and lobbed the smoke grenade through the door. It hit the tile with a metal clatter before, POOF!, a thick cloud of white erupted, swallowing the dining hall.

Mace moved quickly. He burst from the kitchen, running low, the pot gripped tight in both hands. The smoke curled around him, making the world feel surreal, like he was moving through a dream. The moment he reached the entrance of the dining hall, he dropped into a slide, sending the explosive skidding across the floor.

The Broken Arrows had little time to react before, BOOM! The blast rocked the hall, the pressure wave slamming into Mace's chest. Shrapnel tore through the air, slicing into one of the soldiers, sending him crumpling to the ground in a heap. The other two staggered back, disoriented, coughing as the smoke filled their lungs.

Gunfire erupted. The Ghost, despite his wound, was already unloading rounds into the chaos. One of the remaining Broken Arrows dropped, riddled with bullets. But the third one, the last one, was moving.

Mace saw him through the haze of smoke and debris, his silhouette shifting through the wreckage. He wasn't retreating. He was pushing forward. Toward the kitchen doors. Toward the

Ghost. Mace's pulse spiked. His mind screamed move! His fingers closed around his knife.

The Ghost's lesson echoed in his head. A single, clean swipe. Silent. Precise. Mace moved in behind him, his body tightening as he prepared his ambush.

The Broken Arrow soldier never heard him coming. One second he was breathing, the next, Mace's blade sliced deep across his throat. The man stiffened, his hands clawing at the wound as wet, gurgling sounds filled the air. His rifle slipped from his grip as he dropped forward, collapsing in a twitching heap at the Ghost's feet.

For a long moment, there was only the crackling of small fires and the faint drip of blood pooling onto the tile. The Ghost looked down at the body, then up at Mace. He hadn't even seen him move. Slowly, a grin spread across the Ghost's face. He gave a nod of approval.

"Yeah," he said, his voice rough but satisfied. "Fuse suits you."

CHAPTER THIRTY-TWO
"Bullets, Blood and Bodies"

Ty moved swiftly through the shattered remains of the casino, his steps silent, his breath controlled. The stench of gunpowder, blood, and burned fabric hung thick in the air, mixing with the distant echo of gunfire. The once-glamorous building now resembled a warzone, bullet-riddled walls, shattered chandeliers, and slot machines ruined. But another sound caught his attention, cutting the chaos like a razor.

A voice, mocking and cruel. Up ahead, two Broken Arrow soldiers stood over a casino staff member, a middle-aged man in a torn uniform, his hands shaking as he knelt on the bloodstained carpet. Sweat ran down his face as he pleaded for his life, his body trembling in fear.

One of the soldiers chuckled, pressing the barrel of his rifle against the man's forehead. "Got any last words?"

Ty didn't wait. His hands moved on instinct, raising his Glock .45. The suppressed shots cracked like whispers of death, two clean, precise rounds. Blood sprayed forward as both soldiers crumpled, their bodies twitching on the floor.

The staff member flinched, breath hitching in his throat as he stared at the bodies, then up at Ty. His eyes were wide, disbelief and relief evident on his face.

Ty gave him a firm nod. "Go hide. It's almost over."

The man hesitated only for a second before scrambling to his feet and bolting toward safety. Ty ejected his spent magazine, letting it clatter onto the floor before slapping in a fresh one. His heart pounded, but he ignored it, there was no time for fatigue. He pressed forward, his boots crunching over shattered glass as he neared the poker room.

He stepped inside and froze. Brian lay sprawled on the floor, his head caved in by a single, brutal shot. There was no mistaking it, he was gone. The coppery scent of fresh blood filled the air, pooling beneath him in a thick, glistening puddle.

Ty's jaw tightened, but he forced himself to look away. On the poker table, another body lay still. The Reaper. Ty crouched beside him, pressing two fingers against his neck. At first, nothing. Then, a faint pulse, shallow, struggling, but there.

"Damn, you're tougher than you look," he mumbled.

His eyes scanned The Reaper's vest, four rounds had struck the armor, denting and tearing into it, but it had done its job. The real damage was beneath. Ty yanked his knife from its sheath and sliced open the blood-soaked fabric. The first wound was just above the right hip, deep but not gushing. It had missed the femoral artery, lucky. The second wound was near the collarbone, a clean entry with no exit. The bullet was lodged deep.

Ty cursed under his breath. "You're not dying here."

Gritting his teeth, he hooked his arms under The Reaper and heaved him up onto his shoulder. Pain lanced through his muscles, blood soaking into his vest and shirt, but he pushed forward. Brian's body remained where it fell. There was no time for goodbyes.

The hallways blurred past him as he carried The Reaper toward the triage room, boots thudding against the ruined carpet. By the time he reached the door, sweat ran down his temples, and his breathing came in rough gasps. He kicked the door open, startling the medics inside. They jumped, hands half-raised before realizing it was Ty.

"He's still alive," Ty grunted, easing The Reaper onto a cot. "Two wounds, lower right side and near the collarbone. Vest stopped four, but he needs work. Fast."

230

One of the medics nodded, already reaching for supplies. "We'll do what we can."

Ty took a step back, rubbing a hand over his face, his muscles screaming in protest. Sweat clung to his skin, the exhaustion settling in. He rolled his shoulder, wincing at the ache. "I'm way too damn old for this," he groaned.

There was no time to rest. With one last glance at The Reaper, Ty turned and jogged toward the shopping area. Logan's last radio call had come from there. If he was still alive, Ty intended to make sure he stayed that way.

The once-grand casino still stood, battered but not broken. The Broken Arrows had thrown everything they had at it, but the Red 30 gang had held their ground. Now, the few remaining enemy soldiers were being picked off one by one.

The walls, once pristine and polished, were now defaced with bullet holes, black scorch marks, and the grotesque splatter of blood. Ty moved across the casino floor, stepping past the bodies of three Broken Arrow soldiers sprawled near the ruined slot machines. Their weapons lay discarded, their bodies twisted from earlier gunfights.

Nearby, a shattered poker table bore fresh bloodstains. Ty recognized the carnage, it had been the handiwork of The Reaper. He pushed forward, reaching the stairs. His legs burned as he climbed, breath coming heavier now. His mind drifted for a split second to the escalator, mocking his struggle. "Damn thing would be useful right about now."

Reaching the top, he paused, and grinned.

"I'm glad to see you alive," Logan announced from a bench, raising a hand in greeting as Ty slowed his approach.

Ty eyed him, shaking his head. "You look too damn comfortable."

Logan smirked. "You look rough yourself." He winked.

Ty loosened his vest, letting the body armor drop with a heavy thud. His shirt was soaked in sweat and blood, his and others'. "I'll be back," he said before turning toward the nearby golf store.

Inside, he tore off his ruined shirt, using a golf towel to wipe away the grime. Blood had dried against his skin, mixing with dirt and sweat, the rough fabric scratching against his raw flesh. He tossed the towel aside, scanning the racks.

His fingers ran over the neatly folded shirts before grabbing one, soft cotton, a fresh relief against his irritated skin. He pulled it on, relishing the small comfort. Returning to Logan, he dropped onto the bench beside him with a sigh.

Logan stretched, his back cracking. "Radio's busted," he said, motioning toward the two dead Broken Arrow soldiers lying nearby. "Took a hit in a shootout."

Ty nodded. "I see that." He glanced toward the golf store, then back at Logan. "I'm guessing you were also responsible for the big guy in there with a hole in his chest?"

Logan's lips quirked in a half-smile. "Yeah, that might've been my work."

Ty grinned. "Guess you could say that was a hole in one."

Logan burst out laughing, smacking Ty's chest. "That's what I said."

For a moment, amidst the bloodshed and exhaustion, the weight of war eased, just a little.

Mace joined them shortly, startling both men. "You guys look... old. I could've used some help in this fight." He grinned.

Logan grunted, pulling Mace into a tight embrace. "Damn good to see you safe."

Mace nodded. "I'm good, Dad. The Ghost took a round, stomach or back, I couldn't tell. I got him to the medics."

Ty exhaled. "Might've gone through. We'll check on him later. Right now, let's get Logan's leg taken care of."

Mace looked at the fallen soldiers in the hall, then back to his father, "this place is filled with blood, bullets and bodies."

"Where's Owen?" Ty asked.

Logan's face tightened. "I haven't heard from him. Who's got a radio?"

No one did.

"The last I saw him, he was going toward Iron Hawk's position," Mace said.

"That's where we're going then," Logan replied, gritting his teeth as he tested his injured leg.

They moved carefully, covering each other as they reached the hallway leading to the basement level. Mace moved ahead, slipping into the stairwell. Logan and Ty held their ground, rifles ready.

Mace inched forward, only to stop cold in the bottom hallway. He found Iron Hawk, slumped against the wall, blood pooling beneath him. His breaths were shallow, his body riddled with bullets.

"Iron Hawk," Mace whispered.

The warrior struggled to open his eyes. "Protect..." He struggled to push out the words. "Protect... Running Bear." His voice faded with his final breath. His head leaned forward, his chin resting on his chest as he went to sleep for the last time.

Mace clenched his jaw but there was no time to grieve. He pushed forward, moving with caution. He knew the Wolf was present, his every step slow and measured. The halls were vast, doors going into a maze of directions. "Uncle Owen, hang in there, I'm coming."

CHAPTER THIRTY-THREE
"What Must be Done"

Inside the office, Wolf sneered at the turned chair before him, only the elaborate headpiece visible. "I told you I would come for you, Running Bear. Order a complete stand down."

Wolf's anger grew as he starred at the intricate headpiece, with it's vibrant feathers and beads, getting no response in return.

"You have no idea what you've done," Wolf snarled, his hands curling into fists at his sides. "You've left my family out in the cold for years, while you and your people grew fat off this casino money." His voice dripped with venom as he took another step forward. "My grandfather was a warrior, a true leader. He stood beside your grandfather, fought for our people. And what did your family do in return?"

The chair remained unmoving.

Wolf sneered, continuing, "You shut us out. Cut us off. Treated us like we were nothing. We should've been here, running this place, sharing in the wealth, but you and your council made damn sure we got nothing. My father drank himself to death because of you, because we had to scrape by while you played king in your fancy casino." He exhaled sharply, rage darkening his expression.

"I swore I'd take back what was mine. And now, I will." His lips curled into a smirk as he ran a hand over the desk, his fingers trailing along the carved wood. "This place, this casino, it belongs to me now. I'll rebuild my army stronger than before, and no one will dare stand against me." He paused, narrowing his eyes. "And you, Running Bear... you'll get to watch as I undo everything your people have built."

The chair finally moved, slowly turning to face him. Wolf's smirk faltered as the first thing he saw was a raised middle finger leading the way. Then his eyes widened as the man in the chair wasn't Running Bear, it was Owen.

Owen grinned, reaching up to remove the large headpiece and setting it down on the desk with a thump. "Those are pretty, but not very comfortable," Owen said, adjusting his neck side to side. His voice was laced with amusement. "Am I not who you expected?"

Wolf's expression darkened, his jaw tightening as realization set in. His nostrils flared as he clenched his fists. "You," he growled.

Owen's smirk widened. "Me," he said mockingly. "Disappointed?"

Wolf's fury burned hot as he realized he'd been duped. His hands twitched at his sides, his entire body rigid with rage. "You must be the leader of the Red 30 that has been disrupting my plans," Wolf said through gritted teeth.

Owen chuckled. "No, no, I'm not the leader. I can't hit a golf ball straight, so I don't get to participate in much. I'm what's known as the flunky of the group." He stood slowly, his movements deliberate. "The leaders of our group don't see you as a big enough threat to deal with themselves. That's when they call me in."

Wolf seethed, his eyes blazing with hatred. His fingers twitched, itching to wrap around Owen's throat. "You had no business getting involved in this. It wasn't your fight. Your arrogance has cost many lives, and now, it will cost you yours. I have taken out Iron Hawk, The Reaper, and many more. I will find each person in your team, and I will slo...."

"Yeah, yeah, yeah, you're a badass, and you're gonna kill us all, let God sort us out," Owen interrupted, rolling his eyes. "Let's just do this."

With that, he moved around and lunged. Wolf barely had time to react before Owen tackled him, driving him backward with explosive force. They crashed against the desk, knocking over stacks of paper and sending a heavy lamp clattering to the floor. Wolf swung a wild punch at Owen's head, but Owen ducked, ramming his shoulder into Wolf's gut and slamming him against a bookshelf.

Wolf grunted, shoving Owen back and throwing a heavy right hook. Owen turned in time, the fist glancing off his jaw instead of shattering it outright. The force sent him staggering, but he recovered fast, spitting blood onto the carpet.

"That all you got?" Owen taunted, wiping his mouth.

Wolf snarled and lunged again, his fists flying. Owen blocked the first strike, but the second caught him in the ribs, forcing the air from his lungs. The third punch came even faster, a brutal uppercut that snapped Owen's head back. He reeled, blinking stars from his vision as he stumbled toward the desk.

Wolf didn't let up. He grabbed a glass decanter from the bar cart and swung it like a club. Owen barely ducked in time, the heavy glass shattering against the desk behind him.

Owen lashed out, grabbing the closest weapon he could, a thick hardcover book. Without hesitation, he swung it into Wolf's face with a loud crack. Wolf growled, momentarily stunned, but before Owen could capitalize, Wolf charged, tackling him clean over the desk.

Both men crashed onto the floor, grappling, their limbs tangling as they rolled over one another. Wolf landed on top, pinning Owen's shoulders down, his fist rising to strike.

Owen twisted violently, throwing his weight to the side and knocking Wolf off balance. He freed a leg and drove his knee into Wolf's stomach, then hooked his foot behind Wolf's knee, rolling them over.

Now on top, Owen rained down a savage barrage of punches. His knuckles split Wolf's skin, blood spraying with each impact. Wolf roared in fury, bucking like a wild animal, but Owen was relentless.

"You like taking what isn't yours?" *Crack!* A punch to Wolf's cheek split his lip.

"You like feeling powerful?" *Crack!* Another blow sent a tooth flying.

Owen went for another punch, but Wolf caught his wrist, twisting it violently. Owen grunted in pain, his grip weakening just enough for Wolf to throw him off.

Both men staggered to their feet, breathing hard. Wolf's face was a mess of blood and bruises, but his eyes still burned with rage. Owen rolled his shoulders, cracking his neck.

"Still standing?" Owen grumbled. "Gotta give you credit for that. You may be evil, but you're a tough bastard."

Wolf didn't answer. He charged again. Owen sidestepped, using Wolf's momentum against him. He grabbed Wolf's arm, twisted it behind his back, and drove him headfirst into the wooden coffee table. The table shattered under the impact, splinters flying in all directions.

Wolf groaned, dazed, his body sprawled in the wreckage. Owen didn't hesitate to flip Wolf onto his stomach, yanking his arms back. He zip-tied Wolf's wrists, cinching tight. Wolf thrashed, but his strength was spent.

Mace entered just in time to see Owen heave Wolf's limp body into a chair, securing the bonds even tighter. Wolf's chest heaved, blood dripping from his nose and mouth as he glared up at Owen with pure, unfiltered hatred.

Owen caught his breath, shaking out his bruised fists. "Not as fun when you're on the losing side, is it?" he said.

Then, with a smirk, he turned to the large bookcase, knocking firmly against the wood. "It's Owen. You're clear to come out."

The hidden door creaked open, and Running Bear stepped forward, his expression unreadable. He moved with quiet purpose, carrying a wooden box that looked aged, the carvings on its surface telling stories of battles long past. He placed it on the desk, his fingers tracing the edges before he slowly lifted the lid.

Wolf scoffed, shifting in his seat. "Finally," he spat, blood staining his teeth. "The coward shows himself."

Inside, resting on a bed of dark velvet, was a knife. The handle was carved bone, polished smooth with time, and the blade itself gleamed in the light, its edge wickedly sharp. Running Bear lifted it with respect, turning it in his hand as he spoke. Wolf's struggle ceased as he recognized what it was. For the first time, real fear flickered in his eyes.

Running Bear met his gaze, unshaken. "You have always been blind to the truth, Gideon." His voice was calm, steady, weighted with something ancient.

Wolf's jaw clenched at the use of his birth name. He sneered. "You left my family to starve! Cast us out like we were nothing. You built this empire while we rotted in the cold."

Running Bear exhaled through his nose, his fingers tracing the intricate carvings on the wooden box. "Rotted in the cold?" he repeated softly, his dark eyes studying Wolf. "Do you even know why your family was cast out?"

Wolf's expression darkened. "Because you couldn't stand my father. Because he wasn't one of you."

Running Bear shook his head. "No. It was never because he was white. It was because both your father and your mother betrayed our people."

Wolf's scowl faltered slightly. "You're lying."

Running Bear continued, his voice unwavering. "Your mother, a woman of our tribe, stood beside your father not as a loving wife, but as his accomplice. They were thieves, Gideon, stealing from their own people, from their own blood."

Wolf stilled, but his eyes remained locked on Running Bear, as if daring him to continue.

"Your father," Running Bear said, "convinced the tribal council to trust him, to let him oversee government funds meant for our people, money that was meant for housing, for food, for medical care. And your mother, she vouched for him, used her place within the tribe to silence doubts. Together, they siphoned those funds into their own pockets, leaving our sick to die, our elders to suffer, our children to go without."

Wolf shook his head violently, his bound hands straining against the zip ties. "You're making this up."

Running Bear's gaze didn't waver. "Am I? You were a child, Gideon. You didn't see the suffering your parents caused. You didn't see the elders who had no medicine because the funds had vanished. You didn't see the families left without homes, truly left in the cold."

Wolf's breathing turned ragged. He wanted to deny it, to call Running Bear a liar, but something in the old man's voice, something unshakable, kept him silent.

"When the truth came out," Running Bear continued, "we had a choice. To let justice be served through the courts, or to handle it as our ancestors would have. Your parents were given a chance to make it right, to return what they stole, to answer for their crimes and remain on this sacred land."

He paused, his voice dropping lower. "But they ran."

Wolf's lips parted slightly, his breath shaky now.

"They abandoned you," Running Bear said, his gaze piercing. "Just as they abandoned the people they stole from. They left you behind to fend for yourself while they vanished into the world with blood money. They didn't die the way you thought."

Wolf clenched his jaw, his entire body tensing. "You could have taken me in," he growled.

Running Bear studied him. "The family who took you, cared for you. You were given a choice as you grew, to stay and make your own path, or to follow the road your parents took. You chose bitterness, Gideon. You chose anger. And now, you stand before me, repeating their sins, trying to steal what you did not earn."

Wolf's face twisted in rage. "You think you're better than me?" he snapped. "You think you're righteous?" He laughed bitterly. "Look at you now. You're just another old man holding onto a past that's already dead. That knife in your hand? You're no different than me."

Running Bear's fingers curled around the handle of the ceremonial knife, the blade catching the dim light. His voice remained even, his expression unreadable.

"The difference between us," he said, "is that I do not kill for greed." He took a slow step forward, his grip tightening. "I kill for justice."

Running Bear turned to Owen. "Go. Your people need you. I will do what must be done."

Owen hesitated. He had no love for Wolf, no sympathy for the man who had slaughtered without remorse. But there was something in Running Bear's voice, something that sent a chill through him. It wasn't anger or vengeance. It was certainty, a finality that could not be undone.

Owen took a slow step back, then another, before nodding. "Take your time. Let's go, Mace."

He turned, but before he could step through the door, Wolf let out a bitter laugh. "You think this changes anything?" His voice was hoarse, raw, but still filled with defiance. "You kill me, but you'll never kill what I started. My men will rebuild. The

240

Broken Arrows will rise again, and when they do, they'll burn this place to the ground. Every single one of you, your people, your families, you'll all die screaming."

Running Bear didn't respond immediately. Instead, he stepped forward, his grip tightening on the knife. "Your father said something similar before he ran."

Wolf's sneer faltered. "You won't get away with this, you or the Red 30 mercenaries you hired."

"I stood where you sit now, listening to your father's promises of revenge." Running Bear's voice was quiet, steady. "But the truth is, men like him, men like you, you are not builders. You do not create. You do not rise. You only destroy."

Wolf clenched his jaw. "You're a coward, hiding behind your damn traditions. You think you're some wise old man sitting on a throne of lies? You're just another killer."

Running Bear gave him a slow nod. "Perhaps. But unlike you, I do not kill the innocent."

He took another step forward, his lips parting as he began to chant, low, rhythmic, each word carrying the weight of generations before him. The sound filled the room, wrapping around them like an unseen force, ancient and unshaken.

Wolf's bravado cracked. He pulled at his restraints, his breathing growing uneven. "You...."

The first scream cut through the air. Owen and Mace kept walking. Their boots thudded against the floor, Owen's breath slow and measured, even as the sound of Wolf's agony echoed behind him.

By the time he reached the stairwell, a second scream tore loose, ragged and desperate. Owen exhaled sharply and closed his eyes for a moment. He didn't need to turn back. He already knew.

Running Bear had begun.

CHAPTER THIRTY-FOUR

"The Last Judgement"

The Red 30 gang regrouped inside the casino, their boots echoing through the battered remains. The odor of gunpowder mingling with burnt upholstery, a lingering testament to the battle that had raged through the night. They moved cautiously, eyes sweeping across the destruction, their adrenaline still pumping.

"Is it over?" Owen asked as he patted Logan on the back.

Ty exhaled, then yawned deeply. "I sure hope so, I'm ready for a week of sleep."

Poker tables lay overturned, playing cards scattered across the floor like autumn leaves. Bullet-riddled slot machines stood frozen in time, their shattered screens reflecting the cost of betting on war. Glass crunched under their steps, a grim reminder of the firefight that had torn through this once-bustling den of greed and fortune. Shell casings littered the floor, mingling with bloodstains, some fresh, others smeared by the scuffle of boots.

Yet, in the stillness, pockets of normalcy remained untouched. Some tables sat pristine, stacks of poker chips still neatly arranged, as if waiting for gamblers to return. The surreal contrast between chaos and order made it feel as though the casino itself hadn't yet decided whether the war was over.

The first light of dawn crept through the shattered windows, its golden beams cutting through the dust-choked air. The glow stretched across the marble floor, revealing the bodies of the fallen. It was quiet now, no more gunfire, no more screams. Just the weight of survival settling over them.

As they neared the main lobby, a voice cut through the silence. "I caught this guy trying to sneak out." Crackhead's hulking frame loomed over a man pinned beneath him. His thick knee was pressed into the back of Elijah, the Broken Arrows lieutenant, who lay sprawled across the cold floor. Blood dripped from his nose onto the marble, his chest rising and falling in ragged breaths.

"I wasn't sure if I should kill him," Crackhead said, his grin twisted with amusement. "So, I figured I'd wait."

Owen, Logan, and Mace exchanged glances before Logan raised his voice, forcing authority through the pain of his own wounds. "Everyone, listen up." His tone was firm, commanding. "You've survived the night. Each of you is a warrior now." His words carried weight, but he wasn't finished. "But it's not over yet. Split into teams. Sweep every inch of this property. Open every door, check every room. Make sure this place is clear of any Broken Arrows."

Murmurs of acknowledgment rippled through the group as men moved to carry out his orders. Crackhead, however, remained where he was, his knee still planted firmly on Elijah's back. "What about this one?" he asked with a smirk. "Should I put him down?"

Logan nodded, about to give the order, but Mace stepped forward. "Wait," he said. "Bring him outside. I have an idea."

They dragged Elijah to his feet and hauled him toward the exit. The moment they pushed through the shattered doors, the cool morning air hit them like a breath of fresh life. The sun had fully risen now, its warmth brushing against their bloodstained skin, the first sign that the nightmare was over.

Mace grabbed Elijah's chin, forcing him to look at the scene before them. "The Broken Arrows are done," Mace said, his grip firm. "And you can thank the Red 30 for your downfall."

He jerked his head toward the traffic light where their two prisoners remained bound, survivors, though barely. Their heads hung low, their bodies slumped with exhaustion. "Those two? They're all that's left of your army. Maybe it's God's will that they survived."

Elijah clenched his jaw, his bloodied face contorting with hatred. "Where's Wolf?" he spat.

Owen's smile was slow and cruel. "Wolf is being dispatched, tribal style."

Elijah's face twisted in fury, but Mace tightened his grip. "We're letting you go," he said. "Take your men, start a new life. But first, I want to hear you say it. Say the words."

Elijah's breathing was heavy, his pride fighting with his instinct to survive. His hands curled into fists before, finally, he exhaled sharply. "You have defeated the Broken Arrows," he admitted through gritted teeth.

Ty scoffed. "This is a mistake, Mace. We need to finish them."

Mace's expression remained unchanged. "I've earned at least one decision," he said calmly. "And this is it. Let him go."

Crackhead cut the ties binding Elijah's wrists, then handed him a knife. Mace's voice was steady, his eyes cold.

"Don't get any ideas with that knife. Cut those men loose. The second you make a move, you die," Mace said firmly.

Elijah's fingers curled around the handle, his knuckles turning white. But he didn't strike. Instead, he turned and walked away, his steps slow, calculated. Every few feet, he cast a glance back, hatred burning in his eyes.

"Mace..." Logan started, but Mace raised a hand.

"Don't say it, Dad."

Elijah reached the two bound soldiers. His fingers twitched around the knife. His body trembled with rage. He turned back one last time, his voice filled with venom.

"The Broken Arrows will never be defeated!"

"I told you..." Ty grumbled deeply.

Then, Elijah slashed the knife downward, severing the cable tie of the first soldier. A metallic *ping* rang out as the tripwire snapped. For a split second, silence. Then the explosion ripped through the intersection. Flames engulfed them, the shockwave tearing through flesh and bone. The blast sent limbs and debris flying, a fiery roar swallowing their screams. The force shattered nearby windows in the steakhouse, a final, violent punctuation mark on the end of the Broken Arrows, at the same intersection it had first begun.

When the dust settled, all that remained was the blackened, smoldering remnants of what had once been Elijah and his men. The burnt flesh filling the morning air.

"Whoooaaaa!" Owen exhaled, blinking through the settling haze.

Mace turned to Ty with a smirk. "What was that you were saying?"

Ty's eyes were wide with surprise, but his lips curled into a slow grin. "I was just gonna say... I always knew you were amazing, a born leader."

Logan placed a firm hand on Mace's shoulder, giving it a squeeze. "Mace," he said, his voice low, almost proud. "You've really learned to become dangerous."

Mace grinned, turning to the others. "Come on, did you all really think I was dumb enough to let that murdering piece of garbage walk away?"

Crackhead chuckled, shaking his head. "Mace, you sneaky bastard."

Owen eyed Crackhead, arching a brow. "You look like you got hit by a truck. A big one, twice, maybe three times."

Crackhead grinned. "You think you look any prettier?"

The gang shared a quiet laugh, the tension finally breaking as they turned their faces to the sun.

Logan exhaled. "I need medical attention. Crackhead, you too. The Reaper, no, he probably wants to be Grant again, took some bullets."

As Logan turned to head inside, Mace called after him.

"Hey, Dad. One more thing."

Logan stopped, glancing back.

"You can call me Fuse now," Mace said with a smirk. "The Ghost says it's my new nickname."

Logan studied him for a long moment before nodding. "Then Fuse it is."

Owen tapped Ty, pointing across the parking lot. "Look, isn't that Dale?" He said pointing at the elder man who loaded bodies into the truck.

Dale, or Ahyvnywi, held up a hand, a soft wave to the guys. It was one last show of gratitude, as he climbed inside his truck once again, driving away slowly.

"That guy comes and goes like a silent spirit in the wind," Ty said as they all sat on the sidewalk, letting the sun warm them before moving back inside.

Logan leaned against Crackhead, unable to lower himself down. "We're gonna' need a few days for some healing."

CHAPTER THIRY-FIVE
"Summoned"

Logan sat back in the golf cart, his wounded leg stretched out, the dull ache a constant reminder of the fight they had just survived. Though the days of bloodshed were behind them, the weight of what had happened still lingered. He wasn't the type to sit around, and as much as he needed rest, he was eager to be part of something again, part of rebuilding, not just surviving.

Riding alongside the guys, he watched as they worked to repair the fairways, smoothing out the deep ruts left behind by the chase that had torn through the course. He smirked, resting his arm lazily over the wheel. "Broken fairways might be before us now," he said, his voice carrying in the open air. "But as the Red 30 gang, we're gonna help repair them."

His words settled between them, and the others understood, this wasn't just about the grass and dirt beneath their feet. It was about everything. About the country, their lives, the people they had lost. They weren't just survivors anymore, they would be a force for good, doing their part to rebuild in whatever way they could.

The moment passed, and Logan leaned back, grinning as he made a show of relaxing. "Damn shame I can't help, what with my leg and all," he teased. "Hard work's just not in the cards for me right now."

Owen and Ty exchanged a glance before, without warning, Mace heaved a full bucket of water over him. Logan gasped, sputtering as the cold water drenched him. Owen smirked. "Guess you can't catch us either."

Logan wiped his face, shaking his head with a laugh. "You ungrateful little shits." He revved the cart's engine. "You better run," he said as he threw a golf ball at them, the ball smacking off the top of their cart.

Back at Grant's property, Mace crouched beside The Ghost, his hands steady as he worked with the wires in front of him. The controlled chaos of bomb-making fascinated him, the precision, the patience, the delicate balance between destruction and control. It was an art, and he was diving in headfirst, eager to master every technique The Ghost showed him. He liked the name that had stuck to him, 'The Fuse', and he wore it like a badge of honor.

"You're catching on quick," The Ghost said, watching as Mace connected the final wire. "But the real skill ain't just making 'em. It's knowing when to use 'em."

Mace grinned. "Yeah, well, I figure if I'm good at something, might as well go all in, you can teach me all of it."

Before The Ghost could respond, Crackhead's heavy boots thudded against the ground as he approached. "Hey, Fuse," he called out with a grin. "Hate to pull you away from your arts and crafts project, but you're being called in."

Mace wiped his hands on his pants and stood up. "Called in? For what?"

"Running Bear wants to see you all," Crackhead said. "He's got something to say, more importantly, the reward."

That caught Mace's attention. He turned to The Ghost, who nodded. "Go handle your business. We'll pick this up later."

Mace didn't hesitate. He and Crackhead made their way across the property, heading toward the barn where Logan, Ty, and Owen were resting. As soon as they found them, Crackhead clapped his hands together. "Alright, boys, suit up. You've been summoned to the casino."

Ty raised an eyebrow. "Summoned? Sounds dramatic."

"Hell yeah, it does," Owen smirked. "Let's hope it comes with drinks."

Mace cracked his knuckles, feeling a surge of excitement. Whatever Running Bear had planned, he was ready for it. The Red 30 had changed the game, and now it was time to see what came next.

Logan found Grant near the back of the house, kneeling beside his wife as she worked the soil in their garden. The once-thriving patch had suffered during the chaos, but she was determined to bring it back to life, one plant at a time. Grant wiped the sweat from his brow, watching her with quiet admiration before turning his attention to Logan.

"What's up?" Grant asked, standing slowly to stretch his back, careful not to put much pressure on his healing wounds.

"Running Bear wants to see us," Logan said. "We're heading to the casino. Figured you'd want to come along."

Grant exhaled, glancing back at his wife. "Nah," he said, shaking his head. "I'm gonna sit this one out."

Logan raised an eyebrow. "You sure? He might be offering more than just a handshake."

Grant chuckled. "I'm sure. I've spent enough time running around and getting shot at. Right now, I want to be here, with her, helping put this place back together. The fight might be over, but there's still plenty of work to do." He gestured to the garden. "She's been trying to get this back in order, and I think it's about time I did my part."

Logan nodded, understanding the deeper meaning behind Grant's words. "Alright. We'll handle it."

"Take Crackhead," Grant added. "On my behalf."

Logan smirked. "Crackhead as your official representative, huh? That should be interesting."

Grant grinned. "Hey, the guy's got a way with words. Mostly four-letter ones, but still."

Logan chuckled and tapped Grant on the shoulder. "We'll let you know how it goes."

As Logan turned to leave, Grant knelt back down slowly, pulling a stubborn weed from the soil. The garden, and all it stood for, was his focus now. He'd done his fighting. Now, it was time to rebuild, his property and his body.

The Red 30 gang arrived at the casino just as the sun dipped below the horizon, creating darkness over the parking lot. The wreckage from the battle, burned-out cars, twisted trucks, and shattered buses, had been cleared or pushed to the far end, leaving behind an open space that spoke of renewal and hope rather than destruction and devastation.

Red Willow stood at the entrance, waiting for them. Her dark eyes reflected the soft glow of the lanterns flickering inside. "Welcome back," she said warmly, as they entered.

Inside, the transformation was striking. Lanterns bathed the interior in a warm and welcoming glow, the light on the walls that had once been riddled with bullet holes. The damage was already being repaired, the scars of war fading beneath fresh coats of paint and some newly restored furnishings. The Cherokee people refused to let the battle define them, they were moving forward, embracing faith over ruin.

Red Willow led them deeper into the casino, weaving through the rows of tables and slot machines. Their boots echoed against the polished floors as they descended a hallway leading to Running Bear's office.

When they stepped inside, a roar of cheers erupted from the room. The office was packed with members of the Cherokee tribe, their faces bright with gratitude and admiration. Lining the tables was their promised reward, but it was far more than expected. Gold coins glimmered under the lantern light, stacks of ammunition and rifles were neatly arranged, and crates of food supplies stood ready to be loaded. Everything they had asked for, plus some additional for good measure.

CHAPTER THIRTY-SIX
"The Vault"

Running Bear stood at the head of the room, his powerful presence commanding attention. He raised a hand, and the cheers faded into respectful silence.

"You have done more than fight," he began, his deep voice resonating in the room. "You have shown courage. You have shown honor. You have fought not just for yourselves, but for something greater, for a future." He stepped forward, dipping his fingers into a bowl of red and black paint. "And for that, you will not leave here as mere men. Tonight, you leave as warriors, marked by the Cherokee as brothers."

He approached Logan first, drawing a bold symbol across his forehead. "You led your people through fire and death, never faltering, never breaking. From this night forward, you are 'Chief,' a leader among men."

Logan held his head high, feeling the weight of the title. It was more than just a name, it was a responsibility.

Running Bear turned to Ty, marking his forehead with a similar design. "You stood beside him, planning, fighting, ensuring victory before the first shot was even fired. You are 'Iron Hand,' the one who builds the path to triumph."

Mace stepped forward next, his eyes burning with excitement. Running Bear studied him for a moment before nodding. "You are 'Fuse.' It is a name that suits you, and it shall remain. Your energy, your fire, it will be needed in the days ahead. A fuse can bring destruction, but also change. You will help carry the Red 30 forward, igniting the way."

Mace grinned, embracing the name with pride.

Finally, Running Bear faced Owen. He dipped his fingers into the paint once more, pressing a symbol onto his forehead. "You were willing to sacrifice yourself for your people. A shield against the storm. You are 'Stone Guardian,' the protector who does not waver."

Owen nodded solemnly, accepting the honor.

Running Bear stepped back, surveying the men before him. "You are warriors. You are brothers. And wherever the road takes you next, know this, you do not walk it alone."

Crackhead couldn't hold back his large smile, like a kid waiting for his treat, he leaned forward, kneeling slightly to lower his forehead.

Running Bear dipped his fingers into the paint, smirking as he turned to Crackhead. "Now, what do we call a man who's too stubborn to die, too wild to tame, and somehow still standing after everything?" He chuckled slightly, shaking his head. "I'd call you 'Hard Head,' but I think we all know that's an understatement." The room rumbled with laughter.

Then, Running Bear's expression turned more serious. He placed a hand on Crackhead's shoulder as he marked his face with paint. "You are relentless. You are a survivor, a warrior who fights with fire in his soul. With love for others in his heart. Your name will be Unelanvhi Adanvdo, 'Ghost of Thunder.' Because wherever you go, the storm follows."

The Red 30 gang let out cheers, nodding in approval. Crackhead grinned, rubbing the fresh mark on his forehead. "Ghost of Thunder, huh? Damn, I like the sound of that. You hear that Fuse? I'm Crackhead, the Ghost of Thunder."

The room erupted into cheers once more, the celebration carried into the night. For the Red 30 gang, this wasn't just a reward. It was a reminder of who they had become, and the path they would forge ahead.

As the celebration wound down, Running Bear raised a hand, signaling for the Red 30 gang to remain while the others filtered out of the room. The warmth of victory still hung in the air, but the shift in his expression was unmistakable, this wasn't just another speech.

Once the room had emptied, a man entered, a thin figure with sharp eyes and a radio clipped to his belt. His weathered face and tense posture spoke volumes before he even opened his mouth. Running Bear gestured toward him.

"This is Daniel White Crow. He's been handling our communications, keeping track of what's left of the world outside these walls."

White Crow nodded, stepping forward. "What I'm about to tell you isn't just rumor, it's the best information we've managed to piece together from the broken lines of communication we have left." He took a deep breath. "The United States... it's barely holding on."

The room fell into heavy silence.

"We knew things were bad," Logan said, shifting his stance. "But how bad?"

White Crow glanced at Running Bear before continuing. "Worse than we feared. The attacks didn't just hit military bases and major cities. They hit everything, power grids, supply chains, infrastructure. Some places are just... gone."

He hesitated, then listed them. "New York City. Washington, D.C. Most of the West Coast is in chaos. Denver was hit hard. Houston's burning. Chicago is unrecognizable."

Owen exhaled sharply, rubbing the back of his neck. Mace swallowed, his usual energy subdued. Ty's hands curled into fists.

"There are a few places where communications are still coming through," White Crow continued. "Some military outposts. A few government locations. They're trying to regroup, but there's no real chain of command anymore. No president, no clear leadership. Just fragments of what used to be the government, trying to figure out their next move."

"How long before they get back on their feet?" Crackhead asked.

White Crow shook his head. "Years. Maybe decades. They pushed back the invaders, but the damage is done. Rebuilding won't happen overnight. Roads, power, water, it's all going to take time. And even then, it won't be the country we knew."

Running Bear crossed his arms. "This isn't just about survival anymore. It's about what comes next. What we build from the ruins."

The weight of his words settled over them. They had fought to stay alive, fought to protect what they could. But now, the battle wasn't just against enemies with guns. It was against time, against the collapse of everything they had once taken for granted.

"We're going to help," Logan said, his voice steady.

Ty and Owen exchanged a look, understanding that he wasn't just talking, he meant it, they would do whatever they could.

They weren't just survivors anymore. They were builders. And their fight was far from over.

As the weight of White Crow's words settled over them, Running Bear motioned toward the door. "Before you leave, there's someone else you need to meet."

The door creaked open, and a man stepped inside. He was lean, with deep-set eyes that had seen too much, his face lined with exhaustion and desperation. His clothes were worn, his boots covered in dust from long travel.

"This is Aaron McClain," Running Bear said, his tone serious. "He's come a long way to find you."

McClain nodded, glancing at each of them in turn before clearing his throat. "I'm from Pigeon Forge, Tennessee." His voice was hoarse, as if he hadn't spoken much in days. "I've heard the stories. The Red 30 gang, your skills, your fight, your victory." He took a shaky breath. "And I've come to ask for your help."

The room went quiet, the weight of his plea pressing down like a heavy stone.

"Go on," Logan said, his full attention on Aaron.

McClain swallowed hard, his fingers flexing at his sides as if holding back frustration or fear. "It's bad out there. Real bad. Gangs have taken over Pigeon Forge, running wild, terrorizing people, turning the town into their own sick playground."

Owen's jaw tightened. "What kind of gangs?"

McClain hesitated, then spoke the name like a curse. "The Blood Vultures."

Ty let out a slow breath. "Never heard of them, sounds kind of cheezy."

"They're new, the attack on the country has created them," McClain said. "And they're worse than anything we've seen before. They don't just take what they want. They make people fight each other, for sport, for entertainment. They pit fathers against sons, neighbors against neighbors. If you refuse, they kill you. If you fight and lose, they kill you. If you fight and win... they make you do it again the next day." His voice cracked, his hands clenching into fists. "They're breaking people. Tearing families apart. If something isn't done soon, there won't be anything left to save."

Silence filled the space. No one needed to ask if he was telling the truth. The desperation in his eyes, the raw edge in his voice, it was all real.

"I know you don't owe us anything," McClain said, his voice thick with emotion. "But if even half of what I've heard about you is true... we need your help to stop them. Please. Come help us before it's too late."

The Red 30 gang exchanged looks, the weight of his words settling in their minds. They had fought to survive. They had fought for revenge. But now? Now, they were being asked to fight for something bigger. Logan exhaled, glancing toward his men. He could already see it in their eyes. The answer wasn't in question. It never had been.

Aaron let out a weary sigh, rubbing a hand over his face. "I have to begin my return tomorrow evening," he said. "I know this is a lot to ask, and I know the road ahead won't be easy. But if you accept, you won't go unrewarded. We'll make it worth your while."

Logan nodded, his expression unreadable. "We'll give you our answer by noon tomorrow."

Aaron studied him for a moment, then gave a single nod before turning and exiting the room. The heavy silence that followed lingered until Mace broke it.

"That's intense, but before we wrap things up for the nigh or get sidetracked," Mace said, grinning slightly, "I've got one last request, Mr. Running Bear."

Running Bear raised a brow. "Oh?"

"We want to see the vault," Mace said. "I know the cash ain't worth anything now, but we've all wondered what it looks like in there."

A knowing smile tugged at Running Bear's lips. "Is that all?" He chuckled. "Alright then, follow me, Fuse."

"No way!" Ty exclaimed. "He's gonna do it!"

Running Bear led them deeper into the casino, passing through secured corridors until they reached a reinforced steel door. With a smooth motion, Running Bear entered a code, unlocking it with a heavy click. Beyond it lay another room, smaller but lined with more security measures. He stepped to a massive dial, gripping it with both hands and giving it a slow, deliberate turn. A deep, mechanical groan filled the space as he worked the mechanism.

He stepped back, motioning toward the door with his hand. Owen and Mace exchanged a glance before stepping forward, each gripping the vault door's handle. With a collective heave, they pulled it open.

Their eyes widened.

Before them lay a fortress of wealth, shelves stacked high with bricks of hundred-dollar bills, gold bars glinting under the dim security lights, and safety deposit boxes likely filled with who knew what. The air inside carried the scent of paper and metal, of fortunes now rendered meaningless in a shattered world.

"Damn," Ty mumbled.

"Now that," Owen said, shaking his head in awe, "is something to see."

Running Bear chuckled. "Take it in while you can, boys, time's up, I've got one more surprise for you."

He led them back through the corridors, up to the main casino floor. Just before they stepped inside, he lifted a radio. "Turn it on."

A hum filled the air as power surged through the building. Suddenly, the casino sprang to life. Slot machines flickered, reels spinning in an endless cycle of bright neon. Lights glowed, reflecting off the polished tables. Music and mechanical jingles echoed across the floor.

At the center of it all, Big Red stood at a roulette table, grinning. Five large stacks of chips sat before her, each valued at twenty thousand dollars, if money ever meant anything again.

Across the floor, a bartender polished a glass, nodding toward them as he stood ready for orders. A poker table had been set up, another twenty-thousand-dollar stack waiting along with lady luck for each man.

Running Bear spread his arms wide. "The chips may only hold optimism in value for now, but anything you win tonight will be stored in the vault, for your safekeeping, should you return one day." His eyes swept over them, his voice steady. "I already know your answer about Pigeon Forge. You leave day after tomorrow. You are protectors of the innocent, you, Red 30, are warriors. But tonight..." He gestured toward the tables. "Tonight, you celebrate."

For a moment, the war, the destruction, the weight of the road ahead faded. The Red 30 gang laughed as they took their seats, tossing chips, taking turns at the roulette wheel, and exchanging jabs with Big Red. Drinks flowed, toasts were made, and for the first time in what felt like forever, they allowed themselves to breathe.

Happiness, appreciation, and camaraderie filled the air.

Tomorrow, the day after, the next week, soon, they would fight again.

But tonight, they lived as it had all began, Red 30!

EPILOGUE

The Red 30 Gang rode out at the following day, leaving behind the safety of Grant's ridge and the gratitude of those they had fought beside. The battle for the casino had been won, the Cherokee people had their land secured, and Running Bear's tribe could begin rebuilding. But the war for survival was far from over.

Crackhead stood beside Grant as they loaded up, his expression somber. "I owe him," he said simply. "He gave me a place when I had nothing. Somebody's gotta watch his back." Logan locked forearms, nodding in understanding. Crackhead wasn't running, he was standing his ground with Grant. As they rode past the burned-out remains of broken vehicles and bullet-riddled buildings, the weight of what lay ahead settled over them. Their mission had started as a fight for their own survival, but it had become something more. The world was in ruins, lawless and unforgiving, and people were suffering under the grip of those who thrived on chaos.

Someone had to stand against them. Someone had to push back. Logan, Ty, Owen, and Mace didn't look back as they crossed the ridge, heading toward their next fight. The call from Pigeon Forge echoed in their minds, a town overrun, innocent people forced into violence for sport. Another battlefield. Another test of who they were.

The wind whispered through the trees as they disappeared into the horizon, carrying with it the spirit of the Cherokee warriors who had fought before them. They were not alone; they were a brotherhood that would endure. The Red 30 Gang had become more than just a group of men trying to get home. They were warriors now. Protectors of the innocent and their fight had only just begun.

www.ingramcontent.com/pod-product-compliance
Lightning Source LLC
Chambersburg PA
CBHW020554180626
46810CB00007B/2494